THE
WATCHMAN
OF EPHRAIM

ALSO BY GERARD DE MARIGNY

CRIS DE NIRO

The Watchman of Ephraim

de Marigny Gerard

JARRYJORNO PUBLISHING

HENDERSON

Published by JarRyJorNo Publishing
Henderson, Nevada

Edited by Lisa de Marigny and Jared de Marigny

ISBN: 1456575406
ISBN-13: 978-1456575403

Library of Congress Control Number: 2011901491

3 4 5 6   14 13 12 11

*The days of punishment
have come;
The days of recompense
have come.
Israel knows!
The prophet is a fool,
The spiritual man is insane,
Because of the greatness of
your iniquity and great
enmity.
The watchman of Ephraim
Is with my God;
But the prophet is a fowler's
snare in all his ways,
And enmity in the house of
his God. (Hos. 9:7-8)*

In memory of our friend Daniel Afflitto who died in the North Tower of the World Trade Center on September 11, 2001, and for all the other families and friends of victims who lost their lives on that terrible day.

This book is dedicated to Danny's sons, Joseph and Daniel Jr. and to his wife Stacey.

Thanks to all my friends who visit me on my website, Facebook, LinkedIn, Twitter and MySpace ... you know who you are!

Thanks to my Canadian friend and fabulous writer of fantasy, "S&M" ... S.M. Carrière for taking the time to help me fix those pesky ellipses and single quotation marks. Please look for her written works!

My sincere gratitude and appreciation goes to Dean Wesley Smith, a great writer and mentor to neophyte authors like myself, without whose guidance and advice this novel would not have been published. Please check out his written works!

Special thanks to my wife Lisa ... who is my inspiration, my editor, my biggest critic and my soulmate and to my sons Jared, Ryan, Jordan, & Noah (you're my best friends ... got ya first!) ... all my hopes!

THE WATCHMAN
OF EPHRAIM

CHAPTER 1

WORLD TRADE CENTER MALL
NEW YORK, NEW YORK

8:30A.M., TUESDAY, SEPTEMBER 11, 2001
(16 MINUTES BEFORE TERRORISTS CRASHED AMERICAN AIRLINES FLIGHT 11
INTO TOWER ONE)

The shopkeeper smiled at the handsome, well-tailored customer as she finished tying a ribbon around the box of long-stemmed roses he picked out. She noticed his wedding ring and could surmise for whom the flowers were intended. The earthy woman's ruddy cheeks glowed with satisfaction as she affixed the final touch to her handiwork – a big red bow – to the top and center of the lid.

"Will this be cash or charge?"

De Niro handed over his American Express black card as he flipped his cell phone open and hit an auto-dial button.

The shopkeeper raised her eyebrows when she examined the oddly-colored card and read the famous last name embossed onto it. After swiping it through the terminal, her blue eyes sparkled with curiosity as she handed it back to him. De Niro knew the look on her face well. He'd seen it countless times before, and though he bore little resemblance to the legendary actor with the same last name, curiosity got the better of most people.

If I had a dollar for every time someone gibed me with the line, "You talkin' to me ..." I can only imagine what it's like to – be – Robert De Niro.

Smiling politely, he answered her question before she even asked it.

"No relation."

Born Cristiano Stephen De Niro, De Niro had long ago given up teasing people by telling them, "We're cousins."

After deciding whether she should believe him or not, the shopkeeper flashed De Niro a knowing glance. Handing him the box, she added a little too loudly for his comfort, "I understand, Mr. De Niro."

De Niro rolled his eyes and, with a few curious stares from other customers, made a quick exit from the store.

Located behind the "Twin Towers," the florist shop was nestled in the far corner of the concourse, the largest shopping center in Manhattan. The WTC Mall was also a main stop for a number of trains including the PATH that carried people into the city from New Jersey as well as the N, R, 1 and 9 lines that ran from Brooklyn and Queens to uptown. As he passed the entrance to the PATH train platform heading for the Tower One lobby, De Niro detected the familiar smell of the subway below. It brought to mind his harried youth, when he took the train from Brooklyn to uptown to go to work.

The smell of the subway and over-cooked pretzels will always remind me of Manhattan.

He hadn't been to the Trade Center in awhile but De Niro could see some things hadn't changed - his call wasn't going through - so he disconnected it and tried again. Being there brought back so many memories of when he first met his wife, Lisa. At the time, she worked for Cantor Fitzgerald, the world-famous bond house. Lisa landed her job with Cantor right out of college and worked her way up the ladder, eventually becoming the firm's chief market analyst. Lisa and Cris both knew God had a hand in their meeting despite the fact they didn't get off to the best start.

De Niro blushed with embarrassment whenever he thought about how they met. It was at a cocktail hour that kicked off an investment conference in San Francisco, where they both were scheduled to speak. He arrived late and had just walked into the reception area. Lisa greeted him and introduced herself in her usual, confident manner. He offered his hand to her and began to introduce himself, when she interrupted him with just a touch of sarcasm.

"I know who you are."

Winking, she glanced over his head and walked away. De Niro was perplexed until he noticed that he was standing directly under a ten-foot billboard poster of himself, complete with his name in bold, printed under his picture. Apparently, someone working for the event's promotion department thought it was a brilliant idea to plaster the behemoth posters all over the conference center.

After catching up to Lisa, De Niro asked her to dinner. He remembered it like it was yesterday. Before that, he was used to taking women out who were either interested in talking about themselves the whole night or turning the date into a Fortune magazine interview about his net worth. Lisa, on the other hand, captivated him from the start. She was a total knockout but didn't seem preoccupied with her looks; he liked that in a woman. Unlike the vain model-types that ordered a salad and picked the croutons out for fear of gaining an ounce, Lisa had a hearty appetite.

Not only did she polish off what was on her plate; she asked me if I was gonna finish what was on mine!

When he told her to have at it, she casually reached across with her fork, as if they knew each other forever. Savoring the fish from his dish made her flash that beautiful smile of hers. It beamed as much from her golden eyes as from her mouth and was accented with a dimple she said she inherited from her granddad. She proceeded to talk about everything except the two of them, from sports - they both loved the Yankees; he was an avid Oakland Raiders fan, she hated them, to politics - they were both conservative; she was outspoken and active, he mostly kept his views to himself, to how many kids she pictured having when she married - incredibly, they both wanted four.

De Niro recalled how the entire evening passed and she never uttered a word about what she did for a living. When he asked her why, she simply said, "That's what I do ... it's not who I am." De Niro was well aware though, from listening to her speak at the conference, that she knew her stuff. In fact, he teased her that if things didn't work out between them romantically, he was interested in hiring her as a consultant. Without missing a beat, Lisa gibed back that, either way, she didn't come cheap.

As he made his way through the bustling, morning crowd, more memories came back to him and brought a smile to his face. He remembered how when they returned to New York, they began dating, but not for long. Exactly one month after meeting Lisa, De Niro proposed to her. He had taken her to her favorite restaurant downtown on West Broadway, "Barolo," where they had a romantic dinner and polished off the best bottle of their favorite Barolo wine.

Landing back at her apartment, he asked her, hypothetically, what she would say if he asked her to marry him. With her dry wit unaffected by the wine she drank, she replied that she'd ask for a "pre-nup" in case he was only interested in her money. With that, De Niro got on one knee and presented a box to her with the name "De Beers" written inside it. It contained the most beautiful engagement ring she ever saw – a flawless, round, 9-carat white diamond mounted in platinum. He joked to their friends later that that was the only time he ever saw Lisa speechless. They were married in the Bahamas three months later ... almost five years ago.

De Niro was well on his way to becoming one of the youngest billionaire hedge fund managers even before he met his wife. So when they finally decided to have children, the couple traded in their apartment in the city for a magnificent, sprawling estate in Colts Neck, New Jersey. Lisa left Cantor when she was seven months pregnant with Richard, their firstborn, but she continued to maintain her friendships with her colleagues there.

The De Niro's started a tradition of inviting Lisa's Cantor cronies to lavish barbeques at their Colts Neck home. They just had their Labor Day barbecue the weekend before, with dozens of friends from her old firm showing up for it, along with their spouses and kids. It was an extra special occasion because many of them found out for the first time, at the barbecue, that Lisa was pregnant with their third child, another son.

Making it even more special, Lisa's closest girlfriend Stacey, also pregnant, came to the barbecue. The two women started at Cantor around the same time and they quickly became best friends. Stacey was about to go on maternity leave herself. She invited Lisa to meet her at Cantor the following week, on September 11, which was to be her last day. Stacey was having her second baby and the girls were planning to meet up on the 104th floor to say hi to everyone and then go to breakfast.

The idea to buy Lisa roses occurred to De Niro during the limo ride to his mid-town financial firm. It all stemmed from his wife's desire to see him take a more active role in the lives of their two young sons, Richard and Louis. Lisa made him feel terribly about missing so many of the boys' important "firsts," like their first words spoken and their first steps taken. De Niro hated spending so much time away from them, working and traveling, but he reasoned to her that he was sacrificing time with the boys now, so that he could ensure their futures.

Lisa never agreed with his way of thinking though, arguing that the things he was missing couldn't be purchased for any amount of money. Finally, that morning, she put her foot down and insisted that he take their oldest son to his first day of pre-school.

At the time, he wasn't too happy about it, but seeing Richard walk into the classroom and introduce himself to the other boys and girls was priceless to him now. The experience really had a profound effect on him, enough that by the time he left the school, he was committed to spending more time with his boys. He was also definitely going to be there for all of the firsts of their new baby. The flowers were to thank Lisa for making him go and he thought he'd join his wife and Stacey for breakfast, so he could tell both of them all about it.

First, he had to move an important breakfast meeting he had scheduled with an overseas client. De Niro couldn't wait to see Lisa's face when he handed her the flowers in front of all of her friends up on the 104th floor.

As he entered the north tower from the mall, De Niro was having difficulty calling Maria, his executive assistant. He always seemed to have bad cell service whenever he was in the Trade Center, so he headed out of the front entrance. The further he walked from the building, the more bars he started to see until finally, the call went through when he was standing at the curb. It was a beautiful morning outside.

"Good morning, Mr. De Niro's office, Maria speaking, may I help you?"

"Maria, its Cris."

"Good morning Mr. De Niro." Maria Fernandez had been De Niro's executive assistant for the last six years, but no matter how often he asked her to, she didn't feel comfortable calling him by his first name.

"Hey, do me a favor; I'm down at the Trade Center and I want to take my wife to breakfast. Call David Nicholls and ask him if we can meet for lunch instead, today."

"Yes sir. What would you like me to tell Mr. Nicholls if he isn't available for lunch?"

"Well, he's returning to London tonight," De Niro thought out loud, "tell him that we can video conference tomorrow and that I'll buy him a pint next month, after I speak at the British conference."

"Very well, may I ask the occasion?"

De Niro smiled, "Lisa twisted my arm and made me take Richard to his first day of school this morning. It was so much fun!"

"How nice ...!" De Niro could hear the sincere excitement in Maria's voice. "How was it?! Was Richard nervous?"

"Maria, he was amazing! He walked into the classroom and started introducing himself, '*Hello, my name is Richard De Niro. What's your name?*'"

De Niro laughed, "He's not even three years old yet and already he sounded like he was running for President! He reminds me so much of his mother."

De Niro heard Maria laughing on the other end.

"It was really great. I was more nervous than he was. My wife is right, I'm missing too much. I cut my limo loose and bought Lisa flowers to thank her. I'll cab it up to the firm after breakfast."

"That was so thoughtful! Okay, I'll take care of Mr. Nicholls, have a nice breakfast with Mrs. De Niro and tell her I said hello!"

"Will do ..."

De Niro closed his phone and looked up to the top of the tower as he started walking back to it.

I hate tall buildings, I'm glad Lisa doesn't work up there anymore.

CHAPTER 2

ONE WORLD TRADE CENTER
NEW YORK, NEW YORK
8:46A.M., TUESDAY, SEPTEMBER 11, 2001

Making sure not to crush the long box of flowers he was carrying, De Niro entered through the revolving door of One World Trade Center. Starting down the lengthy corridor leading to the elevators, he heard the sound of a large jet. It was loud ... really loud, as if it were flying very low.

That's strange; you never hear planes overhead in Manhattan!

... And then all hell broke loose!

The tall building reeled then shook violently while somewhere high above, a thunderous rumbling caused the people in the lobby to cower. Confused, everyone remained still as the bedlam was followed by a brief, eerie moment of silence. No one had any idea what was happening. Then the rumbling started again, this time rapidly growing louder. A sense that something was fast approaching the lobby filled the air with apprehension.

Standing only a few feet ahead of him, a small oriental woman turned and looked at De Niro with an utter look of terror on her face. Just as she did, from behind her, it seemed like the devil himself spewed hellfire from his mouth! Blinding heat came belching out of the elevators and blasted down the corridor incinerating everything and everyone in its path. No one had time to react. The people closest to the elevators were vaporized while others farther away were set ablaze and literally bulldozed over by the tremendous ball of flame.

The fireball enveloped De Niro, lifting him off of his feet and propelling him backwards with such force that he smashed right through one of the large plate glass windows in the front of the building. When the blistering wind finally released him, the back of his head slammed against the pavement as his body came to rest, and then all he felt was pain.

Trying to remain conscious, De Niro smelled the sickly-sweet odor of burning clothes and flesh, he was on fire! He started rolling on the ground trying to put the blaze out on his arms and legs. Tearing his suit jacket off and throwing the burning garment, he used his hands to snuff out the flames on his trousers.

When he finally extinguished himself, De Niro was lying in the street surrounded by chards of glass and debris that had already begun falling from the top of the tower. An ice-cold sensation started spreading over the burned parts of his face and body when he heard shrieking.

The small oriental lady was rolling around on the floor about ten feet away from him. In agony, De Niro got to his feet and stumbled over to her. The back of her dress was still on fire, so he grabbed hold of it and tore it off of her, scorching his already burned hands in the process. He carried the dazed and badly injured lady over to the curb and sat her down as gently as he could. Both of them were shivering. No words were exchanged by either of them, but De Niro could see the look of gratitude in the pained woman's eyes.

De Niro stood there for a moment, trying to regain his senses and catch his breath when he heard the sound of his cell phone ringing from somewhere behind him. As quickly as he could, he made his way to his smoldering suit jacket and ripped the vibrating device out of the inside pocket. It was hot to the touch and looked partially melted and warped, but remarkably, it was still working. Unable to flip the phone open, he used both hands to pry it open. He saw that it was Lisa calling him. De Niro's heart started racing from a combination of anxious joy and relief as he put the phone to his ear.

"Lisa!"

"Cris, it's me."

"Honey, are you okay?!"

"Yeah, I'm okay. We're not sure what just happened. I'm here at Cantor with Stacey. We think a bomb might have just gone off in the tower somewhere."

De Niro's heart sank. When the phone rang and he saw it was his wife, he hoped that she might have already gone to breakfast and wasn't in the building. For the first time, he thought about what just happened. He remembered hearing the sound of a jet flying really low right before the whole world went crazy.

Is it possible? No reason to tell her a plane may have crashed into the building ... or that I'm injured.

"Honey, listen, can you and Stacey make it to a stairway?"

"Hold on," she replied. Then he heard his wife ask, "My husband wants to know if we can make it to the stairs?"

De Niro heard a number of voices in the background, including at least one male voice, but he couldn't tell who they were. Finally, she answered, "No, Cris, we're all huddled inside a conference room with the door closed. There was smoke coming in under it, so someone stuffed their jacket there to try and stop it, but I don't think we can open that door."

De Niro heard the sound of people coughing in the background as one of the male voices was saying something. Then Lisa continued, "Cris, the smoke is getting worse in here. A few of the men want to break the windows to let air in. We tried to call 9-11 but we can't get through. No one knows what to do!"

De Niro heard the tension building in his wife's voice. One of the things he loved about Lisa was how cool she was in pressure situations. Lisa came from a military family. Her granddad and dad both served with distinction, in the army and her brother was a Navy SEAL. One thing was for sure, as De Niro's dad, a Marine, once put it, Lisa was no "candy-ass." He knew that conditions had to be dire up there for her to sound that nervous.

De Niro felt determination run through his veins but he also felt something else, something he never felt before. His whole life, whenever he put his mind to achieving a goal, he accomplished it, without fear of failure or any doubt, no matter how difficult it might be. Looking up at the towering structure before him now, with smoke pouring out of it and his wife's life at stake, for the first time in his life De Niro doubted himself ... he was afraid.

"Alright, listen, honey, I'm gonna try and make my way up to you. Just stay in that room!"

"Make your way up to me ... Cris, where are you?!"

"I'm right in front of the building ... After I dropped Richard off ... I was going to surprise you ..." De Niro had to hold back his own tears as he heard the sound of tears in his wife's voice, "Oh Cris ... is it safe enough for you to come up—"

De Niro waited a moment for his wife to continue but all he heard was silence.

"Lisa, are you there?! Lisa ... honey are you there?!"

He took the phone from his ear and examined it – there were no lights – it was dead. After popping the battery out and replacing it with no results, he threw the useless device to the ground in frustration. It shattered into pieces joining the rest of the debris scattered everywhere.

Making his way back towards the revolving front doors, De Niro surveyed the area as he went. It looked like a bomb went off in the lobby of Tower One. Virtually every window was blown out and there was wreckage littered and accumulating all over the street in front of the building. As bad as it was outside, inside was a horror scene!

As he staggered inside, De Niro heard screams coming from down the corridor. He stood in shock, in the same spot in which he and the oriental lady were standing just minutes before. There were bodies strewn everywhere, all of them scorched, some smoldering, others ablaze. The screams he heard came from a woman who looked like she was trying to run away from the fire coming from the back of her jacket and skirt. As she ran past him, De Niro wanted to help her but he knew he couldn't catch up to her in his physical state. Besides, all he could think about now was getting to Lisa.

Realizing that the fireball came from the elevator shafts, De Niro entered the stairwell. He gazed up and took a deep breath.

Please Father, let her be alive!

Starting up the stairs in a panic, De Niro overruled the objections of pain that his brain was shouting to him, but after the first few flights it was slow going. As he made it to the 20th floor, he began to see a regular stream of people heading down the stairs. Some were injured while others looked unharmed. He stepped in front of one man who appeared okay.

"Hey, what floor are you coming from?"

The man was repulsed by the sight of De Niro, bloody and burned. He tried to push past him without answering, but even in his weakened state, De Niro's resolve to get to Lisa gave him enough strength to block his way.

"I asked you what floor you came from!"

"The eightieth," the man replied breaking down the stairs the moment De Niro let him pass.

De Niro bent over resting his hands on his thighs and took a few deep breaths. He was exhausted, his head was bleeding and he was shivering from his burns, but he felt new energy course through him.

If he was able to make it down the stairs from the 80th floor, maybe Lisa and the others made their way out of that room and I'll see her coming down the stairs soon, too!

By the time he made it to the 30th floor, De Niro was climbing at a snail's pace clinging to the staircase railings, leaving a trail of blood on them. It took him almost an hour just to reach floor thirty and he was already drenched in cold sweat that stung the burns on his face and back. People continued filing passed, heading down the stairwell, some warning him to turn around.

He heard one lady say, "Its hell up there!"

It was all becoming surreal to him. The people descending

the stairs were so diverse; some were women, some men; some old, some young; and some injured while others didn't have a scratch on them. It also occurred to him that everyone was relatively quiet. The fear and shock on their faces was obvious, but no one was panicking.

Resuming his ascent, De Niro felt a hand on his shoulder. Fireman Keith Tompkins, a tall dark-skinned African American man, wearing full gear with an oxygen tank strapped to his back was, like him, also drenched in sweat. The fireman was carrying a coiled fire hose and he looked as out-of-breath as De Niro was. Tompkins scanned De Niro and saw that he was badly injured.

"Hey buddy, you can't go up there. You need to get out of the building with the rest of these people."

De Niro shook his head in defiance, pointing up the stairs.

"My wife is up there!"

"What floor is she on?" Tompkins asked.

De Niro hesitated, "She's ... she's on the 104th floor at Cantor Fitzgerald!"

For a moment, the two locked eyes, the fireman's were filled with regret.

De Niro pulled from Tompkins' grasp and took a few steps up when he heard a voice break through the static coming from the fireman's walkie-talkie.

"Command post in Tower One to all units, evacuate the building!"

The two men locked eyes again. Both men knew the evacuation order sealed the fates of everyone trapped upstairs. De Niro's eyebrows clenched in anger and defiance. The fireman knew this husband would die trying to save his wife. Before he could turn away, Tompkins tried a different approach.

"Do you have kids?!"

The question caught De Niro by surprise. Up until then, he was only thinking about Lisa. He felt his eyes swell with tears. People pushed past both of them as Tompkins stepped up close to him and repeated the question, "Do you have kids?"

De Niro's throat tightened up so much he couldn't speak. Tears fell from his eyes as the point of the fireman's question pierced his heart; all he could do was nod.

"What's your name?"

"... Cris."

"Cris, my name is Keith. Cris, it's time you thought about your kids. What's your wife's name?"

De Niro couldn't hold back his tears as his emotions overtook him, "... Lisa."

Tompkins leaned over and spoke right into his ear, "What do you think Lisa would want you to do?"

De Niro turned and looked back up the stairs. Blood from the bruises on his head dripped into his eyes as tears fell from them. He bit his lower lip to try and stop it from quivering as he pictured Lisa in that moment, smiling as she always smiled at him, with glittering eyes and her dimpled cheek. Every moment they spent together from the first moment they met, all flashed through his brain. For an instant, everything went quiet and time stopped. He felt his heart beating, pounding ... then breaking. As his wife's image faded, he mouthed the words, *I love you!*

De Niro knew he couldn't make it all the way up to the 104th floor in his condition, but he was content to die trying. That is, until he was reminded of Richard and Louis. He turned back to Tompkins, standing patiently a step below him and nodded in defeat. Understanding, Tompkins discarded the fire hose and put his arm around De Niro's waist to aid him down the stairs.

Thoughts raced through De Niro's mind, too fast for him to make any sense of them as he felt himself descending, mostly being carried by the fatigued fireman. By the twentieth floor, both men were worn out but they pressed on, and by the tenth they were stumbling down the stairs as the last of the people behind them pushed past them. It took them over twenty minutes to reach the lobby. When they finally did, the fireman let go of De Niro and both men collapsed to their knees.

De Niro noticed Tompkins look over to the far corner of the lobby as they both caught their breath. After a moment, the tall man shot to his feet with a look of grave concern on his face. It occurred to De Niro also that something was very wrong. There was no one in the lobby, not a single living soul and it looked like a dust storm had blown down the corridors since he was last there. Tompkins observed that even the temporary command center had been abandoned. He reached down and lifted De

Niro from under his arm.

"Come on, we got to get out of this building now!"

Using the last remnants of his will power, De Niro got to his feet and staggered after his rescuer. As they made it to the front doors of Tower One, it was apparent that something very bad must have happened while they were in the building. There was no way for them to know that the South Tower had already fallen.

De Niro didn't know if his eyesight was blurry and causing everything to look ghostly, but the chalky taste in his mouth made him know it was all too real. It looked like a nuclear bomb was detonated outside! In the distance, people were wandering aimlessly like those who survive a plane crash sometimes do. You couldn't tell the color of their skin because they were all covered with a thick white powder. As far as the eye could see ... the ground, the cars, everything was coated in a dirty, pallid ash.

De Niro and Tompkins started to exit the building when a fireman standing across the street waved his hands and yelled, "GET BACK!"

The two men scrambled back into the revolving doors just in time to hear two loud, horrific thuds. Unsure of what caused them, they wandered out to investigate and realized the situation had turned gruesome. As if in a nightmare, they discovered they were standing amidst the mutilated, flattened corpses of men and women, who had either fallen or jumped to their deaths from high up. Their badly mangled bodies now lay contorted in shallow craters created by the impacts from their fall. De Niro felt sick. He could see that the ghastly site deeply affected Fireman Tompkins too; a man who witnessed his share of horrific things.

Every one of them was someone's husband or wife, mom or dad, son or daughter, all who less than an hour ago were alive and well. Please let none of them be Lisa!

After taking in the total devastation and carnage, De Niro's strength finally gave out. He couldn't keep his eyes focused any longer from his head injury and his knees buckled underneath him from his blood loss and exhaustion. Sweat-soaked and near collapse himself, Tompkins strained to lift him up.

The shell-shocked firefighter lumbered into the middle of West Street with De Niro thrown over his shoulder. Walkie-talkie chatter emanated from all directions as he made his way north through the trashed landscape. West Street was lined on both sides with vehicles of every type, some completely covered in powdery-white cinders.

De Niro was barely able to lift is head up to look around.

What in hell happened? This couldn't all be from a plane crash?

Tompkins made it less than a half-block, plodding through wreckage strewn all over the usually traffic-infested thoroughfare when the ground started shaking under his feet. From behind him, a sound erupted like a herd of stampeding cattle.

Twisting around and peering up towards the top of the tower they just exited, Tompkins couldn't believe his eyes. The once-mighty building was collapsing, its roof, along with its famous antenna racing down towards the ground at a furious pace.

Grunting and breathing heavily with each step, the lanky fireman did his best to sprint away from the crumpling structure. He only made it part way down the street before the menacing cloud billowing from the mountain of rubble - that only a moment ago was one of the tallest buildings on earth – a pitch black, monstrous fog - overtook them.

At the last moment, Tompkins threw De Niro in front of a parked car and then fell on top of him to protect him. Immediately, an enormous storm of soot enveloped them. From within it, building fragments pelted the fireman's heavy overcoat and helmet while paperwork from the desks of people in the tower rained down like macabre confetti during a parade, ending up on the ground all around them.

Blinded, the two men lay in the gutter, coughing and gasping for air as daylight turned to the blackest night. De Niro could feel the cold blackness creep inside his heart as a torrent of wind whistled pass them. The enormity of what just happened and what it meant – hit him.

Lisa was gone.

"LISSSAAA ...!"

"LISSAA ...!" De Niro shouted again, this time his voice broke down from grief.

Tompkins lifted himself off of De Niro and kneeled beside him. His nostrils flared as his eyes, too, became watery; the power of hearing a man crying out for his wife, in anguish, overcame the seasoned firefighter.

Slipping into unconsciousness, De Niro's last thoughts were a prayer.

Please Father; let it be that she didn't suffer!

CHAPTER 3

DOS ESCUELAS PARK
HENDERSON, NEVADA

11:30A.M., SATURDAY, MAY 14, 2011
(ALMOST 10 YEARS LATER)

"WAIT FOR A GOOD ONE, LOUIS!" De Niro shouted to his youngest son.

Both De Niro's boys played for the same team, the Paseo Verde Yankees. 10 year-old Louis was the team's catcher while his soon-to-be 12 year-old brother Richard was one of their starting pitchers. Standing at the plate, Louis heard his dad's advice from the bleachers and nodded in his direction. He smashed the next pitch past the shortstop.

De Niro jumped to his feet.

"WAY TO GO!"

Standing next to De Niro, his brother-in-law, Captain Louis "Mugsy" Ricci USN (SEAL) Ret. used his fingers to emit a loud whistle of celebration. His sister Lisa had given him his nickname when he was very young and it stuck – even his parents called him Mugsy. Formerly Commanding Officer of the Naval Special Warfare Center, where all Navy SEALS undergo basic and advanced training, Mugsy Ricci was just getting used to writing the "Ret-period" after his name.

After just completing his twenty-third year with the SEALS, he surprised more than a few fellow officers and friends with his decision to "hang up his spurs," as they put it. Borrowing a line from one of his favorite movies, "The Godfather," Ricci simply told them that his brother-in-law Cris had *made him an offer he couldn't refuse.*

The truth was, De Niro had called him a few months before, to ask him if he'd be interested in heading an anti-terrorism consulting firm he was about to acquire. If it were anyone else asking or any other position being offered, Ricci would have declined, but it was Cris De Niro doing the asking and the position was ideal for him.

Other than the fact that De Niro was a billionaire and one of the most respected businessmen in the world, he had also been married to his sister ... and family was everything to Italians. As for the job, from the time the Muslim terrorists had murdered Lisa, Ricci was committed to dedicating the rest of his life to fighting terrorism. His service in the SEALS helped him deal with his grief, though he couldn't shake the guilt of not being able to protect his sister and the rest of those who lost their lives on September 11, 2001.

For the first several years after 9/11, Ricci had taken part in countless covert operations with the SEALS in Afghanistan, Iraq and other places to be left unnamed. He was awarded eleven different military decorations during that time, including: the Medal of Honor, Silver Star, Purple Heart, Commendation Medal, and Combat Action Ribbon. A victim of his own success, the Navy also rewarded him with a promotion to Captain and put him in command of the Naval Special Warfare Center. The problem was that running NSWC placed Captain Ricci behind a desk far too often for his liking.

De Niro hadn't explained all the specifics of the position, but his brother-in-law did confirm that he would be completely in charge. All Ricci cared about was that he would have the authority to decide who would take part in any operations - meaning he was going to be back in the game, not just coaching from the sidelines. He found out after accepting the position that it paid three times his captain's salary. Ricci told his brother-in-law he would have taken the job for minimum wage. De Niro replied that he was happy that Uncle Mugsy could finally afford all the gifts he bought for Richard and Louis.

It took Ricci only three months to resign his commission - typically a person had to submit the paperwork six months out. As soon as the Navy gave him their approval, he packed his bags and per instructions from his brother-in-law, used his new corporate credit card to book his moving van and first-class plane fare to Las Vegas McCarran. With his new salary, he could afford to buy a small mansion of his own but De Niro told him he was welcome to stay in one of the estate's guest houses for as long as he wanted.

Ricci liked being close to his sister's boys and he suspected that his brother-in-law liked his company too. He was well aware that De Niro had virtually no social life apart from raising his sons, since Lisa died. He knew that there was only one person who was more devastated than he was about his sister's death ... and that was Cris.

De Niro told him that they were scheduled to fly east to meet the staff of the firm he just purchased, on Monday. That gave them the entire weekend to spend with the boys.

As both men sat back down, an attractive blond-haired woman took a seat on the bleachers right in front of them.

Ricci nudged De Niro.

"Do you know her?"

"Uh-huh," De Niro replied keeping his eyes on Louis at second base.

"What's her name?"

Before De Niro could reply, the boy at-bat hit a long fly ball to right field.

De Niro jumped back to his feet and started yelling to Louis, "RUN!"

Ricci jumped up too. It took him a moment to figure out

what happened.

"GO LOUIS!"

Running as fast as he could, De Niro's youngest son slid under the tag of the opposing catcher, a boy twice his size. After making sure he touched home plate, the umpire extended his arms.

"SAFE!"

The Yankees bleachers erupted in cheers as Louis's run ended the game with a Yankees victory. His teammates stormed out of the dugout and swarmed around him.

While some of the other parents started exiting the bleachers, De Niro remained where he was and motioned for his brother-in-law to join him.

"Hang here for a few minutes. Their coach likes to talk to them in the dugout after each game. Then we'll head back to my house. I invited the whole team and their parents to a back yard barbecue."

Ricci nodded again towards the woman sitting in front of them.

"So, what's her name?"

De Niro sighed with an audible exhale.

"Her name is Lauren, she's a mom of one the boys' teammates."

"Where's her husband?"

De Niro shook his head knowing where his brother-in-law was leading with his line of questions.

"She's divorced."

"Did you invite her to the barbecue?"

The woman stood up and started walking down the bleachers as he asked the question. Moving quickly, Ricci intercepted her and offered his hand.

"Hi, I'm Louis. Richard and Louis ... on the team are my nephews."

"Nice to meet you, I'm Lauren."

"Cris De Niro is my brother-in-law. Do you two know each other?"

Joining them, De Niro answered.

"As a matter of fact, we do. Pay no mind to him Lauren, my

brother-in-law is a former Navy Seal and they tend to be a little ... high strung."

Lauren smiled at De Niro.

"Is that so? Well in that case ..."

Ricci shot De Niro an angry look.

"Uh, Lauren, do you know about the barbecue Cris invited everyone to?"

"Yes, the coach told me about it."

"Will we see you there?"

Lauren beamed a big smile, more to De Niro than his brother-in-law.

"I wouldn't miss it for the world!"

De Niro returned her smile but didn't reply, so Ricci did.

"Great, we'll see you there."

As soon as the striking blond was out of earshot, De Niro punched his brother-in-law in the arm.

"What?"

"What was that all about?"

"Cris, are you blind?! Lauren is drop-dead beautiful ... AND she's available!"

Paying no mind to him, De Niro made his way over to his sons. Fist-punching both, he grabbed Louis around his shoulders.

"Now, THAT'S the way to run bases! Richard, did you see your brother drop it into high gear!"

Ricci wouldn't give up.

"Cris, you have to be blind if you don't move on her at the barbecue!"

"Who are you talking about, Uncle Mugs?" asked De Niro's oldest son, Richard.

"One of your teammate's moms is super-hot and she's coming to the barbecue. I was just telling your dad that he's an idiot if he doesn't try to move on her."

"You didn't say I was an idiot, you said I was blind."

"Same thing," Ricci shot back.

"Is she nice, Daddy?" Louis asked.

"What does *that* matter, Louis?!" Richard snapped at his younger brother.

Ricci admonished his oldest nephew, "Hey Richard, take it easy!"

It was obvious Richard didn't want his dad to even look at another woman. Louis, on the other hand, didn't seem to mind.

Richard glared in fury at his uncle, as De Niro tried to put an end to the whole topic.

"Hey, Mugsy and Richard ... Louis asked me the question. Louis, to answer your question, yes, she's a very nice lady, but I have absolutely no interest in, as your fool-of-an-uncle puts it, 'moving on her.'"

The boys threw their bags into the back of De Niro's Cadillac Escalade and everyone got in.

Ricci buckled himself in and grumbled.

"You're crazy! That woman is drop-dead gorgeous, she's nice, she's hot ... she's got the greatest smile ... the greatest personality and ..."

"... and she's not my type," De Niro interrupted.

"Yeah," Ricci shot back, "and what is your type?"

De Niro didn't reply prompting his brother-in-law to mutter in frustration.

"... yeah, yeah, I know your type ... my sister ... my DEAD sister is your only type!"

De Niro remained quiet. A moment later Ricci regretted what he said.

"I'm sorry Cris ... it's just ... you shouldn't be alone. For the boys, you shouldn't be alone!"

"Don't bring us into it, Uncle Mugs!" Richard shouted from the back seat.

Ricci turned to face the boys.

"But wouldn't you guys like to have a mommy?"

"We have a mommy!" Richard snapped, "She's just sleeping, is all!"

Ricci turned to see De Niro grinning. He threw his hands up in mock defeat.

"I give up. I think you're all crazy!"

De Niro adjusted his rear-view mirror so he could look right at Richard. The boy and his dad's eyes met and De Niro winked at him bringing a smile to Richard's face. De Niro reached over and patted his brother-in-law's shoulder.

"You know, Mugs, I think Lauren was impressed when I told her you were a former SEAL."

Ricci was about to reply when he caught himself.

To that, both boys and their dad laughed and after a moment, so did their uncle.

CHAPTER 4

ESTANCIA DE NIRO (THE DE NIRO RANCH)
HENDERSON, NEVADA
12:30P.M., SATURDAY, MAY 14, 2011

About a year after 9/11, De Niro decided he could no longer live back east. There were just too many memories of Lisa there. His wife was such a charismatic and social person that her presence and her absence seemed to permeate every facet of his existence – from their favorite restaurants and shops to just sitting on the front porch of their home. Their magnificent estate, their beautiful community, their friends and neighbors – none of it brought any joy to De Niro anymore. He knew he had to relocate, especially while Richard and Louis were still young, so he chose a place that made him happiest when he was a boy. His dad was a hard-working man that had only one vice – he liked to gamble. His old man told him though, that once he married his mom, he'd never gamble again unless he could do so with money they didn't need – and then only in a place like Las Vegas, lest he'd be tempted all the time. So once a year, every year, his dad would take his mom and young Cris to Las Vegas. He couldn't remember even one trip when he didn't have the best time.

When De Niro got older he continued to meet his parents out in Las Vegas during their annual jaunts. In fact, it was in Las Vegas during one of those trips that he introduced his parents to Lisa. She and he used to talk about moving there when they got older and the boys moved out. Even after her passing, that dream didn't die in his mind. So one day, after praying for guidance, he just boarded his Global Aviation jet with his boys, flew to Las Vegas and never looked back.

When they arrived, De Niro checked them into a suite at a resort then spent every day looking for property. It didn't take long for several of the top real estate agents to get wind of his search. They each tried in vain to lure him to buy one of their exclusive "golf course" properties, where the estates abutted a picturesque hole of one of the private country club courses near the Strip, but De Niro had other plans. He finally settled on buying a 250,000-acre property southeast of the Strip. Most of the real estate agents thought he was crazy for selecting that parcel of land but it was exactly what he wanted. To the north, it offered a fabulous panorama of the entire Las Vegas valley. To the south there were miles of rough, rugged, hilly terrain, and to the west, magnificent views of the sunset. De Niro had constructed a sprawling hacienda-fortress complete with a 30,000 square-foot ranch-style home, modeled after the posh "estancia" ranch homes that he and Lisa loved so much in Argentina; a 4,000 square-foot guest house and 3,000 square-foot butler's mansion; casita-sized abodes for the hacienda staff members and additional guests, with a community pool and work-out facilities just for ranch staff, and stables for his horses. He converted fifty acres of the land into an organic garden and farm to grow all of his own fruits and vegetables and another one hundred-fifty acres to raise his own cattle, chickens, turkeys, goats and lambs.

There were horse trails leading to all parts of "Estancia De Niro," the name his head "gaucho," Martin Fierro, gave to the ranch. De Niro met Martin in Argentina at a horse and cattle auction a decade ago. Although an accomplished rider himself, De Niro had never seen anyone better with horses – riding them, training them, and caring for them, than Martin. He knew that gauchos were considered undesirables in modern-day Argentina but he never paid attention to stereotypes of any sort. His dad taught him to head the words of Dr. Martin Luther King Jr. - to judge each man by ... *the content of his character* and so De Niro offered Martin an opportunity to come to work for him, to run his stables. At first, Martin turned him down because he didn't want to leave his wife and children in Argentina, but he was overjoyed when De Niro paid to relocate his entire family with him. That made Fierro extremely loyal to "Don" De Niro.

As was all of their staff, Martin was broken-hearted from the murder of Señora Lisa, so much so, that he told De Niro that he would gladly fly to the hills of Pakistan to find and kill Osama Bin Laden himself. Though De Niro turned down his offer, it wasn't because he didn't think Martin had the skills. He knew the man was equally proficient riding a horse, tracking, shooting a rifle and pistol, wielding a knife and tossing a lariat, but De Niro also knew with his Latin blood, he might very well start a war all on his own.

The horse trails also lead to a remote area where De Niro had a compound built deep within the foothills themselves. The only people that knew its location were his sons and his Personal Assistant William Brett, a transplanted proper English butler who Lisa had hired when they first moved to Colts Neck.

William was the butler for a British friend of De Niro's, a member of the royal line, who was known as a playboy and daredevil. While Lisa thought Cris's friend was a bit of an egocentric fool, she was impressed by William. When news reached them of the royal's death in a boat-racing accident, De Niro and Lisa flew to London, De Niro to attend his friend's funeral and Lisa to solicit William to come work for them. Although William was taken care of quite handsomely in his master's will and had no interest in living in the United States, he took a liking to Lisa. As she was prone to do, Lisa finally got her way when she persuaded William by telling him that she was pregnant - with Richard, at the time - and that he could heal some of the loss he was feeling - he practically raised his former master from childbirth and was taking his loss as one would, losing a son - by helping to raise her children.

William had the utmost respect for Lisa and took her death with the heaviest of hearts. After her funeral, his loyalty to De Niro grew when De Niro offered him the opportunity to become his Personal Assistant. William also became fiercely devoted to Richard and Louis after their mother's death. In fact, De Niro would entrust no one else with his sons – even making sure to stipulate that in his will.

Martin and William were the two men De Niro most relied upon. They had both remained with him and his sons through their most trying and depressed times. They not only looked after him but they were fiercely protective of Richard and Louis, partially a result of 9/11. Just as De Niro did, William and Martin both harbored irrational guilt about not protecting Lisa that day. They were two very different men, but they shared an unbridled loyalty to De Niro and the boys. They also shared mutual respect for one another but you could never get either of them to admit that out loud.

Since 9/11, De Niro tried desperately hard to make sense of it all. His Italian-Spanish blood boiled as his old neighborhood temperament demanded revenge, but something else had taken root in his life too. In the middle of the night and in solitude, he found himself on his knees praying to his Father in Heaven, calling out as a boy does for his Father to save him from what lurked in the darkness around him ... and the darkness inside him. Night after night, after tucking his sons in, he'd cry his eyes out. It was as if a deep crater formed in his heart, in the place where Lisa was ripped from it. That hole, as deep as his soul, was filling with self-pity and rage and both were consuming him. De Niro sensed the cold presence of demons in his midst, waiting for an invitation to let them dwell with him. Something had to give ... and it did, on the first anniversary of Lisa's death, on the first anniversary of 9/11, De Niro felt himself die.

While the rest of the country mourned and kept vigil; the masses comforting each other with their tears and their prayers,

De Niro spent the day locked in his room, missing Lisa so badly he could no longer breathe. Not even looking at the faces of his children could save him. He lashed out as someone would if they were suffocating to death, breaking everything in his reach. Shelves once filled with photos of his wife lay shattered and lying around him in tatters. With his arms and hands bloody and his face covered in sweat and tears, he fell into a deep, dead slumber. It was only when rays of sunshine broke through his bedroom window and touched his face the next morning that he realized he was still alive; he had survived the night, but it was more than that.

De Niro felt reborn, not of the same kind that some Christians professed, with their hands poked out to the heavens hollering, *"I accepted Jay-zus and he saved me,"* as if they had already arrived in the Kingdom. De Niro didn't feel like he arrived anywhere, yet. It was more like he was setting off on a new path, one without his soulmate Lisa, but nevertheless one that he wouldn't travel alone. And though the rage inside him didn't abate, over time he believed his newfound faith would teach him how to harness its power. De Niro learned he could live with his wounded heart if he dedicated the rest of his life to honoring her memory. The focus of his life would no longer be just making money; it would be putting all of his vast wealth to work for a purpose. Lisa and he had always given to charities. He continued that giving by setting up a trust in her name but he had to do more. While his primary focus was his sons, he vowed to do more.

The terrorists made it personal on 9/11. As they always do, they targeted civilians. To them, no American is innocent. It didn't matter that they murdered people from over seventy different countries on 9/11, they considered them collateral damage. It didn't matter that some of their own faith would have to commit suicide to get the job done; to them they would be rewarded in heaven. It made De Niro furious. He felt that his country let him down on 9/11 too. To him, democrats and republicans alike politicized our nation's security, their ideologies once again colliding like a train wreck. This time though, the result wasn't higher taxes or unemployment, this time innocent lives were lost. Nevertheless, De Niro was still a patriot, he just didn't feel patriotic anymore – the fireworks on the fourth of July would never burn as brightly to him as the candle he lit each year, in remembrance of his wife and the others that lost their lives on 9/11.

The most difficult thing De Niro had to come to terms with was his faith. At first, he studied scriptures looking for a loophole – some tenet that would allow him to strike back at the people that murdered Lisa, but there were none. In fact, De Niro's God, the Christian God commanded that vengeance was His and His alone. So that he would never forget that, he hung a plaque over his desk in his office that had a verse from the Apostle Paul's letter to the Ephesians engraved in brass. It read, *"Be angry, and do no sin: do not let the sun go down on your wrath"* (Ephesians 4:26). That left no room for interpretation, no room for "old neighborhood" ethics. Revenge was out of the question, if De Niro were to keep to his faith, so he continued to study his Bible and prayed that he would find something that would allow him to channel his rage in a righteous direction. The more he studied, the more he felt that God was giving him the ability to understand prophecy. De Niro focused on prophecies concerning the United States. He learned that since Jacob was renamed Israel, all of his offspring were Israel. Each of Jacob's sons became a tribe and each tribe eventually would become nations of people. Jacob's son Joseph had twin sons of his own. They were Manasseh and Ephraim. The descendants of those two tribes became Great Britain and the United States. The prophecies of Ephraim became his obsession.

De Niro drove around the long circular driveway and pulled up to the front of his sprawling hacienda. There were already several cars parked here and there, most likely parents and kids from the Yankees who got a head start to his home. De Niro's ranch was well known to most everyone in his community. Without Lisa though, De Niro didn't socialize much. She was the one that volunteered in their community and was known by all of their neighbors. As a result, most people who lived nearby were curious to see the ranch and jumped at any chance to visit it.

William was standing outside with a few of the other

hacienda staff. One of them opened the passenger doors to the Escalade as William opened the driver's door. The boys jumped out and grabbed their own bags from the trunk - De Niro and William were on the same page about raising the boys to pull their own weight, including tending to chores and taking care of their things.

As De Niro and his brother-in-law exited the vehicle a young Mexican man named Concho jumped into the driver's seat. Concho was the head mechanic on the estancia. De Niro hired him after he caught him trying to steal one of his most expensive sports cars. While waiting for the police, De Niro engaged Concho in conversation, in Spanish. He was greatly impressed by the young man's knowledge of automobiles in general and of his fleet of vehicles in particular. They both shared a love of finely made machines. By the time the police arrived, De Niro had dropped the charges and offered Concho a job as mechanic. Within a year he was put in charge of De Niro's entire fleet of vehicles. Concho had a small team assigned to him, all of them family members of his. Together they maintained all of De Niro's sports cars, SUV's, one stretch limo, off-road vehicles, farm tractors and equipment, trail bikes, motorcycles, boats - De Niro owned three, a luxury yacht he kept docked in Newport Beach, CA and a speed boat and fishing boat he transported back and forth to Lake Mead, jet skis, as well as De Niro's Rolls Royce Corniche Convertible, his Bentley Azure Convertible Mulliner and his favorite, a midnight blue (with white racing stripes) Shelby GT500 Mustang that Carroll Shelby's Special Performance Plant in Las Vegas rebuilt into a 725 hp "Super Snake."

De Niro liked the passion he saw in the young man.

"¿Hola hombre, que pasa?"

"¿No mucho, cómo es usted jefe? Replied a grinning Concho as he sped away, kicking up a little dust to William's dismay.

De Niro put his hand on William's back as they walked into the hacienda.

"Is everything under control with the barbeque?"

"Yes sir, people started arriving about five minutes ago. I'm having them escorted around the side of the hacienda."

"Very good, did the Tompkins family arrive yet?"

"No, sir. Their plane should have just touched down. I sent Edgar with the limousine to meet them."

"Excellent, it's always great to see my godson."

About a month after 9/11, Fireman Keith Tompkins, the man who saved De Niro's life on 9/11, received a call from De Niro thanking him for his heroism. Tompkins told him it was all part of the job but De Niro would have none of that. As he was on the phone, Tompkins' doorbell rang. De Niro told him to answer the door while he remained on the phone with him. The man at the door identified himself as "Michael Anthony," (De Niro told Tompkins later he got the idea from the old TV show, "The Millionaire") and handed Tompkins a letter containing a note of thanks from De Niro. Inside the note was a certified check for one million dollars, tax-free. It took De Niro more time and effort than he thought it would to convince Tompkins that it wasn't a prank. The two men were close friends ever since, mostly keeping in touch by email, text messages and the occasional phone call. De Niro also made it a point to meet up with Tompkins every year, on September 11. They both attended memorial services down at "Ground Zero," as it was now known, with other survivors as well as family and friends of victims.

Tompkins had honored De Niro by naming his second child after him and asking him to be his godfather. De Niro looked forward to seeing young Cris every year and taking him to a Yankees game with his dad. This was the first time that Tompkins and his family were visiting Las Vegas. Tompkins surprised De Niro with the visit and was intending to stay at a Strip hotel, but De Niro insisted that he and his family all stay at Estancia De Niro. De Niro's brother-in-law Mugsy was staying in the large guest house but he immediately offered it to the Tompkins family and moved into one of the smaller casitas for the duration of their stay.

De Niro walked into his large kitchen and grabbed two Stella Artois tall neck beers from one of his refrigerators. He popped the caps on both and handed one to his brother-in-law. Both men walked out onto the large patio in the back of the house and sat down at one of the tables. William had assigned Aurelio and his brother Arturo, two of the best cooks on De Niro's whole staff, to man the two large grills. They were already turning out steaks, chicken, hamburgers and hot dogs. Aurelio's wife Rosita prepared a variety of Mexican dishes – tacos, burritos, tamales, enchiladas – and she had a fajita station set up along with a table filled with salads, chips, pretzels and dips. To drink, there was beer, wine, sangria, soda, lemonade and water and for dessert there would be ice cream and toasting marshmallows over the grills. Music was playing throughout the whole yard area and Richard and Louis were inviting their friends to change into their bathing suits and join them in their large pool. Some of the other dad's and the coaches came by and clanked their bottles of beer against De Niro's thanking him for his hospitality. De Niro was gracious to everyone but he excused himself when William told him that the Tompkins family had arrived.

"Mugsy, let's welcome Keith and Yvonne."

"This is the first time I'll get to meet them away from the 9/11 services," Ricci said, as he got up from his chair.

Both men made it the front door just as Tompkins, his wife Yvonne, his daughter Kendra and his son Cris were walking from the car. The kids ran right past De Niro after giving him a hug, heading for the back.

"They heard about the party from Edgar." Tompkins said as he shook De Niro's hand. The two men hugged and patted each other on their backs and then Tompkins and Ricci did the same.

"The kids are getting bigger every time I see them. I'm gonna be looking up at my godson pretty soon, I think!"

After kissing and hugging Yvonne, De Niro moved aside to allow Ricci to do the same.

"The boys were so excited that you all were coming to visit."

"I hope we're not an inconvenience, Cris. You know we could stay on the Strip and just visit you here," Yvonne said slipping her arm around De Niro's as he led them to the yard through the house.

"Not a chance. Besides, it's not like we're cramped here." De Niro winked as he said it. "I put you up in the main guest house. There's an SUV parked in the driveway with the keys in it. You can use it to get around town, or if you prefer, Edgar is available to take you anywhere you want to go in the limo."

De Niro motioned William over.

"Keith and Yvonne Tompkins, I'd like to introduce you to my Personal Assistant, William Brett."

William bowed slightly and then offered his hand to both.

"It's a pleasure to meet you sir ... madam."

"If you need anything, just ask for William. He runs things here on the ranch."

"The only thing I need is a nice cool glass of sangria and to see your two cuties!" Yvonne replied as she headed out to the patio.

After the three men fetched an assortment of food onto their plates, De Niro led them back to the table where he and his brother-in-law had been sitting. William brought them three ice-cold tall necks.

"So, I have to say, Keith, I was surprised when you told me you were coming to visit."

"It was long overdue, Cris. Yvonne and the kids have been after me forever to bring them out here. Cris Junior talks to your boys through their X-Box games and all I hear is, 'Daddy, we HAVE to go out there, Richard and Louis say it's SO nice out there!' Besides, I ... wanted to talk to you about something."

"... Everything okay with your family?"

"Everything's fine with us. You saw to that, Cris. The house is paid off, so are the cars and we have college savings accounts set up for Kendra and Junior. I finally broke down and let Yvonne go on a shopping spree for herself. Even with all that money in the bank, I still got indigestion when I saw the credit card bill."

De Niro winked at Ricci as both men laughed. De Niro cut a piece of steak on his plate and savored it in his mouth then he washed it down with a swig of beer.

"I told you years ago to do that. The money's yours Keith. I'm not gonna ask for it back, you know."

"I know. It was the greatest gift ... I just needed time to adjust to it. Yvonne, on the other hand, didn't need any time."

The men laughed again. De Niro took another swig of his beer.

"So, how's life at the firehouse, now that you're a lieutenant and congratulations, again, on your promotion."

"It's got its ups and downs. I don't think I want to make captain. I have another two years before I make twenty, then I think I'll call it quits."

"Well, I'm glad to hear that. I know from personal experience that being one of New York's bravest is one of the most dangerous jobs. They definitely don't pay firemen enough."

De Niro could see that something was on his friend's mind.

"So Keith, what did you want to talk to me about?"

Keith flashed a quick look at Ricci who was busy eating his sizzling steak fajita.

"Could we take a walk, Cris? Do you mind Mugsy?"

Ricci barely looked up from his food.

"Not at all brother, go to it!"

Both men stood up and De Niro nodded to Keith to follow him. De Niro grabbed two more Stellas as he passed through the kitchen on the way to his study. The study in Casa De Niro was the size of a small library, large and airy and lined on all sides with large mahogany book shelves – something else De Niro and Lisa had in common, they loved to read.

De Niro took a seat on one of two sofas that lined a tremendous fireplace. Handing him one of the tall-necks, he motioned to Tompkins to sit on the other, facing him.

"So, what's up?"

Tompkins took a long pull from his bottle of beer, then paused a moment to collect his thoughts.

"Cris, you heard about the mosque business kicking up again near Ground Zero?"

De Niro tried not to show his emotions, only blinking gave away his anger.

"I read about it online."

Tompkins put his beer down on an end table.

"What's your take on it?"

"My take? In what way?"

Tompkins leaned forward.

"Come on, what do you think about it?"

De Niro took a long pull from his bottle.

"I think it would be a desecration ... but I don't think they'll be able to build it there. Understand, they have the legal right to build it, but I agree with Bill O'Reilly, there won't be a construction crew in New York that will lift a finger to build it."

Tompkins sat back and looked away.

"That's not what I'm hearing around the city."

"Really, and just what are you hearing?"

"I'm hearing the media start that whole thing again about how anyone against building the mosque there is a bigot, including survivors of 9/11 and families and friends of victims. I'm hearing the mayor restate that they have the right to build there and I even heard some say that the President will support their right to build it!"

De Niro finished his beer and put the empty bottle on the end table nearest him.

"Keith, there's no question they have the legal right to build a mosque there. We don't need the President of the United States to tell us that. The question is, is it morally right, morally appropriate to build it there."

"Cris, can you believe they're saying that there are families of 9/11 victims that are for the building of the mosque? It gets me sick!"

De Niro leaned in.

"Keith, they have a right to feel any way they want to feel, but that's not the point here either. If the building of the mosque that close to Ground Zero upset even one family or friend of a victim, it shouldn't be built. It would incite discord between Muslims and many non-Muslims and the hurtful nature of it will be seen as a profound dishonor by anyone attached to it. I thought that even the Muslim backers had backed off of the idea."

Keith leaned back in.

"Cris, they did, until someone came forward to finance it. I hear that they're gonna use Iranian money to build it. Some are saying that it will end up being a recruiting center for terrorists ... and can you imagine the parades they're gonna have in all those Muslim countries when that mosque goes up! I mean, it's like building a friggin' shrine to Emperor Hirohito at Pearl Harbor!"

De Niro's face flushed with rage, but after a moment, he flashed his friend a small smile.

"... and you're telling me this, why? You want me to fly to New York and go ten rounds with the Imam?"

Tompkins replied without breaking a smile, "Something like that."

De Niro's smile disappeared for a moment then he flashed it again.

"Keith, I was joking. They have a legal right to build it there but there's still a lot for them to do. Even if they did raise the money to build it, which I'm not sure they did. They only paid for the property, so far."

"And what if they did raise the money?"

"Then they'll still have to find construction crews to build it and permits to build it ... and deal with the picketing that will inevitably surround the building."

"Cris, you're not listening, from what I hear, they're gonna have powerful allies ... the mayor of New York, for one ... not to mention the President!"

"Keith, the President made his thoughts known about the subject, but I don't think he'll do more than that. If I was one of his advisors, I would be advising him not to get involved in what is really a local affair, but even if he does weigh in again, President Obama isn't going to grab his tool belt and start pouring the foundation, you know."

Both men were interrupted by a knock on the door, followed by Ricci walking in the room.

"Sorry to bother you guys, but Cris, the boys wanted to know if they can break out the ice cream and marshmallows now."

De Niro looked at Tompkins with a tongue-in-cheek expression.

"You want some ice cream?"

Tompkins rolled his eyes, shaking his head.

"No, I don't want ice cream, Cris. I want you to fly to New York and buy that building back from them!"

"What building? Ricci asked as he took a seat on the arm of the sofa next to Tompkins.

De Niro scowled then looked over at his brother-in-law.

"Keith wants me to fly to New York and try to buy the property back from the Imam who wants to build the mosque at Ground Zero."

Ricci raised an eyebrow in Tompkins' direction.

"What makes you think they want to sell it?"

Tompkins glared at Ricci for a moment, then stood up in frustration and leaned his arm on the large fireplace mantle.

"I don't know. Maybe Don De Niro over here can make them an offer they can't refuse."

Ricci folded his arms in mock thought.

"Yeah, and I can be like ... Luca Brasi. Let's see, maybe I can cut off one of the horse's head's that pull those carriages around Central Park and put it in the Imam's bed ..."

Tompkins pointed at Ricci as he looked at De Niro.

"SEE, THIS is why I wanted to speak to you in private!"

De Niro laughed quietly as he stood up and winked at his brother-in-law.

"Keith, for one, for them to purchase that property, they knew in advance the resistance they were going to meet. They wouldn't have gone into it if they intended to just sell out right. As a matter of fact, I think I read somewhere where someone already approached them and offered them four times what they paid for it and they turned the offer down. For another, I think it's too premature. I told you, as far as I know they only purchased the property; they still have to raise the money to demolish what's there and build their mosque."

Tompkins walked up to De Niro, put his hand on his shoulders and looked him straight in the eyes.

"Cris, for all my friends ... all the firefighters that lost their lives ... for all those innocent victims ... and for Lisa ... these people can't be allowed to build that mosque there."

Mentioning Lisa wounded De Niro. There weren't many people that De Niro would have allowed to mention her name in that context, but Keith Tompkins was one of the few that could. He also knew that his friend wouldn't have mentioned his wife's name in a casual fashion. This meant a lot to Tompkins as it did many others ... including him.

Tompkins spoke first.

"All I'm asking is for you to go to New York and ... do what you do. Look into it whatever way you feel is right. Then maybe you can speak to a bunch of us ... survivors and families and friends of victims. We've been keeping in touch about this and I sort of told them that you and I were friends and that you'd look into it for us. Everyone respects you Cris. Just let us know what you think."

De Niro stood in thought a moment. *What can it hurt?*

"Alright, Mugsy and I have business in the east anyway. I'll see if I can talk to a few people and get a handle on what's really going on, but no promises Keith! There's probably nothing I can do but let a few people know I'm against it being built so close to Ground Zero. I think speaking to the Imam or his wife will be a waste of time, their minds are made up, but I was friends with one of Mayor Giuliani's advisors. I'll meet with him and see if we can coax Mayor Bloomberg's support away from it."

Tompkins smiled broadly and put his arm around De Niro.

"Fantastic. I knew you'd come through brother!"

"Mugsy and I will be flying east Monday. Why don't you tag along? We'll stop off first in Virginia. Mugsy, I'll have you get things rolling there on your own, on Monday. Keith and I will fly up to Teterboro and take care of business in Manhattan. We'll stay in the city overnight then fly down to you on Tuesday morning. You can fill me in, introduce me to your new staff and we can give Keith here a tour of our new company. Then we can be back in the air right after lunchtime and be back here in Vegas before Yvonne even knows Keith is gone."

"With the way that woman gambles, I bet she won't even know I left!"

All three men laughed.

CHAPTER 5

THE WATCHMAN AGENCY
(FORMERLY LIBERTY DEFENSE CONTRACTORS)

OFFICE OF THE PRESIDENT
ARLINGTON, VIRGINIA
2:00P.M., MONDAY, MAY 16, 2011

"Charley, do you have a minute?"

The voice of Les Pastak, Executive Vice President of what had been known as "LDC," Liberty Defense Contractors, a counter-terrorism consulting firm, emanated from the intercom of Charley Santappia. Santappia's title was Director of Operations but no one was sure if they were going to keep their jobs after the billionaire hedge fund manager, Cris De Niro bought their firm out the week before.

The first to go was the firm's founder and CEO Nick Gerolitis, but that was part of the acquisition deal. All of the details of the deal weren't known, but the gossip was that De Niro paid Gerolitis twenty million dollars for his firm. All

Gerolitis told everyone - by email - was that it was an offer he couldn't refuse and wished everyone at LDC well before he packed his things and left.

Santappia was formerly Major Charles Santappia, a highly decorated United States Marine who joined LDC right after 9/11. Counter-terrorism firms were in great demand after 9/11 and so they all went on a hiring spree, plucking many warriors from America's armed services, luring them with large salaries and perks, but Santappia didn't need any luring. He was a patriot that knew his time serving in the Marines was coming to an end but decided he still wanted to "fight the fight" to defend the nation. Pastak, on the other hand was Gerolitis's brother-in-law. A lawyer by trade, he never served a day in the military. Most of the former military men had no use for the Executive VP. Pastak had taken it upon himself to move into the president's office the moment Gerolitis moved out of it. Since then he'd been acting like he was President though he was never appointed acting-President by De Niro. Some air was let out of his balloon-ego when he received an email from De Niro stating that he was on his way to put the new president in place. The message didn't say that he was naming Pastak president but Pastak was convinced that no one else could be given the position. In any case, he wasn't about to pack up his things and move out of the office. He figured that his initiative would probably impress the new owner. Charley had a feeling Pastak wanted to see him to try and get his ducks in a row.

"Sit down Charley," Pastak pointed to a chair as he buzzed Debbie Lynch, former Executive Assistant to Gerolitis. She didn't like taking orders from Pastak any more than Santappia did.

"Debbie, could you make me a latte and bring it into me ... and I want to know the moment De Niro's car enters our gates."

There was a pause, just long enough for the Executive Assistant to express her indignation - it infuriated Pastak. Just as he was about to repeat his order, her voice came through the phone speaker.

"... yes ... sir."

Santappia suppressed a smile as Pastak looked up at him.

"Charley, before De Niro arrives, I wanted to talk to you, so we could sort of align."

"Align, how so, Les?" Santappia knew it grated Pastak when anyone but Gerolitis called him by his first name. He could see Pastak's face turning red from it already.

"What I mean to say is that I'm sure there are changes that De Niro may want to make in our firm. Some people will probably be let go and the rest of us may be moved around within the organization. I just think that if we show a unified front, we may be able to influence him to put the right people in the right positions."

Santappia tried hard not to show his anger with Pastak's disrespectful tone whenever he uttered the new owner's name, specifically omitting the "mister" whenever he referred to him and for his attempt to manipulate De Niro, but he thought it best to hear him out.

"… And just who are the right people for the right positions, Les?" His question lit Pastak's face up with a devilish smile.

Pastak leaned back in his chair.

"Well Charley, I think it's a foregone conclusion that I'll be named president. After all, I'm sure De Niro isn't going to take the helm here, himself. Since I was the second in command, it's just common sense to promote me to CEO. Now, as for who will become my Executive VP … that's what I called you in to talk about."

Santappia tucked his hands under his thighs for fear that he would reach across the desk and choke Pastak.

"I know you have seniority here over the other directors, but … a few of them are younger than you are and … quite frankly Charley, I never considered you on my team."

Santappia couldn't conceal his anger anymore.

"What EXACTLY are you saying Les, spell it out!"

"Yes, Les, I would like you to spell it out too!" The comment came from just beyond the door to the office.

Pastak rose to his feet from behind the president's desk with a look of shock on his face as Santappia remained seated, just twisting his head around to see who was walking into the office. It was Mugsy Ricci followed by Debbie Lynch with a latte in her hand.

Pastak looked at Ricci but directed his enraged comments to Lynch.

"Debbie, I thought I told you to let me know when—"

"Mr. Pastak, you ordered me to alert you when Mr. De Niro's car entered our gates," Lynch interrupted. "This is not Mr. De Niro. Gentlemen, this is Captain Louis Ricci, United States Navy, retired."

Now Santappia stood up, this time unable to suppress his smile. He winked at Lynch as he offered his hand to Ricci.

"Please to meet you, Captain. Would you be Captain Mugsy Ricci, by chance?"

"The one and only ..."

"Please, call me Charley, Captain."

"I will and it's Mugsy, Charley."

It was obvious that the two men both liked each other from the start. Pastak, on the other hand, had been standing behind the desk with a look of confusion on his face while the two men were introducing each other. His confusion finally wore off being replaced with anger at everyone else in the room.

"Excuse me; we were having a private meeting here. Debbie, please show this gentleman out of my office and then I want to speak to you after I speak with Mr. Santappia, is that clear?"

"Belay that order Ms ..."

Lynch offered her hand, "Debbie Lynch, sir, I was Executive Assistant to Mr. Gerolitis."

"Pleased to meet you Ms. Lynch, Ricci said, shaking her hand.

"Excuse me!" Pastak raised his voice.

"Please Captain, call me Debbie."

"EXCUSE ME!" repeated Pastak even louder.

"Okay. Debbie, belay that order."

"EXCUSE ME!!! Pastak repeated one more time, this time banging his palms against the desk as he did.

Ricci finally turned to face the enraged man.

"Les, may I call you Les?" Before Pastak could say no, Ricci went on.

"Les, my name is Captain Ricci. I'm here on behalf of Cris

De Niro to inform you that, effective immediately, I've been appointed by him to take the helm of this firm as President and CEO."

Ricci handed Pastak a sealed envelope.

"This is the letter of authority signed by Mr. De Niro, stating such."

Ricci could have continued but he decided that it would be more fun to pause and give the utterly beside-himself Pastak the opportunity to read the letter. After reading it, Pastak looked up at Santappia with the look of someone who just realized he didn't win the lottery after all and Santappia countered with a mock shrug of his shoulders. Apparently he was enjoying this as much as Ricci was.

Pastak blinked a few times then tossed the letter onto the desk and picked up the phone.

"This is outrageous! I've been acting in the capacity of president since my brother-in-law left!"

"In fact ... I'm calling my brother-in-law now and I'm going to get this straightened out."

Ricci stepped close to the desk and put his index finger on the button to disconnect the call then took the phone out of the shaking man's hand and hung it up.

"Les, I want to point out the errors in judgment you just made. First, your brother-in-law no longer owns this firm. MY brother-in-law Cris De Niro does. Second, I think you were trying to intimidate me by picking up the phone, my phone, by the way ... and as long as I'm pointing errors out, moving yourself into this office ... my office ... without authorization from me ... BIG error in judgment!"

Pastak's face turned white as snow as he looked around at both Lynch and Santappia. Both stood behind Ricci staring at him with blank expressions.

"I ... I want to speak to De Niro. I want—"

"MISTER De Niro, Les!" Ricci cut him off. "From now on, you refer to him as MISTER De Niro and you refer to me as Captain Ricci. Are we clear?!"

There was silence until it occurred to Pastak that Ricci was expecting him to answer.

"Yes ... sir, Captain Ricci, but I still want—"

"You can speak to Mr. De Niro tomorrow, when he arrives here," Ricci cut him off again. "For now, I want you out of my office."

A look of abject fear appeared on Pastak's face.

"... out ... out of your office, yes sir. You mean, just leave your office now? ... where should I go?"

"Les, for now, just leave the room. After I speak to Major Santappia and Ms. Lynch, you can come back, retrieve your things and move them back into your office while Major Santappia and Ms. Lynch join me for a late lunch. I would invite you, but I want my office ready for me to move into when I return."

Pastak's relief when he realized he wasn't being fired covered up some of his embarrassment.

"Yes sir, Captain."

Just as he was about to walk out the door, Debbie Lynch called out to him.

"Mr. Pastak, you forgot your latte!"

CHAPTER 6

THE "GROUND ZERO" MOSQUE
(IN A LIMO PARKED IN FRONT OF THE PROPOSED SITE)
45-51 PARK PLACE
NEW YORK, NEW YORK
2:30P.M., MONDAY, MAY 16, 2011

"It's not exactly being built on top of ground zero, is it," De Niro remarked. Sitting in a limo with him was Keith Tompkins and Joe Carbone, a former advisor to Mayor Giuliani.

"That's not the point or the perception it will make Cris and you know it!" exclaimed Tompkins.

"What do you think, Joe?" asked De Niro.

"Your friend is correct, Cris. Two blocks is just too close to build a mosque. That is, if your intent was to create peace and harmony between Muslims and non-Muslims."

"I see," replied De Niro, "so, playing devil's advocate, just how far away would be acceptable to most people, for them to build their mosque?"

"Most people I know say that if the street had debris blown onto it from the collapse of the towers, no mosque should be built on it!" replied Tompkins.

De Niro nodded then exited the limo with Tompkins. He told the driver to take the former mayor's advisor wherever he wanted to go then to meet the two men down by Ground Zero. Before pulling away, Carbone lowered the window in the back of the limo.

"Cris, I didn't have to tell you that they have the legal right to build here. As far as this Mayor is concerned, he supports their right. I can also tell you that I've heard from reliable sources inside the White House that the President still supports their right to build here."

"This isn't a question of legal rights though, Joe. It's a question of wisdom, is it wise to build here ... and motives ... what are they trying to accomplish by building here?"

"Well, I told you Rudi's feelings on the matter. He believes it's insensitive to build it here. Do you want me to set up a meeting between you and him?"

"No, there's no reason. Thanks Joe, for taking time out of your busy schedule to meet with me on such short notice."

"Never a problem Cris, tell the boys I was asking about them."

"Will do. Say hi to your wife from me."

De Niro patted on the hood of the limo as Carbone raised the heavily tinted window, signaling that the driver could pull out.

De Niro and Tompkins started walking up to West Broadway on their way to Ground Zero as a man sitting in a van parked across the street punched an auto-dial button on his cell phone.

(In Farsi) "This is Payam. You wanted to know of anything unusual. There was a limo here with three men in it. We've taken pictures of each and are running them through the facial recognition software now. The limo is rented."

The reply was in English with a slight British accent.

"How long will it take you to identify the men?"

Payam replied in American English, "It could take some time. We had the limo followed but two of the three men are on foot now. Should we follow them?"

"Yes, follow them and send me the photos now of the three men."

Payam spoke in Farsi to the two men in the back of the van.

"The photos are being sent to you now."

"Good, I want to know where all three men go."

As the photos appeared on his iPhone, the man on the other end of the phone immediately identified one of the three men.

"Payam, which two men are walking?"

"The tall black man and the man in the blue suit are walking, they turned south on West Broadway. The older man remained in the limo."

The man on the other end of the phone thought for a moment; then replied.

"I think I know where they are heading. Follow them anyway but keep your distance. Call me on my cell phone when they arrive at their destination."

The man ended the call by simply hitting the disconnect button. Then he hit an intercom button.

"Have my car brought around."

Aref Sami Zamani stood up from his desk in his lower-midtown office and headed for his private elevator, followed by his aide, Bahman Fard who used a keycard to open the doors to the elevator. Fard was curious.

"Sir, our plane is being readied for takeoff in less than two hours. Shall I notify the flight crew that we will be delayed?"

Zamani smiled at the tact his aide used. He knew that Fard was curious as to where they were going but knew better than to boldly ask. *Bahman is even cunning with me. He looks like an accountant but he will kill on my command without a hint of remorse.*

"That's not necessary, this won't take long."

Zamani saw the look of frustration on Fard's face and decided not to keep him in suspense.

"You are wondering what I saw in those photos, Fard, and where we are going now?"

"Sir, I—"

Zamani held his hand up to quiet his aide, then he handed him his iPhone.

"Do you recognize any of those men?"

Fard looked closely at the small screen and used his finger to move between each photo.

"This one looks like ... that hedge fund manager ... De—"

"De Niro, you are correct Fard. It is Cris De Niro and we are going downtown so that I may meet him before we leave."

The doors opened to the elevator and both men walked out of the building and straight into their waiting limo. Fard was still confused.

"But sir, do we not have to wait for Payam to call back to tell us where he is?"

Just then Zamani's phone rang, Fard handed it back to him.

"Yes ... I figured he would be there, what about the other? And the one who remained in the car? You are sure? Very well, return to Park51 and resume your watch."

Zamani placed his phone in his suit pocket, then answered Fard's question.

"I know where he is. He is at the Ground Zero site paying respects to his deceased wife. What I do not know is why he was parked in a limousine outside of Park51 with an activist fireman and an advisor to the former mayor."

Fard's curiosity turned to concern.

"Sir, is it wise to meet him in this way, just showing up unannounced and in of all places, at Ground Zero? Did you not want to keep your ... interest ... in Park51 unknown to everyone?"

Zamani ignored Fard's questions, instead he shared his thoughts.

"If a man like Cris De Niro joins the opposition to the Mosque, he could bankroll them himself. They have not had any real financial backing to this point. With this man's wealth, he could broaden and deepen the investigation into the financing of Park51."

Fard knew better than to repeat the questions to which he had not received answers, but he was still curious about one thing.

"Sir, with respect, why would we care if this man bankroll's those infidels? There is no question, we have the legal right to build there and that money can be raised from other Muslims to build it."

Zamani marveled at how his aide could be both so intelligent and so short-sided.

"Fard, with enough money and a financial master like this man De Niro investigating, it's possible that he could discover our financing of our other operations in the west."

Zamani looked out the window as they approached the site where the World Trade Center once was. He felt great pride in seeing the sky where the towers once stood.

"I will admit that Park51 would be another triumph for us. Some in our cause believe that it is a great decoy, away from our more ... important activities in the United States. Others, like me believe it is an unnecessary distraction away from our more militant actions."

"Then why did you agree to back it financially?"

Zamani's face turned red with anger.

"Fard, just as our President does, I heed the bidding of the clerics in Tehran ... not to do so would be ... unwise."

Straightening his tie, he got his anger under control.

"Nevertheless, we cannot allow the spotlight that this American may focus on it to grow in intensity, to the point where it illuminates operations we need to keep cloaked in darkness. Besides, I have always wanted to meet him. He is something of a legend in the global financial circles."

Fard nodded his understanding then peered out his window.

"Sir, is that not him standing by that wall?"

Zamani ordered his bodyguard/driver to pull to the curb. He stepped out of the car then ordered both of his bodyguards to wait outside by the car while he approached De Niro.

Zamani knocked on the limo's window, motioning for Fard to lower it.

"You will wait in the car, while I go speak to him. Do not be concerned, Fard. I will keep my identity from him. I think it is an acceptable risk for me to see if I can determine what this man De Niro's interest is in Park51. I'm sure those back in Tehran would want to know."

CHAPTER 7

THE VIEWING WALL AT GROUND ZERO
CHURCH STREET, NEW YORK, NEW YORK
3:00P.M., MONDAY, MAY 16, 2011

De Niro and Tompkins stood silently for several minutes looking out over the site where almost 10 years before, both men met, on that fateful September morning.

After they had been standing there for some time their limo pulled up at the curb behind them.

Tompkins walked over and told the driver to wait there. Then he approached De Niro, who seemed to be lost in thought. He put his hand on De Niro's shoulder. De Niro started speaking to him without turning.

"You know Keith, that's exactly what you did when you first met me in the stairwell – you put your hand on my shoulder. I can still remember it like it was yesterday."

"So can I, brother, so can I ..."

De Niro turned to face his friend.

"If it weren't for you, Richard and Louis would have lost both of their parents that day. I'm not sure I can ever thank you enough for what you did."

"Cris, you did more than thank me, you enabled me to take care of my wife and kids for the rest of their lives. I should be thanking you, broth."

De Niro smiled at his friend but then let the smile fade from his face.

"Take the limo back to the hotel. I want to stay here awhile. I'll catch a cab later and meet you for dinner."

"You sure you're alright?"

De Niro shook Tompkins hand, "I'm sure. I'll see you later."

De Niro turned back to look out at what was now a construction site. *To me, this will always be a burial ground. It's where the lives of my wife and unborn son ended and all those others. Part of me died with them and resides here. This is a place I never want to visit ... but can never leave!*

De Niro didn't even notice the limo with Tompkins in it drive away, nor did he notice the other limo pull up with three men stepping out of it. He paid no mind to the person who took a position next to him.

"It will be a remarkable complex when it is built, will it not?"

De Niro turned to see who was talking to him. It was a man about his age, taller than him, dressed impeccably in an English-tailored suit. The man was dark-skinned, obviously Middle Eastern but with crystal blue eyes. His face was adorned with a meticulously trimmed moustache.

"I apologize if I'm intruding on your privacy."

De Niro's squinted eyes showed a bit of annoyance but then he resumed looking back out over the site.

"That's okay."

"You are Mr. Cris De Niro, are you not?"

De Niro turned back to the stranger, this time showing more than a bit of annoyance in his eyes.

"Mr. De Niro, I meant no offense. I attended a conference some years ago where you spoke."

That calmed De Niro down some but left him curious. *I'd definitely remember if I met this guy, just from those eyes of his.*

"... And who might you be?"

The man bowed his head slightly. "My name is Prince Farouk al-Hassan. I am visiting from Kuwait. As a matter of fact, I was about to fly home when I decided to see the famous Ground Zero for myself."

De Niro nodded.

The two men stood silently for a few minutes; then Zamani spoke again.

"Mr. De Niro, would you mind if I asked you a question of a personal nature?"

De Niro looked straight into Zamani's eyes.

"Shoot."

Zamani hesitated for a moment.

"Ah, you Americans and your colloquialisms, shoot, yes, well ... I wanted to ask you what your feelings are on the ... what do you Americans call it ... the Ground Zero mosque? May I ask, are you for or against it being built?"

De Niro looked at the man before him; *he's asking me questions about the Ground Zero mosque less than an hour after I was parked in front of it. This guy obviously is unaware of the innate cynicism of an Italian born in Brooklyn. I'll play along though.*

"Are you sure you're not a reporter Prince Hassan?"

"A reporter ...?"

"You know, a journalist looking for a quote for some article you're writing."

Zamani played up his part.

"Mr. De Niro, I assure you, I am not a reporter. I merely thought I could get a real American's viewpoint instead of just listening to what they tell us on Fox News. I will admit, I do not think that most Muslims really understand why there are such negative feelings to a mosque being built so far from where we are standing. If I have been indiscrete, I apologize."

"No need to apologize ... Your Royal Highness. If you really want to know, I think building a mosque that close to this place is indiscrete."

"... But you realize they have the legal right to—"

"Prince Hassan, the disagreement is not over the legal right to build there; it's a question of the wisdom of building there. The United States is a country unlike any other on earth. We're a true melting pot of nationalities, religious and ethnic backgrounds. On top of that, we have a democratic form of government that, although it is ruled by the majority of opinion, is sensitive to the rights and opinions of our various minorities. Our very nature is to be tolerant and understanding and our laws reflect that nature. That's why the owners of that property have the legal right to build a mosque there. However, there is a spirit of responsibility and moral or ethical judgment that each citizen of this great county should have, with respect not only to one's own rights, beliefs and feelings but to the rights, beliefs and feelings of their fellow Americans."

Nodding his head in the direction of the construction, De Niro continued.

"This place is known as Ground Zero because the two towers fell here, but the rubble, including the dust, to which so many of the victims were reduced, was scattered for many blocks, including to the block where they are proposing to build the mosque. In effect, I believe all of the surrounding blocks that were covered with, what very well could be those human remains should be considered Ground Zero too. So to me, they are proposing to build a place for Muslim worship on Ground Zero. As a friend of mine once said, it is tantamount to '... building a shrine to Emperor Hirohito at Pearl Harbor.' No, Your Royal Highness, the question is not one of legality, but one of wisdom."

Zamani stood quietly for a moment. *Although an infidel and an enemy, this man is obviously intelligent and shrewd ... and quite possibly dangerous to our cause. It makes it even riskier for me to try and find out his intentions. I must be careful.*

Zamani asked in a light tone, with just a hint of sarcasm.

"So, do you intend on joining the others who will hold up picket signs in front of that property?"

"You understand that they too have the legal right to do that, Your Royal Highness – but that's not exactly my style." De Niro paused before adding, "Nor is flying a plane into a building filled with innocent people. We each have our ways of expressing dissension."

Zamani raised his eyebrows but knew he could not press the question further.

"I see. I can understand your feelings, Mr. De Niro. They are quite understandable for someone who has lost loved ones here."

De Niro didn't reply, but he also didn't miss the fact that this man knew a whole lot about him.

"Well then, I will leave you. Thank you for sharing your thoughts with me, Mr. De Niro."

De Niro watched as the man got back into his limousine, followed by the two burly men that looked like his bodyguards getting into the front seats. He whistled for a cab as the limo pulled away. *What was that all about? One thing's for sure, my dad taught me to know when someone is pissing down my leg and telling me it's raining.*

As soon as Zamani got into the limo he pulled his iPhone out and hit an autodial button.

(In Farsi) "Payam, I want you to find out what you can about the man in the blue suit. His name is Cris De Niro. He may try to look into the funding for Park51 and he has many connections. Alert all of our friends here; if they receive any inquiries from him or his associates, I want to know about it immediately. Oh and Payam, find out where he lives, if he has any relatives, what businesses he owns. I will be out of the country for a week, but you can reach me on my cell."

Fard waited for his boss to put his phone into his pocket.

"Is there a problem, sir?"

Zamani stared out the window as their limo drove north on West Street, heading for his Gulfstream G650 (G6) which was fully fueled and waiting for them at Teterboro airport.

"Americans, Fard ... they are arrogant and decadent but they can also be tenacious and resourceful. Like a dog, sometimes they can be very difficult to shake off once they are onto your scent."

Zamani rested his head back and closed his eyes, then added, "Sometimes the only choice with which one is left ... is to shoot the dog."

CHAPTER 8

THE WATCHMAN AGENCY
EXECUTIVE CONFERENCE ROOM - ALPHA
ARLINGTON, VIRGINIA
10:00A.M., TUESDAY, MAY 17, 2011

The entire executive staff of the newly named, "The Watchman Agency" were sitting at the long, sleek, mahogany conference table. To the right of the head of the table were, in order: Mugsy Ricci, Karla Matthews and Les Pastak; and to the left: John Francis, Charlie Santappia, and Michelle Wang. Debbie Lynch was sitting at the opposite end of the table and De Niro was standing at a small podium just beyond the head of the table. De Niro called the meeting to order.

"Good morning ladies and gentlemen. For those of you who don't know me, my name is Cris De Niro. As you all know, I have recently acquired Liberty Defense Contractors and as you may have seen by the new signs being hung all about, it has been renamed, The Watchman Agency.

"Before I explain the reason for the name change, let me first introduce each of you to one another, along with your new titles and job responsibilities. In some cases you may have been promoted into your new position and in other cases, your title might have changed along with your new role within the agency. Each person in this room has been chosen because our new president and I both feel you are the best at what you do. You will also notice that I have brought in two new people, both of whom I have known for a long time and for which I have the utmost respect."

"Let me begin by introducing the new president of The Watchman Agency, Captain Louis "Mugsy" Ricci United States Navy, retired. Mugsy Ricci was one of the most decorated members of the elite Navy Seals. He was last stationed as Commanding Officer of the Naval Special Warfare Center. Captain Ricci will speak with all of you later, but for now, let me say that I am confident that you will all find him to be a fair but firm leader."

"Sitting across from Captain Ricci, some of you may have recognized, is Mr. John Francis. John will work in the capacity of the newly created position of Chief Information Officer for The Watchman. "Johnny-F," as he is known to his friends and my friendship go all the way back to our childhood in the Ridgewood section of New York. Some of you may know of his fantastic accomplishments and success but that doesn't tell even half of his story. Most of what John has worked on for the last several years is considered top secret. In his role here at The Watchman, John will be tasked with super-charging our information gathering and data crunching. I will also do my best to see to it that he has a blank check when it comes to any technology he wants to acquire for this agency ... my knees just buckled when I said that."

The room erupted in laughter, except for Pastak who forced a fake smile concealing his anger. His position at the table revealed his spot in the pecking order, which was basically just over the Executive Assistant. What he didn't realize was that both the Chairman and the CEO considered Debbie Lynch to be more valuable to the agency.

"To Captain Ricci's right is Karla Matthews. Karla has been promoted from Director to Vice President of Government Relations. Her responsibilities will encompass all of our agency's relations not only with the United States government but also with any other governments and sovereignties with which we may interact. Karla is a Rhodes Scholar, among other things and has a number of years of experience and success working within various areas of the State Department.

"Across from Karla is Major Charles Santappia, United States Marine Corps, retired. As my own dad was a Marine, I know firsthand that, 'once a Marine, always a Marine.' Charlie was a highly decorated member of the second Marine division. He has vast experience commanding and taking part in all types of military operations, from peace-keeping to special operations of which, if he told us about them, he'd have to kill us all."

The room filled with laughter again.

"Charlie has been promoted from Director to Vice President of Operations. His duties include tactical command of all operations of The Watchman conducted inside and outside of these walls."

"To Charlie's left - is Michelle Wang, The Watchman's former Director of, and now new Vice President of Intelligence Services. Michelle came to the former agency from a successful career at Langley, where her human Intel expertise, in particular, went underutilized. Here, we will fully utilize that experience."

"Rounding out our executive staff, you all know Les Pastak whose title and responsibilities have been refined. Les is now Vice President of HR and General Counsel for our agency. And last but certainly not least, Debbie Lynch who formerly served as Executive Assistant to the former president and who continues in that role for our new CEO and president. Debbie is the linchpin of this agency."

"Now let me give you a little insight to why I acquired this firm, what I hope to accomplish with this A-Team of talented individuals and the reason why I renamed the agency, The Watchman."

"After my wife Lisa died in the North Tower of the World Trade Center on 9/11, my life underwent a number of changes.

One of which, the most important of which was my rededication to my Judeo-Christian faith. To help me deal with the loss her loss, I turned to the Bible. I was drawn to one Old Testament prophecy concerning modern day Ephraim, aka the U.S.A. It captivated me. In the book of Hosea, the prophet spoke of the *Watchman of Ephraim*. In biblical times, watchmen, mostly soldiers but not always, were stationed in various places in a city and were responsible for keeping watch and reporting what they saw, to the kings and elders. Their duty was not to fight; it was to inform, particularly of some impending danger."

"I felt that, of all the failures on 9/11, the biggest failure was that no warning was given. In my view, America had no watchman. While democrats and republicans argued along ideological lines – for and against the use of human intel – for and against the use of torture for interrogation – for and against Guantanamo Bay – for and against whether terrorists should be given rights and privileges outlined by the Geneva conventions, whether they were enemy combatants or just misguided zealots, etcetera. I knew that while the federal government acted like the "silly doves" spoken of in the Bible, America's enemies continued relentlessly to plan the next attacks against innocent American civilians on our soil."

"It is my intention to make this agency, the watchman for our country. Our job will be first, to keep watch over all of our national borders; second, when necessary, to warn our government of any threat; and third, in any instance where we, in this room, believe that our country is not acting to protect American citizens, American property and American territory … we will do whatever is necessary to protect and to defend our nation and its citizens."

"Ladies and gentleman, we are not here to replace the military and civilian law enforcement agencies of our country. We are here primarily to advise them and to serve them in whatever capacities we can … but in any case; we will NOT ALLOW … another 9/11! We will NOT ALLOW another terrorist attack on American soil, not if we can help it, not if we can do something about it!"

"If any of you have a problem with anything I just said,

speak now or come to me after this meeting ends. We'll do all we can to find you a job with someone else. There will be no hard feelings, but for the rest of you who feel up to the challenge ... Godspeed and God Bless! "

Everyone in the room stood and applauded, including Pastak, but his only reason for standing was so as not to be the only person left sitting. Pastak was fuming from what he considered to be a major snub and demotion, so much so, that he hardly heard anything De Niro had said.

"I would like to invite Captain Ricci to step up here and say a few words, Mugsy?"

De Niro shook his brother-in-law's hand then took a seat at the head of the table as Ricci stepped up to the podium.

"Thank you Cris and God bless you and everyone in this room. Ladies and gentleman, I'll make this one short and to the point. I'm honored to be chosen for this position with this agency and to lead what I believe to be the finest staff that I have ever commanded.

"Over the next days and weeks we'll get to know one another and we'll get a feel for how we all do our jobs. Please feel free to come to me anytime, day or night, if you need any assistance, advice or guidance. Those who know me know that I'm not a micro-manager, neither is Cris. We both believe in choosing the right people for the job and then letting them do their jobs. We've chosen you and now I'll leave it up to each of you to choose your staff. Please have everyone in place by Friday and notify Les's HR department with any new appointments, so they can make the necessary pay-grade changes. Please also submit your new department roster to Debbie as soon as possible."

"I've never been one to like to sit through long meetings so I'm pleased to announce that everyone in this firm will begin using our proprietary project management system. You may be asking yourself, 'what proprietary project management system?' Well, by the time this meeting adjourns every member of this firm will have The Watchman PMS, otherwise known as 'Big Brother,' running on every one of their desktops, laptops, notebooks and handheld devices. Johnny-F, our new head of IT didn't waste any time '... bringing us into the 21st century,' as he put it."

The room filled with laughter.

"The IT department will immediately train everyone on the use of Big Brother, but in a nutshell, it keeps us all connected and informed. Everyone, I mean everyone is mandated to update Big Brother with their status and location at all times. There will be tiered security levels built into the system, so no one need fear disclosing top secret and covert operation status. New SOP[1]'s are contained in Big Brother. Please become familiar with them. That will be all for now, again, thank you – now let's protect our country!"

"Mugsy, John and Charlie, I'll meet you in Mugsy's office in five, Michelle would you stay a moment?" De Niro added as everyone stood up, a few shaking hands and making small talk.

Everyone left the room except for De Niro and the VP Intelligence Services. De Niro closed the door to the soundproofed room. Both remained standing.

"Michelle, I'd like you to do me a favor, if you would."

"What do you need, Mr. De Niro?"

"Please ... call me Cris. Michelle, is there a way for you to monitor large withdrawals from overseas banks and/or deposits into domestic banks?"

"It depends on a number of things, including the size of the transactions, the nature of the transactions ... whether the money is being wired or withdrew and deposited in cash or check, and on the banks themselves, among other things. I should also point out that it's a relatively easy thing to do if we have legal grounds and a court order. Then we can compel the banks to comply. Why, what's up?"

De Niro reached his hand behind his neck, as if he were reconsidering his request.

"Well, the fact is there's no real reason. I mean no tangible reason ... I'm not making any sense, am I?"

Wang smiled warmly, "Mr. De Niro ... Cris, you'd make more sense if you just spit it out and told me, what's on your mind?"

De Niro continued to rub the back of his neck then stopped and looked into Wang's eyes.

"Okay, I'm sure you know about my ... wife dying on 9/11."

"Yes sir, I do."

"Well, I became close friends with the fireman, Keith Tompkins that saved my life that day."

That caught Wang by surprise.

"Sir, I didn't realize ... were you also at the World Trade Center that day?"

De Niro hesitated then replied.

"Yes ... I was. Anyway, Keith came to me with a request and like I said, we're close friends. You heard about the mosque they want to build near Ground Zero being back in the news?"

"Yes, something about they're trying new ways to raise money for it."

"Well, Keith and a number of other survivors and friends and family of victims are against a mosque being built anywhere near Ground Zero ... and so am I."

"I can understand that."

"Well then, here it is. I want to look into any funding of the mosque."

"Look into the funding ... why?"

"Well, like I said, there's really no material reason, just suspicions ... perhaps fears, that the Park51 project may be funded by ... Islamic radicals."

De Niro noticed Wang's eyebrow rise.

"I know. Sounds like a conspiracy theory raised by folks who are still very angry and hurt. To tell you the truth, it's difficult for me to use pure reason without emotion when it comes to anything about 9/11. I'll tell you this though, if there's even a small chance that Islamic radicals are intending to fund that mosque, I want to know about ... and I'll take it from there!"

Wang remained where she stood, crossing her arms in front of her.

"We'd have no legal grounds to get a court order, Cris."

De Niro continued to look into Wang's eyes.

"I know."

After a moment, Wang softened her stance. *There's something about him that's ... sincere, not vindictive. I'd probably investigate on my own, if it were my husband who died. I won't do less for him.*

"How far do you want me to go to investigate?"

"I don't want any laws broken ... at least, I don't want us to get caught, if we did happen to break one ... and I want the minimum amount of people involved. I'd like to keep this between you and me for now. I was hoping there might be a technological, passive way to handle this."

Wang put the tip of the back of her pen in her mouth and strolled a few steps.

"There might be. I'm not totally up to speed on the full capabilities of Big Brother, but from what I already understand about the system is that Johnny-F enabled it to do dynamic and robust data mining. Perhaps, after he shows me how to set up my own queries, I can have double-B help us ... follow the money."

De Niro smiled, "Excellent, but Michelle, really, err to the side of caution. Don't do anything too intrusive ... and try not to let this favor of mine take you away from the other things you have to do around here, for too long ... understood?"

Wang followed De Niro to the door and just before he opened it, replied, "Got it!"

As De Niro made his way out of the room he was intercepted by Pastak.

"Mr. De Niro, may I speak with you?"

"Sure Les, but if this has to do with your new position here, you need to speak with Captain Ricci, he's in charge here now."

"But sir, I ... didn't get off to a good start with Captain Ricci and—"

"Les let me stop you there. First, let me repeat, Captain Ricci is in charge here, not I. I'm aware of your initial introduction with Captain Ricci and I want you to know that, despite it, Captain Ricci still suggested that not only you stay with the company but he insisted that you keep your pay grade. Under the circumstances, I think that's fair, don't you? In any case, if you have a problem with your new position, let Captain Ricci know as soon as possible. If you don't Les, I suggest you just get on with it. Do your job and I'm sure things will be fine between you and him."

Pastak could see that the conversation was over. It was obvious to him that he was being conspired against. *They probably think I'll leave, but I won't give them the satisfaction. I'll do my job alright; just enough to keep everyone off my back. That is, until I can figure away to get ahead, here or somewhere else!*

"I'll ... do that. Thank you, sir."

De Niro sighed with a deep breath as he watched Pastak disappear into his office then he walked into Mugsy's office. Ricci and Santappia were already there, Mugsy sitting behind and Santappia sitting on one of the two chairs in front of his desk. De Niro took a seat in the other chair.

"Mugs, Les just approached me. I'm still not sure he's happy with his new situation here."

"What did he say?"

"I didn't give him a chance to say anything. I told him to talk to you. Are you sure about him?

"No, I'm not Cris, but the bottom line is that, with all the changes we're making here, replacing him could severely impede our ability to get everyone settled in their new positions, on our timeline. He is competent running human resources. I'm not sure how good he is as our corporate counsel, but I'm hoping we won't need legal counsel to get this ship sailing."

De Niro didn't reply, so Ricci went on.

"Listen, once we get everyone in place and up and running, if he's still not with the program, I'll get him replaced. Who knows, we didn't cut his pay and there aren't many places he can go and get paid the same, so maybe, he'll just fall in line."

There was a knock on the door and then Debbie Lynch walked in followed by John Francis.

"Can I get anyone anything?"

Ricci answered, "No thanks Debbie, just hang the 'Do Not Disturb' sign on the doorknob for a bit. We'll need a few minutes without interruption."

"Got it," Lynch said as she closed the door behind her.

Francis spoke up.

"Sorry I'm late; there was a small line of people waiting to talk to me outside the conference room."

"I bet half wanted to shake your hand and probably the other half wanted your autograph," De Niro quipped.

"Only two wanted my autograph, for your information, the

rest wanted me to walk them through Big Brother. It looks like we have an aggressive team here; everyone wants to get right to work. I had to grab a few of my managers and get them to start the training with the department heads."

De Niro got up and took a seat on the couch next to Santappia. Ricci and Francis joined them. De Niro started.

"John, how far along are you with the new security measures here?"

"I haven't started them. Cris, give me a break, I haven't even hung my hat yet in my office here. I thought the first priority was to get Big Brother installed."

"It was, but we're gonna need at least this office and maybe the conference room sound-proofed, bug-protected and secured a.s.a.p."

Francis nodded.

"Understood, I'll get on it right after we break here."

"Not so fast," replied De Niro, "I need you, Mugsy and Charley to fly home with me. I have something to show you and we can talk safely once we get there. We take off at noon. We'll have lunch on the plane. Why don't you gentlemen go get things squared away, here, with your staff – my car is waiting outside to take us to the airport whenever all of you are ready. "

Francis smiled.

"Vegas huh, I haven't been there since the last Comdex show. Guys, I gotta tell you, I met the finest-looking ladies over at Wynn after the first night of the conference—"

"So that's why you couldn't come and visit with me and the boys?" De Niro interjected. "I thought you told me you were 'all tied up' when I called you, at your hotel room?"

Francis blushed, "Well I was ... literally. You see, one of them, this pretty-little oriental ... she was an acrobat in one of those Cirque De Soleil shows. Anyway, she was showing me one of the illusions they do in the show with these ropes—"

All three men laughed.

CHAPTER 9

ABOARD DE NIRO'S PRIVATELY-OWNED QSST
(QUIET SUPERSONIC TRANSPORT)
AT 60,000 FEET SOUTH OF JEFFERSON CITY, MO
CRUISING AT 1,056 MPH (MACH 1.6)
12:00P.M. (LOCAL TIME), TUESDAY, MAY 17, 2011

Co-pilot Doug Miller collected the empty food trays from De Niro, Mugsy Ricci and Charley Santappia as they sat in the high-tech cabin section of De Niro's new aircraft, the QSST. John Francis's lunch still sat on his tray though, untouched.

De Niro patted the uniformed co-pilot on his back.

"Thanks Doug. Captain Douglas 'Charger' Miller, USAF, retired, I'd like you to meet Captain Louis Ricci, USN, retired and Major Charles Santappia, USMC, retired."

"You make us sound like a bunch of geriatric patients with all those 'retired' after our names, " Ricci gibed as he shook Miller's hand.

"Doug and the Captain, Colonel O'Rourke, USMC retired

have just joined our team. The colonel will take charge of all of our flight operations."

"Wait a minute; did you say O'Rourke, as in Colonel James O'Rourke? You mean Duke's flying this plane? Santappia asked with excitement in his voice.

"You two know each other?" asked De Niro with a little disbelief in his voice.

"Let's just say that we were roommates back in the day."

"More like brig-mates. How the hell are ya, Charley?" O'Rourke said as he entered the cabin from the cockpit, offering his hand to Santappia first, then the others.

"Duke!" cried Santappia as he shook the big man's hand with vigor.

"Brig-mates?" asked Ricci.

Santappia's face turned a shade red.

"Well, I was fresh out of boot camp and on weekend liberty from Lejeune[2] and ended up in this longshoreman's bar in Baltimore when a bunch of their rank and file decided to see for themselves if Marines were as tough as the movies make them out to be. I'm embarrassed to say that I wasn't living up to the Marine Corps image, partially because there were six of them and partially because I had two single-malt scotch highballs in me."

Everyone laughed.

"Well, just as one of the larger ones was about to perform oral surgery on me with his knuckles, Duke here came barreling over like John Wayne himself and proceeded to toss all six of them out of the bar – three through the door and three through the bar's storefront window."

O'Rourke took over.

"Word got around about it and suddenly everyone was calling me 'Duke,' all because of Charley here."

"Wait a minute, what about the brig?" asked De Niro.

Both men smiled as Santappia replied.

"Oh yeah, well, right after Duke tossed the last one out the window, I decided to thank him by buying him and me, another round of that single-malt I was drinking. Before we finished it

---

though, Baltimore's finest burst through the doors and arrested us. The sergeant was an old jarhead so he decided to contact Lejeune and the next thing we knew, we were both thrown into the brig."

"What are the odds you two would meet up here in the clouds," De Niro asked rhetorically.

"It's a small corps, Cris," Santappia replied as he winked at O'Rourke.

"Can I ask another question, if you're back here, whose—"

"... Flying the plane? Mr. Francis sir, he insisted and he said it would be alright with you."

"So that's what he's been doing up there in the cockpit," replied De Niro. "Can he fly my $80 million baby?"

"To tell you the truth, I'm not sure what kind of pilot he is, but he sure does know everything about this aircraft."

"That's Johnny-F. He knows everything about ... everything," replied De Niro.

"Well, if you gentlemen will excuse us, Doug and I will get back to driving this plane. That is if Mr. Francis will allow us to."

De Niro, Ricci and Santappia all walked to the back cabin where they sat around a small conference table and after a few minutes Francis joined them from the cockpit.

"Man-oh-man that was fun ... I gotta get me one of these. How much did you say you paid for it?"

"$80 million, but it's not being offered to the public yet. My friend owns the company that built it."

"Well, tell your friend that I want one ... of course, I'll expect a big discount for being one of your friends ..."

De Niro ignored Francis, directing the rest of what he was saying to Ricci and Santappia.

"I had to get a bunch of clearances to fly it over the U.S. because it flies faster than the speed of sound. The government is afraid it'll shatter windows, but the truth is it's got the sonic signature of 1/100th that of the 'Concorde."

"Just how fast is this bird?" Ricci asked as he gazed out of one of the cabin's portholes.

"She can do Mach 1.8 and has a range of 4,000 nautical." Francis replied with a touch of awe in his voice.

"The best is that she'll fly New York to Los Angeles in 2.2 hours and New York to Paris in less than five." De Niro added.

"Hey, this girl can even make it from New York to Tokyo in 9 ½ hours and that includes a fuel stop in Anchorage!" Francis added with glee.

"That means if I did the calculation right, we'll be landing in Las Vegas an hour before we took off from Dulles, with the time difference!" Ricci remarked, impressed.

De Niro got up and closed the door to the cabin.

"We didn't fly it east because the Colonel and Doug took it to have some new avionics equipment loaded into the cockpit. I told them I want every bell and whistle for this girl."

De Niro returned to his seat at the head of the conference table.

"Okay Charley, the reason I had you tag along with us, other than to meet your old roommate, was to discuss a special unit that Mugsy and I have been contemplating creating. Mugsy will fill you in as it was his idea."

"Charley, when Cris told me about his mandate for The Watchman to do 'whatever is necessary' if the government doesn't when our country or its citizens are in imminent danger - he challenged me to come up with a means to accomplish that. Obviously, we would need a paramilitary arm but then I started thinking along those lines—"

"And you were faced with certain legal and regulatory dilemmas," Santappia interjected.

"Exactly, The Watchman is an intelligence-gathering agency. In our normal course of business we deal with highly sensitive and confidential Intel and information. If we introduced the type of paramilitary unit that we would need to do whatever is necessary – and neither Cris nor I are even sure what that might entail yet – we would have to subject The Watchman agency to government supervision and scrutiny. That's not something we want to do."

Santappia thought hard for a few moments and then replied.

"So, what we need is a black ops arm."

Ricci looked over to De Niro who answered.

"That's the conclusion we came to, also. Charley, this unit

would have to be so dark that only the four of us should even know about its existence."

Santappia nodded his understanding then turned to Ricci.

"Have you selected any members for the unit yet?"

Ricci looked again at De Niro but then replied with a smile on his face.

"Only who we want to command it ..."

The statement showed how much both men respected and trusted Santappia and that didn't get past him.

"Cris left it up to me and I'm leaving it up to you."

"How big do you picture this unit to be?"

"Not too big, maybe two or three squads with the ability to scale up a bit – stock the squads with all specialists."

Charley didn't waste a minute.

"Three squads then and I know just the three men to lead each – Riggy, De May and Pescalitis – all three were CWO5[3]'s. I served with all of them overseas. We all chewed the same dirt. All three of them are top gunner specialists, as good as they get."

"Can you get a hold of them?" asked Ricci.

"I sure can. In fact, I just heard from Riggy. His name is Vic Rigoni. We've always kept in touch. He just called me to tell me that he hired De May and Pescalitis to work in his machine shop in Brooklyn. Riggy's an accomplished mechanical engineer and inventor. The three of them joined the corps together and all three left the corps together."

De Niro jumped in.

"Charley, do you think they'd be interested in the situation we'd be offering? I'll be the first to admit that it may fall ... outside certain legal and regulatory—"

"Sir, I don't mean to cut you off, but, number one, I didn't hear you say that and number two, the three of them have spent their entire careers being asked to do things outside those same parameters by the U.S. government. All three are patriots and besides, all three have been jarheads for so long, they couldn't function as civilians."

Smiling De Niro winked at his brother-in-law. Ricci replied,

---

3   A CWO is a Chief Warrant Officer in the USMC.

"Okay, get a hold of them and tell them you want them to fly out to Vegas. I'll contact Debbie and have her send them three first-class tickets as soon as you tell me when they can make it. If you have to discuss salaries—"

"That won't come up, trust me. These three will jump at this opportunity and they'd all tell you they'd do it for nothing. It's what they were born to do."

"Are they married?" De Niro asked with concern.

"Oh yeah, all three are married. Riggy's a granddad, his daughter just had his first grandson. The other two have adult kids."

"Will their wives be okay with this?"

Santappia couldn't stifle his laughter.

"Sir, their wives would probably chip in for you to get them out of their hair. Those ladies have been married to Marines for so long, they all know the drill."

De Niro grinned as he nodded to the satellite phone on the table.

"Okay, call them from here ... and Charley, call me Cris ... please."

As Santappia started making the calls, De Niro turned to Francis.

"John, is there a way for this black ops unit to utilize Big Brother without anyone even at The Watchman knowing about it?"

"Not a problem, Cris. I've done the same thing for ... certain government agencies that I'll leave unnamed. I'll make it so that not even my own tech department will be able to know that this unit is using the Double-B."

"Excellent. I've already made arrangements to finance and supply the unit outside of The Watchman, so at the end of the day there will be no direct link between the unit and the agency, except for their utilization of Big Brother."

"... and that, no one will know about except for the four of us, I can guarantee that," asserted Francis. "One thing more though, how do we refer to this unit?"

De Niro got up and grabbed an unopened bottle of Macallan Scotch whiskey from the galley. The bottle had the year "1926" emblazed on its label. He opened the bottle and began pouring the silky, dark liquid into four sparkling, highball glasses, as Francis spoke up.

"Cris is that what I think it is?"

"I don't know John, what do you think it is?"

"That looks like a bottle from the Macallan Fine and Rare Collection, 1926, 60 years old ... around $30,000? I had a taste of it once in a hotel in Atlantic City, after I made seven passes at the craps table. A dram cost me $3,300!"

De Niro pushed a glass in front of each man.

"This bottle cost $38,000."

De Niro looked at his brother-in-law with a combination of sadness and happiness in his eyes.

"Lisa bought it for me at an auction that was raising money for children afflicted with cancer. We were saving it for a special occasion."

The men's smiles disappeared from their faces as they each bowed their heads slightly as a sign of respect.

De Niro fought back the tears that welled in his eyes then he took a deep breath to compose himself.

"If she were here, she would consider this a special occasion, as do I. Gentleman here's to the birth of ARCHANGEL, the unit that'll be like the sword of Gideon for The Watchman."

The four men clanked their glasses and said in unison, "ARCHANGEL!"

CHAPTER 10

ESTANCIA DE NIRO
(UNDERGROUND COMPLEX 10 MILES SOUTH OF THE MAIN HOUSE)

HENDERSON, NV

1:00P.M., TUESDAY, MAY 17, 2011

Cris De Niro, Mugsy Ricci, John Francis and Charley Santappia got down from horses they rode from De Niro's stable.

Francis spoke first as he patting the desert dust from his clothes.

"That was fun Cris, don't get me wrong. I love horseback riding, but next time do me a favor and warn me when you're gonna make me ride to Arizona ... so I can change out of my Ferragamos!"

The others laughed as Francis looked around.

"May I ask where exactly we are?"

De Niro grabbed a canteen of water hanging from his saddle and took a swig, then handed it to Francis who did the same.

"Well, for one thing, we're still in Nevada, in fact we're still on my land."

"You gotta be kidding—"

"And for another thing," De Niro cut him off as he looked down at a portable GPS tracking device in his hand, "we're standing at the entrance of the complex I told you about, on the plane."

The three men looked around, but all they could see was barren desert, foothills, cactus and sagebrush. Above their heads, the sky was cloudless and deep blue and the sun was blazing.

De Niro paused a moment amused by their confusion, then he pulled a small remote from his pocket and hit a button.

"Gentlemen, welcome to 'Coyote's Den!'"

The sound of large servo motors could faintly be heard as suddenly, a 12-foot wide swatch of the desert floor, complete with cactus and brush attached, began rising up in the air, exposing a long, concrete ramp leading down. Lights along the walls of the ramp automatically turned on, illuminating what looked like the entrance to a fairly large warehouse-like underground facility. The men stood in silent awe, all except Francis.

"Would ya look at that? ... the southwestern version of the Bat Cave!"

De Niro had the men lead their horses down the long ramp. At the bottom, they saw the concrete bunker in its entirety. It was basically laid out with a number of rooms built into the walls surrounding a 120,000 square-foot central area. The walls, floor and ceilings were constructed of reinforced concrete but the rooms were finished in stucco and wood. Surprisingly, to the men, the air wasn't stagnant and the temperature of the entire underground facility seemed to be comfortable.

De Niro answered some of the questions he was sure they would ask.

"I had a state-of the art ventilation and air conditioning system built into it. We're also using solar power as our primary electrical delivery with battery, AC and natural gas back-up. As far as I can tell, it can't be spotted from satellite and the crew that I used to build it thought that they were building a nuclear bomb shelter."

Ricci clapped his hands a few times to hear the echo, "I think this place might be able to survive a nuke attack!"

De Niro showed the men around. He led them into each room, one housed the electrical systems, there was a small cafeteria, two conference rooms, a dozen small living quarters, two bathrooms complete with showers, a half-dozen offices and a small recreation room. There was also a room filled with security equipment and monitors that appeared to have the capabilities to show every square inch of the entire 250,000-acre ranch.

After showing them the security room, De Niro walked over to Francis.

"John, I want you to turn this place into NSA[4]-West."

"Is that all?" Francis replied with a bit of sarcasm. "Cris this is a big Bat Cave, for sure, but NSA has 10 acres underground, with 20,000 employees, a pretty large percentage of which are mathematicians and the second most powerful supercomputer in the world. Besides the fact, all that tax money we pay is their monopoly money. I know you're rich but their food budget has a 'B' after the number!"

De Niro shrugged his shoulders, a little frustrated.

"... Point taken. Then, how about a mini-NSA? John, I want you to build us the best intel-gathering and analysis facility outside of Fort Meade."

Francis looked around and everyone could tell his brain was working overtime. They all stood quietly for several minutes watching Francis use his hands to frame certain areas of the facility, like a Hollywood director would to shoot a scene in a movie. The whole time he mumbled to himself until finally, he stopped mumbling and took a deep breath and let it out.

"Okay—"

De Niro flashed his widest smile.

"Cris wait, first let me explain. The only way to tackle a project this size is in phases ... and we're talking beaucoup dollars and time."

De Niro was more perturbed about the time element than

---

4   The National Security Agency/Central Security Service (NSA/CSS) is a cryptologic intelligence agency of the United States Department of Defense.

the money.

"How much time do you think you'll need?"

Francis laughed as he turned to Ricci and Santappia.

"He's a piece of work, isn't he? I tell him it's gonna cost a bundle and take time and he asks me how long instead of how much?"

De Niro repeated his question.

"John, how long ..."

Francis stared at his old friend for a long minute then finally shook his head in mock-defeat.

"If you give me the keys to your vault, I could probably expedite phase-one and get a functional system up in 90 days, but for a system with the size and scope of what you're talking about, we could be talking 6-months to a year, depending on the availability of the toys and the boys that play nice with them."

De Niro nodded his understanding as he turned to lead the men back to the horses.

"Fair enough, consider this the green-light to get started."

Francis jogged to catch up to him.

"But Cris, what about The Watchman and the Big Brother install and ramp-up with the staff there – which gets priority?"

De Niro winked at Ricci and Santappia as the three of them watched Francis struggle to mount his horse. Once the computer genius steadied himself, he simply answered.

"Both!"

CHAPTER 11

ZAMANI IMPORT-EXPORT CORPORATION
LOWER MIDTOWN MANHATTAN
NEW YORK, NEW YORK
6:00P.M., MONDAY, JUNE 27, 2011

Aref Sami Zamani sat behind his large ebony and Carpathian elm desk when his Skype® phone rang.

(In Farsi) "Yes?"

"This is Payam. I am sending you the intel on the man De Niro now."

On cue, Zamani heard the soft ringing tone of an email entering his Inbox – Subject: De Niro. There was nothing written in the body of the email just an Adobe Acrobat® file attached. Zamani opened the attachment and started reading a full dossier on De Niro as he spoke.

"I have it. Things went well in Tehran. Our leaders have given us permission to move ahead with the wedding. As the infidels concentrate on Cordoba[5], the celebration will be great in *Antioch*."

"Understood, what are your orders?"

"You see where this man De Niro lives?"

"Yes."

"Go there with your men and perform reconnaissance. I want to know all there is about the level of security at ... Estancia De Niro, as it is named. I hope to be able to provide you with details about De Niro's movements and the movements of his children. I want you and your men to remain there and ready an infiltration plan. I may need you to interrogate him before eliminating him. Placing a gun to his children's heads may inspire him to be more forthright with you. Have the plan ready by the time of the wedding. I don't want to take the chance that he survives the bomb and our men. He and his agency are too much of a potential threat. I don't want Cris De Niro around after *Antioch*"

"Understood"

Zamani's Executive Assistant, Bahman Fard had been standing at the other end of Zamani's desk.

"Sir, our leaders have allowed you to name our holy actions in the west, but why did you choose *Antioch*?

Zamani smiled and leaned back in his chair, pleased with his subordinate's question.

"Fard, how knowledgeable are you of history, of the holy battles fought by those of our faith during the Crusades?"

Fard hesitated then replied with meekness.

"I am ashamed to say, not as knowledgeable as I should be sir."

Zamani blinked his eyes as a sign of condescension.

"You are not alone. It is sad that so many of the true believers are so ignorant when it comes to the history of our faith and of the many heroic battles fought in the name of Allah."

Fard bowed his head in embarrassment as Zamani leaned forward and spoke as a professor would to a class of students.

---

5   "Cordoba" or the Cordoba Project is the name given to the mosque planned to be built just blocks away from Ground Zero.

"In 1268 Baibars[6] besieged the city of Antioch which was badly defended by the Christian knights and abandoned by most of its inhabitants. The people of the city begged Baibars to spare them if they surrendered but the knights would not give up the city. The knights were led by a man named Simon Mansel, who was Constable of Antioch. Mansel was captured in the failed cavalry attack against the Muslim army and Baibars ordered him to command the knights to surrender, but they would not."

Zamani stood up and looked out the window behind his desk. He peered down at the Midtown Manhattan crowds walking to and fro below, as he continued.

"The Christians have never changed, Bahman. Even after over 700 years, their weak peoples beg for mercy and want to surrender while their stubborn and arrogant leaders and their armies try and fight hopeless causes."

Fard stepped up next to Zamani and joined him looking down at the crowds of people.

"What happened then?"

The question made Zamani smile.

"Baibars secretary described it in a letter. He wrote,

Death came among the besieged from all sides and by all roads: we killed all that thou hadst appointed to guard the city or defend its approaches. If thou hadst seen thy knights trampled under the feet of the horses, thy provinces given up to pillage, thy riches distributed by measures full, the wives of thy subjects put to public sale ; if thou hadst seen the pulpits and crosses overturned, the leaves of the Gospel torn and cast to the winds, and the sepulchers of thy patriarchs profaned; if thou hadst seen thy enemies, the Mussulmans trampling upon the tabernacle, and immolating in the sanctuary, monk, priest and deacon; in short, if thou hadst seen thy palaces given up to the flames, the dead devoured by the fire of this world, the Church of St Paul and that of St Peter completely and entirely destroyed, certes, thou wouldst have cried out "Would to Heaven that I were become dust!" [7]"

Zamani smiled at the look of shock and amazement on Fard's face as he continued.

"Baibars reneged on his pledge to Antioch's inhabitants.

---

6   "Baibars" was the Sultan of Egypt and Syria.

7   (Gabrieli, 1984).

Instead of sparing them, he ordered the gates shut and massacred everyone in the city. It is thought that 17,000 Christians were slaughtered and another 100,000 enslaved in that holy siege."

Zamani sat again at his desk prompting Fard to take his seat at the other end.

"I chose the name *Antioch* for our great campaign out west because I intend on doing what my predecessor Baibars did seven centuries ago. We will attack an American city with what they most fear; a nuclear bomb and then we will close the gates to that city and kill all the survivors of the blast. Even as we speak, our fighters and the former Spetsnaz mercenaries we hired will soon pour into the United States – to deliver our wedding gift. Then we select our target. Of the six cities our leaders have chosen, one now jumps out to me. This man Cris De Niro lives in it, Las Vegas. I believe I can persuade our leaders to not only allow me to pick the name for this great campaign, but also the target."

"What about this man De Niro, sir? Is he that much of a threat to us?"

Zamani hit the "forward" button on the email that Payam had sent him about De Niro, forwarding it to Fard. An instant later, Fard's iPhone made the familiar sound of receiving an email.

"I just sent you all the intelligence that Payam dug up on our friend Mr. De Niro. I sent Payam and his men out to his house to prepare a home invasion. I will have them interrogate him to find out if he has any other powerful allies that we should know about. Then they will eliminate him. I want you to find out all you can about this counter-terrorism company he just purchased in Virginia. You ask me if this man is that much of a threat to us, Fard. A man with his wealth, that lost his wife on 9/11 and who now owns a counter-terrorism firm ... and we find him parked outside Park51!"

Zamani banged his desk furiously.

"I told our leaders that Cordoba could backfire on us. While Bin Laden concentrates his efforts on Westerners in European cities, our plans in the United States are moving forward unfettered. I'm afraid that the level of our success here and overseas has made our leaders begin to underestimate Americans. AMERICA IS NOT EUROPE! They will only be pushed so far! We thought because we could use their system of laws against them that that would be enough. Some of our leaders thought that the Americans would just stand around and watch us humiliate them because we have the legal right to do so. I reminded those in Tehran and Pakistan that the BRITISH thought that too and so did the JAPANESE!"

Fard remained quiet, allowing Zamani to compose himself.

"If you want to know the truth, Bahman, I worry more about a man like De Niro than I do about the entire United States government. The United States can be such a foolish nation. With their political correctness, they value an individual's freedom over the security of their country and we laugh as they do. That's why we can live and work here and hide right under their noses without them having a clue of what we're doing. While they claim victory for finding a Pakistani immigrant with a car full of explosives in Times Square, I and others of the faith plan their systematic destruction."

"It is men like De Niro that have the means and the intelligence to uncover the truth about who their real enemies are. They are not bound by rules and laws like the government agencies are ... and he did not strike me as one who is ... politically correct. Now he invests in a counter-terrorism firm. His turning up at Park51, troubles me. The timing of it is too close for us to take any chances with him. We must proceed under the assumption that this man is a threat. While Payam will give me leverage over him personally, I want you, Bahman, to find a way to infiltrate his company ..."

Zamani searched for the name on his screen.

"... The Watchman Agency. Perhaps there are some dissenters inside his agency that are not pleased with their new boss. Use whatever means you need, but I want someone inside his firm as our ally, as soon as possible!"

"Yes sir."

Fard exited Zamani's office and while on the elevator to the building's lobby, used an iPhone app to book a one-way, first class flight to Virginia.

CHAPTER 12

EXECUTIVE CONFERENCE ROOM
THE FOSTER LAFAYETTE, PENTAGON CITY
ARLINGTON, VA
8:45A.M., SUNDAY, JULY 03, 2011

Les Pastak looked at his watch as he entered the luxury hotel
... *good I'm early.*

Searching through the contacts in his phone, he tapped his
finger on one and a moment later his call connected.

"Larry, its Les. I'm here at the hotel. Hold on a second ..."

Pastak asked the cordial, young lady at the front desk
where he could find Mr. Bahman Fard and after looking at her
computer screen she gave him directions to a small conference
room located down one of the corridors. Pastak headed to it as
he resumed his phone conversation.

"Okay, tell me again, this guy Fard is who ... they're an
overseas security firm ... British ... okay and you know for sure
that they're looking for someone to head their U.S. operations

... Larry, you made sure they know not to call The Watchman to check on me, right ... good, you told them how much I'm looking for ... good, plus an expense account, right ... sounds good ... okay, I'm standing outside the door, let me go, thanks."

Pastak turned his phone off, so he couldn't be traced then he straightened his tie and knocked on the conference room door before entering.

"Mr. Fard ... I'm Les Pastak."

"Welcome, Mr. Pastak, please ... sit down, anywhere is fine."

Pastak took a seat directly across from Fard who was sitting with a manila folder opened in front of him, in the center of a small conference table, facing the door. Fard pretended to be reading something contained in the folder; then he closed it and flashed a subtle smile.

"Are you familiar with our firm, Mr. Pastak?"

"Actually, no, not really, except for what Larry ... Mr. Woods, from the executive recruiting agency told me about you ... that you're a British security firm looking to expand here in the States."

"That is essentially correct. We are more of a corporate intelligence firm comprised of over a dozen components, currently located throughout Western Europe, East Asia and the Middle East. It is not surprising that you are not familiar with us as we like to maintain a low profile as much as our clients do. We predominately cater only to Fortune-20 corporations as well as several sovereign banks. We conducted just over one-billion Euros of business last year, which positions us as one of the larger firms in the corporate intelligence and security industry, in all of the largest markets except the United States."

Fard observed the impressed look on Pastak's face, so that confirmed one of his suspicions. ... *he's money-hungry. Now I must see how discontented he is with De Niro.*

"Well, I know that Larry Woods is one of the finest executive recruiters out there and he thought your opportunity ideally matched what I'm looking for—"

"... and what is it that you are looking for, Mr. Pastak?" Fard purposely cut him off.

"Well, Larry told me that you are aware of my salary and

benefits expectations—"

"Yes, yes, but is that all you have been looking for? What about the job itself, does anything about it particularly attract you to it?"

Pastak folded his arms while he decided how frank he intended to be with Fard. Fard only allowed a few seconds to go by before reaching down for his attaché case, opening it and placing the manila folder into it.

"Thank you for coming down, Mr. Pastak."

Pastak unfolded his arms.

"Wait a minute, is that all? You didn't let me answer your question."

Fard took out his phone and made believe he was checking his messages as he replied.

"It is apparent to me that you are not being entirely honest with me, Mr. Pastak, or in the very least, you are not being very open with me."

"Mr. Fard, I assure you, I have been totally honest with you."

Fard acted like he was typing a message on his phone, just to keep Pastak in suspense, then he put his phone away and with a touch of impatience, replied.

"Mr. Pastak, in the spirit of being open and honest, will you share with me why you would be interested in leaving your current firm."

Pastak fumbled over his words.

"Well, like I said, your offer ... I mean your opportunity is what I'm looking for ... the money is right ..."

Fard stood up, as if unimpressed with his answer. In desperation, Pastak searched for what he thought Fard wanted him to say.

"... and I will finally get to run things, my way!"

With that, Fard stared at Pastak and placed his attaché on the table.

"Is that also important to you, Mr. Pastak, to get the opportunity to run things? Because that is exactly the attitude of the person for which we are looking to head our operations here."

"Absolutely, in fact I should have mentioned it first, Mr.

Fard. It's really my primary reason for wanting to move from my existing situation."

Fard could tell that he was setting the hook, now it was time to reel this fish in. He returned to his seat.

"Perhaps, you should have, Mr. Pastak. You see, your resume is fine, your education, your experience are all sufficient - but without knowing the driving factors of why you would change from your present job to our company, I cannot make a determination of whether those same circumstances would once again manifest themselves in your new position with us."

Pastak looked confused to Fard. *These American infidels may all be as greedy as this one, but they cannot all be as dim-witted as him. I better make this easy for him.*

"Mr. Pastak, I will ... how do you Americans put it ... show my hand. Since Mr. De Niro acquired your agency, he has shown signs of wanting to fish in our pond, you understand? We had no competitive problems with your former boss and in fact we had conversations with Mr. Gerolitis about the possibility of our acquiring LDC, but apparently Mr. De Niro has bolder ambitions. We are specifically interested in hiring you to go - what is the term ... toe-to-toe, with your old firm and your old boss. Is this something you feel you can do?"

Pastak unconsciously rubbed his chin. He definitely thought he was better able to run the agency then was De Niro or his former-SEAL brother-in-law, but something about the term "toe-to-toe" made his underarms start to perspire. He knew of De Niro's reputation as a tough Brooklynite with brains and his estimated $9 billion+ net worth. Cris De Niro was not someone that Pastak wanted to spar with.

Fard finally went in for the kill. *I'll appeal to this pig's greed and ego at the same time.*

"Well then, I can see that you're hesitant, Mr. Pastak. There is a lot at stake for both you and our company. We have estimated the market share that our U.S. operations can establish within two years, with the right man at the helm, at around $150 million. All I can do is to assure you that we believe you are the right man for the job and we are willing to support you with the full weight of our company and its resources, in order for you to succeed."

Fard paused for effect.

"I am even prepared to offer you a signing bonus of $1 million, predicated on a few reasonable benchmarks ... and ... if you would accept an assignment before jumping ship, as it were."

Pastak was overwhelmed. He joked nervously, "$1 million ... who do you want me to kill for that?"

Fard flashed his subtle smile again.

"No, no, no, nothing so drastic, but I will ask you, straight-to-the-point, what is the state of your current relationship with Mr. De Niro? I want to know if there are any loyalty issues or any other kinds of issues that would prevent you from running Mr. De Niro's new flagship into the proverbial ground. Please, be completely honest with me, Mr. Pastak. If there are, there will be no hard feelings and rest assured that this meeting will have never taken place."

"Mr. Fard, for $1 million dollars I'd beat my own mother in business ... after all, it would let me give her much better Mother's Day gifts, wouldn't it?"

Fard was confused by the statement until Pastak started to laugh. *Between their vernacular and their humor, Americans are almost unintelligible to the rest of the civilized nations.* Fard forced a silent laugh.

"I really need you to answer the question, Mr. Pastak."

Pastak stared at Fard and then after a moment, threw his hands in the air.

"Okay, you want to know what I think of Cris De Niro. I think he's a pompous ass who is the poorest judge of character and talent. I also know that I got the short end of the stick when he bought the agency. I was supposed to take over when my brother-in-law left! Instead, he gave my office to HIS brother-in-law! It's too bad your company didn't acquire us!"

Fard replied quickly.

"So there is no love lost between you and him?"

"Love ... no Mr. Fard, there is none."

"Would you be willing to prove that, Mr. Pastak?"

"... and how can I prove that to you, Mr. Fard?"

Fard opened his attaché and produced a manila envelope.

He opened the envelope and carefully placed ten stacks of $100 bills on the table in between him and Pastak, along with what looked like an employment contract. Pastak couldn't help staring at the money.

"Mr. Pastak—"

"Les ... call me Les, Mr. Fard," Pastak interjected, still staring at the cash in front of him.

"Yes, of course, Les. I was authorized to offer you ... this advance of $100 thousand, with this Letter of Engagement that spells out the $1 million signing bonus, the benchmarks you need to meet, to earn it, and your salary and benefits along with your job description as head of our U.S. operations, if you would agree to the following. For the next ninety days, before you leave The Watchman, we would merely like you to inform us of any ongoing or just-starting operations that they are conducting, particularly in the Midwest and western United States. That is the area of our primary focus for expansion."

Pastak sat back in his chair.

"You're asking me to commit corporate espionage, Mr. Fard."

Fard waited a full minute before reaching to collect the cash on the table. As he did, Pastak quickly reached across and grabbed his hand, removing it from the cash and turning it so that he could shake it.

"As long as after reviewing it, I can confirm that this employment contract is all in order ... and as long as all I have to do is tell you basic information of any western operations ... no names and no details ... we have a deal Mr. Fard."

Fard smiled, this time more than subtly.

"Welcome aboard, Les."

Fard took the manila folder out of the attaché and allowed Pastak to use it to carry the cash. As soon as Pastak left the room, Fard took out his iPhone and punched an autodial button.

(In Farsi) "It's Fard, sir. It went just as you thought it would. He said he wants to review the Letter of Engagement first, but I get the feeling that he'll probably sign it as soon as he gets to his car."

"Very good Bahman ... return here. Between what that infidel may divulge to us and what Payam tells us, we should be able to deal with Mr. De Niro quite nicely, if the need arises."

Zamani disconnected the phone and then took a moment to look at the photo of De Niro he kept stored in his iPhone. As part of his belief that one should know one's enemy, Zamani had studied the Christian Bible. As he stared at his adversary, one line in particular came to him, from the book of Proverbs … *When your fear cometh as desolation, and your destruction cometh as a whirlwind; when distress and anguish cometh upon you.*

CHAPTER 13

THE COYOTE'S DEN
ESTANCIA DE NIRO
HENDERSON, NV
9:45A.M., MONDAY, JULY 04, 2011

Motion detectors located at the entrance to the covert installation, now called "The Coyote's Den" alerted the three members of ARCHANGEL that someone was outside. Flashing red lights mounted all around the facility and an annoying beeping alarm that sounded similar to a smoke detector needing its batteries changed, engaged simultaneously.

"We got company!" Vic "Riggy" Rigoni shouted unnecessarily to the other two men as he raced into the "sec-com," security and communications room next to his quarters. Riggy looked at the correct screen amidst a bank of monitors.

Emerging from the bathroom shirtless, with half of his face covered in shaving cream, Karl De May's size filled the doorway.

"Who is it?"

"It's our fearless leader."

A moment later, Spiro Pescalitis, a man much smaller than the other two, came jogging out of his quarters with a cell phone held against his face.

"What happened, did De May try to cook again?"

The large man grabbed the smaller man around his neck, prompting Pescalitis to add, with a make-believe choking tone, "Now I got you right where I want you!"

The sound of the large servo motors at the entrance could hardly be heard from inside, as they lifted the "hatch," the name the men gave to the camouflaged door. After a moment, they heard footsteps echoing from the ramp leading into the Den and finally Charley Santappia emerged.

"What are you knuckleheads up to?"

All three men walked over to him and shook his hand, then De May disappeared back into the bathroom.

"We're just about ready to go, if Karl ever finishes shaving," Riggy replied.

Santappia walked over to the equipment delivered during the night.

"It's amazing. With Johnny-F in charge of this project and Cris De Niro's financial backing, this place is getting built about ten-times faster than any government agency could do it."

"That's what happens when you keep the politicians out of it," Riggy added, "... and, Johnny-F and his installation team are as incredible as they are eccentric. I thought us old warhorses had our quirks ... but Charley, you have to see those guys. We can hardly understand them when they talk, but man, can they work! Twelve-hour-plus days, six days a week and they hardly ever take a break. They work while they eat, they work while they drink. We even hear them having conversations with each while they're on the bowl!"

"I know what you mean. It's the same way in Virginia. His IT army buzzes around like a swarm of bees, going from one flower to the next. I was with that agency for awhile and I can tell you that they got more done in two months with Johnny-F in charge than we did in two years, before Cris bought us ... and everything works! Big Brother is gonna be invaluable to us, in the field. I just hope the bad guys wait until we get our battlestar fully operational."

"Well, this is the last of the equipment. John told us that his super-nerds will arrive back here bright and early tomorrow. He estimated that they'll need a week to install, another week to de-bug and barring any unforeseen problems they'll be ready to train the three of us, by week three. By that time, the three of us will have our final personnel recommendations for you to look over. Then it'll probably take us another two or three weeks, minimum to get everyone trained and cross-trained."

Santappia nodded his understanding.

"How is it going, finding the people you want?"

"Well, we made a master list of everyone we want and the three of us have been keeping busy locating all of them, via back channel. Per your orders, we won't contact any of them until you vet them."

"Okay, I spoke with Captain Ricci and we decided on a hybrid-architecture of a SEAL platoon for ARCHANGEL. SEAL platoons consist of 16 SEALs; two officers, one chief, and 13 enlisted men. Their platoon can be divided into two squads or four elements. ARCHANGEL will be slightly different. The Captain and I will act as the two officers, and each of you will be in charge of one squad, making a total of three. Each squad will be comprised of six men - that's including you three. So the total compliment of ARCHANGEL will be 20, counting me and the Captain, and I'm counting us because there will be times when we split into five four-man elements and Captain Ricci and I will each lead one of the elements."

Riggy gave Santappia a cold stare.

"Don't worry, Rigs, the Captain and I both promise to train with you guys whenever we can. One other thing, you're all former Warrant Officers but you have seniority over De May and Pescy, so you'll act as Master Chief with ARCHANGEL. Once we get up and running, I want at least one squad here at all times. We'll rotate squads to man the Den 24/7/365. If all goes smoothly, we can begin to recruit in September and be a hundred-percent staffed by the end of the year. I'll leave it up to the three of you to create a rotation schedule. Oh yeah, and in keeping with our angelic branding, the squads will be named – MICHAEL, GABRIEL, and PADAEL."

Rigoni smiled.

"Angels with dirty faces ... and bad dispositions."

Pescalitis walked over to the two.

"Hey, I just got off the phone with my son, he said, everyone's psyched and they're about to board the shuttle bus to leave for the ranch."

De Niro invited the four men's wives and kids and in Rigoni's case, his baby grandson to spend the weekend in Las Vegas so that they all could attend a 4th of July party, at the ranch. There were a total of 12 of them, plus the baby, so they just fit on his new QSST. Everyone was blown away by the flight on the beautiful aircraft and even more blown away when they arrived and were shuttled to the Bellagio, on a shuttle bus, just for them. De Niro paid for suites in the beautiful resort for everyone.

The men spent Friday and Saturday with their families, but Riggy, De May and Pescalitis returned to the Coyote's Den late Saturday night, to receive more equipment being shipped to them. Work had to get done virtually around the clock, except from sunset to sunset on the Sabbath's, in keeping with De Niro's Judeo-Christian faith. So far, it looked like Johnny-F's timetable of three months for the Den to get operational was feasible.

Rigoni smiled.

"I can't wait to show Cris, my grandson. He asked about him a few times."

"Hey Charley, I know you said Cris is worth a bundle, but this weekend has to be costing him a chunk of change!" Pescalitis added.

De May came walking out of the bathroom trying to stretch a t-shirt over his barrel chest.

"My wife is getting so spoiled. She told me, 'Karl, I know your work is dangerous so please, don't get yourself killed, at least until after next year's 4th of July party!'"

The men laughed. Santappia checked his watch.

"Okay, let's saddle up. By the way, coming out here this morning was my first experience on an ATV. I must say ... very cool!"

"I thought De May and I were going to have problems 'cause of our size, especially King Kong over there," said Riggy, "but we didn't have any problem with them."

"Good, 'cause other than using them around the ranch, they may prove useful in the field. Cris said we can take them with us whenever we need them."

Pescalitis came walking back to them, already wearing his helmet.

"Guys, do you want to stand around here some more or can we get a move on? I got my floating lounge chair already picked out. I scoped it out the last time we were at the ranch and by the time we get there, there'll be a set of tall necks shouting my name!"

CHAPTER 14

THE MAIN HOUSE
ESTANCIA DE NIRO
HENDERSON, NV
12:45P.M., MONDAY, JULY 04, 2011

De Niro's 4th of July party was already in full gear by the time Keith Tompkins showed up with his wife Yvonne, their kids and someone Keith was looking forward to introduce to his friend.

After everyone hugged, Tompkins made the introduction.

"Cris, this is the little lady I told you about. Cris De Niro ... Moriah Stevens. That's Dr. Moriah Stevens. Moriah is the best vet east of the Mississippi. Just ask my kids. About a month after we met, Princess, our golden lab swallowed a rubber ball and Moriah rushed over to our house and pulled the ball out with salad tongs."

De Niro couldn't help laughing as he extended his hand, which made the pretty woman in front of him blush even more.

"Welcome to Estancia De Niro, Dr. Stevens."

"Thank you Mr. De Niro and thank YOU Keith, for that disgusting introduction!"

Keith's wife Yvonne elbowed her husband in his ribs.

"Keith, let's go say hello to William and the boys. You've done enough damage here."

De Niro's eyes sparkled with quiet laughter as he watched his friends walk into the house. Then he turned back to the pretty lady.

"Please, call me Cris."

"Okay Cris, if you call me Moriah ... and you DON'T call me if your dog starts choking."

De Niro laughed out loud again.

"Not to worry Moriah, we don't have a dog. Follow me, everyone's out back."

Moriah's beauty didn't go unnoticed by De Niro. *Now I know why Keith wanted me to meet her ... wise guy!*

Tompkins met Moriah at the 9/11 memorial the year before. He tried, that day, to introduce her to him, but De Niro ducked out before he got the opportunity. Moriah hadn't attended any of the previous memorials, since losing her husband on that fateful day. Her husband had been a passenger on the ill-fated American Airlines Flight 11 that crashed into the North Tower – the same tower where De Niro's wife Lisa lost her life. Since last year's memorial, Tompkins had been telling De Niro about her, but other than feeling compassion for her, De Niro showed no interest in meeting her. Tompkins thought bringing her to the 4th party was the perfect opportunity to introduce them.

Moriah could have been a model; in fact she had been, to help put her through veterinary school. Standing 5'4", with dirty-blond hair, emerald green eyes and an hourglass shape, she wasn't exactly a runway model, but that didn't bother her a bit. She had only been married a year when she lost her husband. Now, she was a 36 year-old widow with no children, although she considered her two dogs, Callie (a large German shepherd) and Booboo (a miniature American Eskimo), and her two cats, Samson and Delilah, to be her kids. Like De Niro, Moriah had shown no interest in the opposite sex since her husband died, though the opposite sex showed a lot of interest in her. Nary had a day gone by, since she stopped wearing her wedding ring, without at least one male, young or old, tall or small, rich or poor, black, white, green and every skin color in between, flirting with her. Moriah was usually cordial, but with the more aggressive ones, she was able to carry herself well, reminding them that she was trained in neutering males of all species.

Dr. Stevens didn't keep a large circle of friends; instead she devoted herself to her veterinary practice located in lower Manhattan. The friends she did have, all tried unsuccessfully to set her up on blind dates - which is why she not only surprised all of them, but surprised herself, saying yes to Keith when he invited her to meet De Niro.

What am I doing here? Is it the fact that he's a billionaire a few times over, or was it the photos Yvonne showed me of him ... or is this just a sign that I'm ready to "move on with my life," as everyone puts it. In any case, he does seem nice and ... he's better looking in person than in the photos.

De Niro led Moriah onto the back porch and introduced her to everyone, including Richard and Louis, with Richard giving her the evil eye, William and the staff, Mugsy and his date, Santappia, Riggy, De May, Pescalitis and their wives. Everyone with the exception of William and the staff were in the pool.

"Okay, now that that's out of the way, what can I get you to drink?"

"Whatever you're drinking is fine, thanks. You have beautiful boys and this ranch is absolutely spectacular!"

De Niro walked over to one of the dozen coolers placed all around the yard and popped the tops on two Stella Artois tallnecks. He handed one to Moriah and they clinked them together. De Niro spoke first.

"Happy 4th Moriah ..."

"Happy 4th Cris ..."

Both took long pulls from their beers as William walked over with a large platter of hot dogs, hamburgers, grilled chicken, and steaks. He carefully placed it in the middle of the large rectangular table. He was followed by Aurelio's wife Rosita who wheeled over a table with salads, condiments, chips and tortilla.

"We have two of the best cooks west of the Pecos, Aurelio

and his brother Arturo."

De Niro pointed over to the two men manning the grills who waved back with spatulas in their hands.

"And this is Señora Rosita ... Aurelio's beautiful wife!"

The small, chubby dark-skinned lady giggled as she nodded to Moriah.

De Niro switched to Spanish as he winked at her, "Rosita, this is Dr. Moriah who is here in case any of our animals swallow rubber balls."

Rosita burst out in laughter. It was Moriah's turn to show off her language skills.

(In Spanish) "That's such a pretty dress, Rosita. Did you buy it here in town?"

Rosita replied in English.

"No, señora, I bought it in Mexico City last year. Thank you so much!"

Impressed, De Niro continued in Spanish.

"You speak Spanish with a slight Puerto Rican accent, did you know that?"

Moriah replied in English.

"I took Spanish at Cornell[8] but I interned in Spanish Harlem. That's where I really learned to speak the language, although, I acquired the accent, in the process. Where did you learn to speak Spanish?"

"My paternal grandmother, Carmen taught me. She was born in Barcelona. We still have people there."

Richard and Louis ran over dripping wet followed by some of the other children. Rosita intercepted them and sat them all at another table, then placed a platter similar to the one that William brought out, on their table. They were followed by all the adults who were in the pool, led by Mugsy.

De Niro quickly grabbed a plate.

"Quick, before the Cavoni clean this platter too, what would you like?"

Moriah laughed.

"You speak Italian too?"

---

8   The New York State College of Veterinary Medicine at Cornell University located in Ithaca, New York.

"My mother taught me."

William walked over and whispered into De Niro's ear, "Sir, Ms. Wang, calling from Virginia, is on the home telephone. She asked to speak to you."

"Thank you William, I'll take the call, in my study. Moriah, if you'll excuse me I'll be right back. William, please serve Dr. Stevens first, before the wet vagabonds raid the platter."

"Hey, we're towel dry," Ricci exclaimed, making everyone laugh. Ricci walked over to De Niro.

"Something up?"

De Niro decided it was time to let his brother-in-law know.

"It's Michelle on my home phone. I'd like you to sit in on the call, that is, once you dry off and make sure what's-her-name gets something to eat; then join me in my study."

"Her name is Courtney, Cris ... at least that's her stage name."

De Niro entered his study and closed the door behind him; then he took a seat behind his desk and picked up the receiver.

"Michelle, its Cris, what's up?"

"Sorry to call on your home phone, Cris, I tried your cell but got your message."

"No problem, that's on me, I left my cell inside the house. Things have a way of melting when you leave them outside, out here. You can always call on this line, though. My Executive Assistant William Brett is familiar with all of Watchman's staff. So what's up, did you turn anything up?"

"Well, something turned up, but it doesn't have anything directly to do with the mosque, at least I don't think it does. You know how we've been monitoring large cash flows into Mexico from the Middle East, as part of our consulting contract with DHS[9]?"

"Sure, they wanted us to help them crack down on any foreign terrorists trying to infiltrate the U.S. via Mexico. Apparently, they had intel that Al Qaeda might be paying the cartels up to $25,000 a piece for every person they helped to smuggle across our southern border."

"Correct. Well, with the help of Big Brother we just got a lead. $25 million American was wired into a Banco Santander account from an account kept in Qatar's leading investment bank. The curious thing is that the account belongs to a Sharia-compliant private equity firm that was on the list of firms that you wanted me to keep an eye on ... and so was the bank in Qatar. The money was said to be an investment that the firm was making into a Mexican logistics warehouse operation."

Ricci quietly entered De Niro's study and closed the door behind him.

"Michelle, Captain Ricci just walked in, I'm putting you on speaker."

"Hi Michelle."

"Hi Captain."

Ricci look quizzically at De Niro.

"Mugs, I asked Michelle a few months ago if she'd do me a favor and look into ... any financial transactions that might take place between firms that might be supporting Islamic terrorism and ... the Ground Zero mosque project."

Ricci was not amused.

"Cris, you asked a person on my staff to do you a personal favor using resources of the firm you put me in charge of ... and you didn't let me know?"

De Niro breathed a sigh of relief, "For a moment there, I thought you were going to reprimand me for the ... legal uncertainty of my request."

Ricci's face turned red with anger, "Hey Cris, she was your wife, but she was my sister too!"

De Niro walked over to his brother-in-law and gave him a quick but sincere hug, "I know Mugs, you're right; I should have told you. I just didn't want to involve anyone else."

Ricci patted De Niro on his back then took a seat.

"So fill me in."

"Michelle was saying that Big Brother kicked out a lead on $25 million American that was paid by one of the Sharia-compliant private equity firms that I had her keeping tabs on, to a Mexican logistics warehouse operation. We're not sure if there's any tie-in with the mosque though. Michelle, Cris again, why did double-B tag this particular transfer. There's nothing illegal or particularly odd about a Sharia-compliant PE company investing in that kind of company. Logistics warehousing is one of the approved by Sharia law industries."

"That's what we thought too Cris, until Big Brother produced some compelling info. It couldn't immediately track the individual investors in the Middle East but it did dig up some disturbing intel on the Mexican side. Apparently, this warehouse operation is suspected of being used by one particular cartel to transport their narcotics into South America and the U.S. The warehouse operation is owned by a few layers of holding companies, but there is also suspicion that those companies may be owned wholly or partially by that same cartel's leader."

"Michelle, its Ricci, which cartel is suspected?"

"Hold on ... the Pacifico cartel ..."

"Pacifico is run by Tuco Ramirez," Ricci replied, more to De Niro than to Michelle, "he's considered the boldest and most violent of the new wave of Mexican drug lords."

Michelle's voice jumped in.

"Captain, I'd like permission to send two of my operatives, one to Qatar and one to Mexico to investigate. Double-B has done all it can do, now we need to put feet on the ground and find out who the limited and general partners are of the private equity firm, and we also need to find out more about that Mexican warehouse operation."

"Michelle, sounds like it could be dangerous, especially on the Mexican side. Are you sure you want to send them both in solo?"

"I'm sending two of my most experienced agents, one is Saudi Arabian, the other is Mexican, both naturalized U.S. citizens drafted by Langley over a decade ago."

Both men detected a hint of defensiveness in Michelle's tone.

"Neither of them should have any trouble. We're already working on their covers. This is a simple fishing expedition and they're both experienced fishermen. They'll know if they're entering rough seas, trust me. They'll both have standing orders to return to port, at the first sign of trouble."

"I do trust you Michelle, make it happen."

"Thanks Captain, sorry if I sounded testy there."

"Not a problem, get back to your July 4th festivities. Where are you, anyway?"

"I'm by my sister's house in Richmond. Hey, tell Johnny-F that Big Brother did its job; double-B even sent me a text message to my cell when it found the dirt on the warehouse."

"Will do, I'll talk to you tomorrow."

"Happy 4th, Michelle and thanks for the head's up," De Niro added.

"No problem Cris, same to you."

De Niro hit the disconnect button. As soon as he did, Ricci spoke up.

"What do ya think?"

"I don't know. If it is something ... it may be something we need to worry about. According to DHS, the cartels supposedly are only charging about 25 grand-per to smuggle a foreign alien over the border. So, if that's a payment to smuggle bad guys into the U.S. that would pay for an army of them. Or else—"

Ricci finished his sentence, "Or else that's not all they're paying to smuggle in. Michelle's right, we need to know."

De Niro thought out loud, "That was odd though, one of the firms that I thought might be interested in funding the mosque, we find transferring $25 million into the account of a company suspected of having ties with a Mexican drug cartel."

Ricci patted De Niro on the back, "As you like to remind me Cris, sometimes God works in mysterious ways. Sometimes you set traps for mice and you snare a rat. I guess we'll see where this leads."

"On both ends," De Niro added.

Both men got up to leave the room. Ricci opened the door but then shut it again, right before De Niro was about to walk out.

"By the way Cris, she's hot!"

De Niro knew exactly who he was talking about.

"Mugs, don't start!"

"I'm not starting; I'm just saying ... she's hot!"

De Niro opened the door and spoke over his shoulder as he walked out.

"Coming from a guy that's dating a girl with a stage name, I appreciate your opinion, Mugs."

Moriah was no longer at the table, by the time De Niro walked out. He looked around the pool for her and saw that everyone else was having a ball. Someone had turned the music up and everyone was singing along to Lynyrd Skynyrd's "Sweet Home Alabama." Before De Niro even asked, William walked over and told him what he wanted to know.

"Dr. Stevens walked over to the stables, sir."

De Niro was about to try and act uninterested, but he knew William knew him too well. So he simply replied, "Thanks William."

As he approached the stables, De Niro could see Martin Fierro, his head "gaucho," standing at the opened gate.

"¿Que pasa, Martin ...?"

Martin replied in English. He was practicing English with William and was proud of his progress.

"The señora took Beauty out for a ride. I told her I go with her but she say not to bother, she just go down the path and back. Here she comes!"

Both men watched as the beautiful lady came trotting up the path, her blond hair in total contrast to Beauty's jet-black mane and body. As she approached she reined the powerful animal into a graceful sidestep.

De Niro thought out loud, "She can ride, can't she ..."

He wasn't expecting a reply, but Martin stepped up next to him.

"Si, señor, she rides like the Chinitas[10] back home in Argentina ... except señora Moriah is a lot better looking than they are!"

Martin winked at De Niro as Moriah stepped down from Beauty.

"Muchas gracias Martin, Beauty lives up to her name!"

"De nada, doctora, you are welcome to ride Beauty, anytime."

Martin led Beauty back into the stable as Moriah walked up to De Niro.

"I hope it was okay to take her for a ride. I couldn't resist. She's a beautiful animal."

"Hence her name," De Niro replied with a smile on his face.

"Martin is amazing too. You know, I think he knows more

---

10   Chinitas is another name for a female gaucho.

about animals than I do."

De Niro didn't reply right away. For a moment he felt something he hadn't felt in a long time, but when it came to him what it was, it made him feel sick. His reply was a little obvious.

"My wife ... thought he was amazing too."

Moriah noticed.

"Keith told me about ... Lisa. I'm so sorry, Cris."

Almost 10 years had passed but De Niro's eyes still watered at the mention of his wife. De Niro turned from her, extending his arm in the direction of the main house. Moriah started walking at his side.

"Keith told me about your husband too. I'm very sorry, Moriah. I understand he was on the plane that struck Tower One; my wife was on the 104th floor of Tower One when the plane hit."

The music and laughter from everyone in and around the pool was faintly audible, contrasting the somber conversation they were having. De Niro didn't feel much like rejoining the party, at that moment. He could tell that Moriah felt the same way.

"Would you like to take a walk? There's a path in the other direction that will take us to the top of one of the ranch's larger foothills. You can see almost the whole spread when you look south and the entire Las Vegas valley if you look north, from up there."

Moriah looked relieved.

"I'd love to."

As they walked, they talked a bit about Lisa and her husband and about the boys and her animals, but neither brought up 9/11. It took them almost a half hour to reach the summit.

"It's so beautiful up here, Cris! You're right about being able to see everything. I bet we can see California from here!"

Moriah put her hand over her eyes to act as a shade.

From behind her, De Niro softly grabbed her by her shoulders and turned her slightly.

"California is that way."

A chill went down Moriah's spine from his touch. She hadn't been touched that way or rather; she hadn't reacted from being touched that way since that terrible day. She stiffened just enough for De Niro to notice.

De Niro backed away. When he did, Moriah turned and walked up so close to him that the tips of their noses almost touched.

Neither said a word for what seemed like an eternity. Finally De Niro stepped back and pointed in the direction of the Strip.

"You have to see the Strip from up here at night, it's an amazing sight."

Moriah tried to identify the feelings she had, from De Niro backing away from her. She finally realized it was disappointment. She was so used to being pursued that she was completely unaccustomed to someone backing away, especially when she wasn't putting up any resistance. It occurred to her in that moment that she hadn't even felt that way with her husband, because he also had come onto her when they first met. It was too much to think about all at once so she decided to try and cool down and lighten up.

Doing her best Mae West impression, she smiled and replied, "You want me to come up and ... see it sometime?"

De Niro stood silently for a moment, which sent a wave of embarrassment over Moriah.

"Okay, I have NO IDEA where that came from."

De Niro started to laugh which made Moriah laugh. Their laughter grew until both of the eyes filled with tears. Nothing more about the intimacy that sparked between them but didn't ignite needed to be said. One thing they both felt, the two had gone from strangers to friends, on that hilltop.

"Well, how about it. How long are you staying in town?"

"I leave tomorrow morning early. I have to be back at work by Tuesday morning."

"So soon ...?"

"Well, we've been in town since Thursday afternoon. Keith said he tried to get a hold of you since we arrived but he you weren't around."

De Niro immediately felt badly. He purposely had blown Keith off expressly because he didn't want to meet Moriah. Now he regretted that he had and that made him feel guilty. He decided not to share any of that with her.

"Well, you'll just have to come back. When can you take off again?"

Moriah's frustration was evident in her voice.

"Not for awhile. I usually only take off the week leading up to September 11 and the end of the year—"

"That's perfect," De Niro interjected. "Come out and stay on the ranch the week before 9/11 and you can fly back to New York with me and the boys. We attend the memorial every year."

Moriah hesitated.

"Come on, you haven't even seen a small portion of the ranch yet and you'll get to ride Beauty again ... and I bet you never have flown faster than the speed of sound."

De Niro's smile was ear to ear. Moriah could tell that his intentions were pure and his friendship, sincere. She appreciated the latter, but as for the former ...

"How could I possibly pass up a chance to ride that beautiful horse again?"

De Niro nodded with pleasure as he offered her his arm and together they started back down the path.

"Come on, by this time, I'm sure everyone's looking for us."

Catching De Niro by surprise, Moriah leaned towards him and kissed him gently on his cheek.

"What was that for?"

Playing coy and turning from him as only a woman can do, she replied, "That was for showing me where California is!"

CHAPTER 15

THE WATCHMAN AGENCY
OFFICE OF THE V.P. OF H.R/GENERAL COUNSEL
ARLINGTON, VIRGINIA
9:45A.M., TUESDAY, JULY 05, 2011

Walking into his office sipping a latte he stopped to buy at Starkbucks, Pastak made a beeline to his desk. As soon as his system started up, he typed something into his Google search bar and after clicking on a few links he picked up his phone and dialed the number that appeared on his screen.

"Hi, is this the Mercedes dealership near the Ballston Common Mall? Your sales department please ... Hi, I'd like to make an appointment to come down to your showroom ... tonight, around seven, if that's okay ... well, I'd like to take a look at the SLR McLaren you had showcased ... yes, I'm aware of the price ... Pastak, P-a-s-t-a-k ... what was your name ... fine Ken, I'll see you at seven."

Pastak hung up his phone and spun around in his chair. He

felt giddy. In fact, he felt even better than when he thought he was taking over LDC. *I already have 100 thousand reasons why I should feel this good and soon I'll have one million. All I have to do now is throw this Fard character a bone ... and after all, who could that hurt? I don't owe anyone here anything, anyway!*

He clicked on a photo of the $425,000 automobile and the interior appeared on his screen. As he leaned in closer to take a look, his intercom buzzed. Without looking away, he tapped the answer button.

"Pastak ..."

"Les its Michelle, do you have a minute?"

Pastak clicked on another photo of the car.

"I'm a little tied up right now, Michelle, what's up?"

Wang was infuriated. ... *tied up right now? Probably checking sports scores on ESPN.com!*

"Les, I need to bring you up to speed on two international ops that just got underway."

That caught Pastak's attention. He closed the car dealership's website.

"Give me five; I'll meet you in your office."

Pastak hit the disconnect button. *Could it be ... could I be this lucky?! Oh man, I hope it's enough to let me keep the mil!*

Wang's door was open but Pastak still knocked on the doorframe.

"Come in Les, grab a seat. I just hired two new agents for intel-gathering operations. They're agents that I've worked with at Langley; I know them both a long time. They've done some freelanced work for LDC in the past. I tried contacting you—"

Pastak's face turned red with anger.

"Wait just a minute, Michelle; you don't have the authority to hire anyone without my approval!"

It was times like this that Wang was especially proud of her Chinese heritage. She learned how to keep her temper in check, from her parents. My dad used to say, *"Hyenas laugh, baboons scream and fools raise their voices in anger."*

She folded her hands in front of her and rested them on her desk.

"Les, apparently you haven't read the new SOP's Captain

Ricci put into place last week. If you had, you'd know that because of the aggressive timeline to bring the agency up to the new standards, in time-sensitive situations, all VP-level staff has been given the authority to hire, on the spot – as long as (a.) Captain Ricci and (b.) the VP of Human Resources ... you ... are informed within 24 hours of the hiring. I informed Captain Ricci already and I'm informing you now. The men were hired early this morning and are already in transit."

Pastak tried to reel back his anger. The truth was that from the moment he was told of his "new" position within the agency, he'd spent all of his time looking for another job and no time reading the new SOP's. *What am I getting so angry about? I'll be out of here soon and driving my new convertible! Then all of these people and their reckless procedures can go to hell!*

"You're right. I haven't gotten around to reading them; I've been tied up with other things."

Wang decided to let that go.

"Not a problem. As I was saying, I tried contacting you Saturday morning to let you know that I may need these two men, but I got an unavailable message from your cell. Did you turn it off Saturday morning?"

Pastak remembered that he did turn his phone off before he met with Fard. It was against agency rules for any senior executive to turn their cell phones off, for any length of time. Normally no one would be reported for such a trivial matter, but Pastak didn't trust any of them anymore, Michelle included.

"Actually, my battery failed and the phone went dead. I didn't notice it until later that morning."

Probably more like, you forgot to charge it, dimwit! Apology accepted!

"Well, here are their files. Like I said, we used them both in the past, so at least we have their personal information. I'm not sure if any of it needs to be updated though."

Wang handed Pastak two manila files. Pastak opened them both and took a quick look at the photos attached to their dossiers. *Majed Ahmed Aziz al Saud – a Saudi ... and Jesus Garcia – a Mexican ... If the Mexican was sent to his homeland, that would count as a western operation!*

"You said they're both in transit. I may need to contact them to confirm their personal information, so I'll need operational access through Big Brother."

Johnny-F had built in many different tiers and types of security access into Big Brother. One such type was Operational Access, which gave the user complete access to all information pertinent to a particular operation. That included all personnel information, which included GPS-tracking info on any personnel attached to the operation.

Wang hesitated which gave Pastak his opportunity to smack her down and return the favor. He looked up from the folders.

"Michelle, unless the new SOP changes include prohibiting the VP of HR to do his job in a timely manner, I suggest you give me op-access immediately."

"I just don't understand why you can't wait until they return to the U.S., Les."

"And exactly when will that be, Michelle?"

"I can't say exactly—"

"Hey Michelle, how about, I don't tell you about the new SOP's and you don't tell me how to do my job."

Wang was furious. *I take it back! Its times like these that I wish I weren't Chinese, so I could feel okay about jumping across my desk and strangling this jerk!*

Wang never felt comfortable letting anyone but essential individuals know about covert operations. She understood the need for Pastak to verify the personal info for both agents but not the urgency. She couldn't deny though that he did have the authority to request ops-access and unless she had a specific reason to deny such access, she had to give it to him.

Wang typed something on her keyboard. After a moment, she looked up at him.

"I just gave you O-A access to Operation India-Golf 070510."

Pastak stood up and smiled.

"Thank you, Michelle."

As soon as he got back in his office, Pastak accessed the operation files on his laptop. He scanned the monitor until he found what he was looking for then he hit a new auto-dial button on his cell, one he just created.

"Mr. Fard, its Les. I have good news. Where and when would you like to meet ... okay, can we make it after say, nine tonight ... I have an appointment at seven I need to keep ... very good, I'll try to get there by nine and oh, Mr. Fard, you'll need to bring your checkbook."

CHAPTER 16

THE FOSTER LAFAYETTE HOTEL
BAHMAN FARD'S SUITE
WASHINGTON, D.C.
9:15P.M., TUESDAY, JULY 05, 2011

Pastak tucked one manila file under his arm, took the ticket from the valet and headed into the five-star hotel. He checked his watch as he stepped onto the elevator. *Not bad, I made good time here. Days don't get much better than this!*

Fard was already contacted by the front desk and informed of his impending guest, so he was standing at the door of his penthouse suite, when Pastak knocked.

The two men shook hands as Fard closed the door behind him.

"You have information for us?"

"I do."

Fard extended his arm towards one of the plush couches.

"Please, make yourself comfortable. May I offer you

something to drink or eat?"

"After our business, here, is done, I'll pay for a bottle of this hotel's best champagne, but scotch would do, for now."

"I'm sorry Les, but I have no alcoholic beverages to offer you. Would you like me to order you room service?"

"That's not necessary. I forgot you're prohibited from drinking alcohol aren't you. You're Muslim, right?"

"Yes, that's right."

"I'll just have what you're having then."

"I'm having tea."

"You know what, nix that. I'll just have a bottle of water, if you have one."

Fard fetched a bottle from the other room, placed it on the table in front of Pastak and took a seat on the couch next to his.

"We're impressed with your rapid progress, Les. Frankly, we didn't anticipate that we would hear from you so soon or I would have remained here in town. I hope this is something worth my flying in from New York on such short notice."

"Yeah, well, to be honest, I didn't anticipate that I'd be contacting you so soon either, but something fell in my lap this morning that I think you'd be interested in."

Pastak leaned over and handed Fard the folder containing Jesus Garcia's personal information. He gave him a few moments to look it over.

"Why are you showing me this man's information?"

"... Because he headed to Mexico this morning on an I-G mission."

"I-G mission ...?"

"I-G stands for intelligence-gathering. You *do* consider Mexico part of the west, don't you Mr. Fard?"

Fard knew that Zamani had only been concerned with possible counter-terrorism operations post their cell's infiltration into the U.S. from Mexico. Any investigations south of the border, prior to their incursion into the States were unanticipated and potentially troublesome. *Zamani won't be happy about this! I need to know everything this fool can tell me and then I need to contact Zamani as soon as possible!*

"We do. Where exactly will this ... Garcia be investigating and exactly what is he investigating?"

"Now Mr. Fard, you remember our agreement. I was only asked to provide you with general information."

"Les, telling us that this man is gathering intelligence in Mexico is too general to benefit us in anyway. I'm afraid we'll need to know exactly what this man is investigating and exactly where he'll conduct his investigation, for it to be of any value to us."

Pastak rubbed his chin with concern.

"Just what is our interest in knowing those things, Mr. Fard? How could knowing what Garcia is investigating benefit ... us ... in any way?"

Fard took a slow sip of his tea then placed the cup back onto the saucer he was holding in his other hand.

"Of course our agreement does not dictate the need for me to explain that to you in any way, Les ... but I will, in any case. One of the reasons why we decided to open operations here in the United States, now, is because we were recently contacted by the Mexican government to perform an investigation on one of their drug cartels. They wanted us to look into this cartel's so-called legitimate business holdings both inside and outside of Mexico. The contract would be multi-year and very lucrative, enough for us to establish permanent operations here. The problem is that after we sent them our proposal, we didn't hear back from them. We have reason to believe that Mr. De Niro might have ... how is it put ... undercut our pricing. We had negotiated a binding 90-day clause with the Mexican government where we were supposed to be afforded the opportunity to match anyone else's offer with our own counter-offer."

Pastak jumped in, "So, if The Watchman sent someone to investigate—"

Fard finished his sentence, "The Mexican government would be in breach of our agreement. In that case, we could sue them, but we're not interested in a law suit. We're interested in securing that business. All we need to do is produce compelling evidence that The Watchman is conducting an investigation, on behalf of the Mexican government. If this man is looking into any of this cartel's businesses then we can use the proof that he is, to ... persuade the Mexican government that it's in their interests to cancel their contract with The Watchman and sign one with us."

Pastak looked concerned.

"Mr. Fard, I'm not privy to client-level info. Even my operational access won't allow us to know on whose behalf The Watchman is conducting this investigation."

"That's not a problem Les. You see, we already have a complete list of all of the legitimate holdings of this cartel in Mexico. All we would need is evidence that this man Garcia is investigating any one of them. Then we can convince the Mexican government that our attorneys will be able to connect the dots, so to speak, in court and prove they're in breach of contract."

Pastak stood up and paced around nervously.

"I should have had you order me up that scotch!"

"What's the matter Les?"

"The matter is Mr. Fard, making you aware of an ongoing investigation, in general terms is one thing. It could be explained away if something goes wrong. But telling you details, especially pertaining to an agent's whereabouts during a covert mission ... that could be construed, at minimum, as industrial espionage or worse! I know about these things, I'm an attorney, remember?"

Fard finished the tea in his cup then stood up, placed the cup and saucer on the cocktail table and extended his arm again.

"Les, please take a seat."

Pastak stopped pacing and stood staring at Fard for a few moments then finally returned to his seat on the couch. Once he sat, Fard also sat again.

"Why are you anticipating that something will go wrong? Nothing will go wrong! I assure you that the information you provide us will be held in the strictest confidence by our company and the Mexican government. There will be no way for anyone at The Watchman to even discover that you have told us anything. The Mexican government will simply find a way out of their contract with them, probably just exercising their 30-day right to terminate."

Pastak wasn't convinced.

"They may not be able to discover anything externally, but I'm not sure what they're capable of doing with their new proprietary computer system. The man that installed created it and installed it is a genius. For all I know, I'm leaving digital footprints inside the ops files that could lead them directly back to me."

Fard was becoming impatient.

"Les, you must have known there was an element of risk involved, but the level of risk to you is small compared to your level of reward."

"Yeah, well, speaking of that reward, I'm NOT going to even think of taking that much of a chance with only being paid the advance! If I decide to give you the info you want, I'm not doing so until AFTER the remaining $900 thousand is deposited in an account I opened in the Cayman Islands."

It was Fard's turn to jump to his feet.

"That is an unreasonable request!"

Pastak jumped to his feet.

"Is it?! Well, those are my terms, take them or leave them!"

The two men stood with their eyes locked. After a few tense moments, Fard flinched first.

"I don't have the authority—"

"Well then I suggest you GET the authority right now or I walk out that door."

I would love nothing more than to slit this infidel's throat ... but I'm sure I'll get that chance soon enough. I have no choice; I'll have to call Zamani.

"I have to make a phone call."

Pastak extended his arm towards the next room.

"Be my guest."

Fard walked all the way into the bedroom before hitting the speed dial on his iPhone.

(In Farsi) "It's Fard, sir. I'm here with the infidel. Sir, he has information that The Watchman has sent one of their agents to Mexico to gather intelligence. The problem is that he's running scared. He wants the remaining $900 thousand deposited into an off-shore account before he'll give us the target of the investigation or the agent's location ... yes sir, I think that's possible ... very well ... I understand ... I think we have to also, it's too close ... I'll take care of it."

Fard walked back into the living room area. Pastak was sitting again on the couch.

"I've been authorized to pay you the rest of your bonus, Les."

Pastak blinked his eyes a few times then slowly a smile appeared on his face. Fard began making the transfer from his iPhone.

"Please provide me with the account number, to where you want the funds transferred."

Pastak jumped up and walked over to Fard.

"May I? It'll be easier for me to enter it in."

Fard handed him his iPhone and Pastak entered the account number then handed the phone back to him. Fard then reluctantly hit a button transferring the money. When it was completed he showed Pastak the confirmation on the phone's screen.

"Now Les, we have held up our end, it's time for you to hold up yours."

Pastak nodded then typed his username and password into the Big Brother front-end on his phone. Then he entered the access code Wang gave him for Operation India-Golf 070510. As soon as the screen populated with data he handed his phone to Fard. Fard began transcribing the information onto a legal pad.

"This system is quite impressive, Les. I have never seen a system so ... dynamic before."

After copying all of the operational info, Fard looked it over and after a moment began shaking his head.

"No, this is not enough. Just knowing the company he's investigating isn't enough, Les. This company has too many locations. He could be at any one of them using phony credentials and in disguise. You said their system has the ability to track the agents assigned to the missions. You'll have to give me Garcia's transponder number so we can locate him."

"Mr. Fard, couldn't you just show the Mexican government that info as proof?"

"No, Les. That's just it; all we would be showing them is information. They could simply dismiss it and say that we fabricated it."

Pastak's nervousness reemerged.

"But—"

"Les, there is nothing to worry about. The transponder number will just allow us to locate Mr. Garcia so that we can take photos of him. Those photos will be enough to corroborate the info you gave me. Your name will never even be brought up and no harm will come to Agent Garcia."

Pastak hesitated.

"Les, you really must live up to your end, you really must!"

Pastak exhaled audibly then took his phone back from Fard and typed into it for a few moments. When Garcia's transponder number appeared on the screen, he handed his phone back to Fard who wrote it down. As soon as he did, he escorted Pastak to the door.

"Thank you Les, you've held up your end."

Pastak stopped just outside the door and looked down the hall to make sure no one was there.

"What do I do now?" Should I hand in my resignation?"

"No-no, not yet, just continue about your business there. You don't want to bring any suspicion onto yourself. Once this business is over with, you can hand in your resignation."

That seemed to make sense to Pastak, so he nodded in agreement.

"Oh and Les, try not to use your new savings just yet. Again, we don't want you to do anything that might bring undo suspicion onto you."

Pastak's look of disappointment was evident.

"Understood ..."

CHAPTER 17

AV. NAFTA 69
PARQUE INDUSTRIAL STIVA AEROPUERTO
66600 APODACA, NUEVO LEÓN, MÉXICO
11:45P.M., TUESDAY, JULY 12, 2011

Agent Jesus Garcia sat in a rental car parked across from the company's Monterrey distribution center. Because of its proximity to the United States border, Monterrey acts as a vital operations host to an array of domestic and international companies. That allowed Garcia to easily blend into the crowded business center using the cover of a Tex-Mex interested in setting up manufacturing operations there. He spent his days being shown available factory space for rent and made sure to lunch each day close to the suspected drug lord's warehouse. That allowed him to "chew the fat" with a number of truck drivers who picked up and delivered from the facility. Garcia was experienced enough to know what to ask and what not to ask. It was much safer to pay for a few bottles of cerveza and let the beer inspire the drivers to tell him what he wanted to know.

It took him a week to establish his cover and talk to the right driver. He received his first piece of real intel at lunch, when a driver named Pedro asked him if he'd be around that night. Pedro told him he had instructions to make a late-night delivery and would be free afterwards to show him a few of the local clubs. Garcia wasn't able to find out much more about the load he was delivering at lunch, but figured he could get Pedro to tell him about it once he bought a few rounds for him at the club.

Garcia's car was the only one parked on the dark street just outside the front gate of the well-lit facility. There was a manned guardhouse protecting the entrance to the large parking lot. Garcia used the time he had to wait, entering notes into Big Brother, via his iPhone. He logged off as soon as he saw Pedro's truck pulling up next to his car. Pedro rolled down his window.

(In Spanish) "It's good to see you, my friend. Hey, follow me. I'll tell the security guard that you're my ride home and he'll let you in. Then I can give you a quick look at what I'm hauling before I take you to the hottest club in town!"

Garcia was careful not to show emotion. *That would be perfect, but experience has taught me to always look a gift horse in the mouth. Could this be a set up? But how, I didn't come close to blowing my cover?*

The smile on Pedro's face grew wider. This time he spoke in broken English.

"I thought you were interested in what I was hauling. To tell you the truth amigo, I'm curious too. We can take a quick peak. This time of night no one's around near the loading dock until I call for them, so it'll be safe. I tell you what, whatever it is, there were a lot of *gallitos*[11] about when they loaded me. Who knows what's back there!"

Garcia still didn't reply. *I gotta make up my mind and quickly. The only way this could be a set up is if my cover is blown, but I'm sure I didn't blow it ... and I've never been wrong about that before.*

The driver got impatient.

(In Spanish) "Jesus, you gonna come or not? If not, just wait for me here. It'll take me about twenty minutes to get unloaded then I'll come out to you."

---

11   "Gallitos" means tough guy, commonly used in Mexico.

Garcia made up his mind and replied, in English.

"Lead on amigo. I don't want to keep the women waiting any longer than necessary."

Pedro's smile returned, this time wide enough for Garcia to see all of his gold teeth. Pedro pulled up to the guard shack and after a moment Garcia saw the guard waving him through. *Maybe this'll be okay. They don't all have to be difficult.*

Garcia followed the driver's truck past a dozen closed doors, then pulled up next to the truck as it backed up to the first dock with its door opened. Just as Pedro said, Garcia didn't see a soul around, inside or outside. Pedro jumped out of his cab and waved Garcia over to join him at the back of the truck. As soon as Pedro opened the back of his truck, he jumped up into the trailer and then he helped Garcia up into it.

"It's a little dark back here, but I don't want to chance turning the spot light on. Let's just take a quick peek into this big one right here."

Pedro handed Garcia a crowbar.

"Here, you pry the nails up and I'll hold the flashlight."

Garcia looked at the wooden crate. It was wide and long enough to put a king-sized mattress inside of it and about two feet tall. He started prying the nails up. *I know they hide drugs in virtually everything, I wonder what's inside this.*

As soon as he pried the last nail up, he turned to Pedro. He could hear him speaking but he couldn't see him, blinded by the flashlight.

"Go ahead, lift the top off. I'll keep an eye out and let you know if anyone's coming."

Garcia's heart started racing. *Something's not right about this—.*

"Hurry up amigo before someone comes!"

Garcia said a silent prayer as he lifted the top off. He was shocked to see just a large, thick plastic tarp inside, *it's a setup!*

Reaching his hand in his jacket for his pistol, Garcia turned quickly, but he was completely blinded by Pedro's flashlight. He tried to take aim in the direction of the light but it was too late. Agent Garcia only remained alive long enough to hear the first of two silenced bullets fired at his forehead. He fell backwards, lifeless into the crate he had just opened.

Pedro wasted no time wrapping Garcia's body in the plastic and tying it tightly around the dead man, with rope already attached to grommets along one end of the tarp. Then he quickly replaced the crate's lid and used the crowbar to hammer the nails back down. When he was finished he barked orders in Spanish to someone standing inside the loading dock, apparently there the whole time.

"Follow me out in his car, he left it running. I'm gonna tell the guard, they loaded me with the wrong load and I have to return it. Keep your face as concealed as you can as you pass the guard shack. Then drive the car downtown and park it where I told you to and lose the keys. Make sure you don't touch anything with your hands. Keep your gloves on the whole time. Understood?"

The man in the loading dock jumped down and did just what he was told to. The guard didn't even look his way as he past the guard shack. Once outside the gate, Pedro turned right and the man in Garcia's car turned left. He drove the car to La Colonia Independencia, just south of the river from the Macroplaza. The area was considered one of the most dangerous areas in Monterrey. As instructed, the man parked the car, got out and walked to the river where he tossed the car keys into the deep. Then he hit a number on his speed dial, connecting him with Pedro.

"It's done."

Pedro replied with no emotion.

"Good. Now go home."

As soon as that call disconnected, Pedro hit an autodial on his phone.

"Tuco, it's done. I'm heading for my next stop ... no problems ... I'll take care of it when I get there."

Pedro put his phone away as he turned onto the "Nacional" aka the National Highway. He headed south with Agent Jesus Garcia's body lying in his crate coffin. His destination was property owned by the cartel in the south of Mexico, where they grew illegal drugs. Garcia's body would join the dozens of other bodies, all murdered by members of the cartel. The cartels' thugs thought it was humorously ironic that pot would grow from the remains of drug enforcement agents. Inside Agent Garcia's pocket though was his iPhone ... and it was beeping.

CHAPTER 18

THE WATCHMAN AGENCY
OFFICE OF THE PRESIDENT
ARLINGTON, VIRGINIA
3:00P.M., THURSDAY, JULY 14, 2011

Michelle Wang was getting nervous and that wasn't something she was accustomed to feeling. Throughout her years in the CIA, she was known for her coolness in tense situations. She always attributed that to a manic work ethic and attention to detail, so when she moved forward, she did so with total confidence.

She also always felt she erred to the side of caution when it came to sending people into the field. She used a very simple rule, one she knew she had in common with Christians ... she did unto others as she would have them do unto her – in other words, she never sent an agent into a situation that she wouldn't enter into herself. That included the intelligence-gathering missions on which she just sent Agents Majed Ahmed Aziz al Saud and Jesus Garcia. She did the diligence, chose the right individuals for the job and weighed the risks. In the end though, she knew there was always an element of time and chance. In all her years of sending agents into the field, she had never lost one. She was wondering now, sitting in Captain Ricci's office, if that perfect record made her careless. Ricci watched her for a few moments, staring at her laptop screen with blood-shot eyes.

"Garcia's last communication was a log entry Tuesday night. He reported that he was following up on a lead he received, from a driver who delivered to the warehouse in Monterrey. He thought he might get a chance to peek at the driver's freight. His last log entry was time-stamped just before midnight on Tuesday. He should have followed up yesterday! Captain, I'm sorry, I should have brought this to your attention sooner ... I just don't know what could have happened. I mean, I've worked with Jesus many times in the past. He was always so careful and he always let me know when he thought the situation was risky. In this case, he just didn't give me any indication—"

"Michelle, you're not to blame. When did you sleep last?" Ricci interrupted her as he hit the intercom button on his phone.

"Debbie, I want to see all executive staff in conference room alpha in five."

Ricci got up from his desk, but Wang remained seated, deep in thought. Ricci put his hand to her shoulder.

"Listen to me. We both know stuff happens out there. Our job now is to find out what happened. This isn't about blame. There is no blame. To me there is only success or failure and reasons for both. Now we have an agent out there that hasn't reported in ... we need to find him and that's all there is to it! And Michelle, you have to get some sleep. I know how it is. You want to sit by your phone and laptop all night, but that doesn't help Garcia or anyone else. Find a way to sleep and that's an order!"

Wang nodded then followed her boss out the door.

By the time Ricci and Wang walked into the Executive Conference Room – Alpha, most of The Watchman staff were already seated. Ricci took his seat at the head of the table and jumped right into it.

"Ladies and gentlemen, we have a situation. One of our

agents, Agent Jesus Garcia has not reported in, since late Tuesday night. If you haven't already done so, please sign in to Big Brother and access Operation India-Golf 070510. It's been declassified for everyone in this room."

Ricci paused to allow everyone time to access the operation files while Debbie Lynch was already projecting images of Agent Garcia and overhead photos of the warehouse in Monterrey, onto a large screen.

"As you can see, a week ago, two agents were dispatched on intel-gathering missions in connection with a lead generated by Big Brother. Double-B alerted us to a $25 million payment from a middle-eastern investment firm into a logistics warehouse operation purported to be owned and controlled by the Pacifico drug cartel. The missions were deemed low to moderate risk fact-finding and up until Tuesday evening, there was nothing to indicate otherwise."

Charley Santappia was first to ask a question.

"Missions in Qatar and Mexico and they were deemed low to moderate risk?"

Wang answered with an air of defensiveness in her tone.

"I deemed them low risk, Charley. The agents I sent in were highly experienced, spoke the language and in the case of Agent Garcia, he was native to Mexico. He reported no problems with his cover or blending in. He wasn't even poking around as much as he was listening ... that's how all of my people are trained, so there shouldn't have been a problem with his cover."

"I still think we could have sent each of them in with a couple of my men, for security."

"This isn't one of your sniper operations, Charley! My people know how to hide in plain sight. There's no need for them to have anyone babysitting them. In fact, my agents would cry bloody murder if we tried to send them in with bodyguards!"

Santappia didn't reply, realizing that Wang's nerves were getting the best of her. He could sympathize. He knew how it was to feel responsible for sending people into harm's way.

Ricci also gave Wang slack, he'd been there too. There was another reason. To put it in old nautical terms, he liked *the cut of her jib*, not to mention she was a beautiful woman to boot.

Instead he started addressing the others.

"Okay, first, let's see where we're at. Michelle, what were the results of trying to contact Agent Garcia?"

Wang took a deep breath and composed herself.

"Beginning at 08:00 hours yesterday and repeated every hour since then, I've attempted to contact Jesus by email, and text message, via double-B. I've also attempted to call his cell every hour on the hour with no results."

"What about his location via GPS?"

"He squawked his location at the warehouse in Monterrey when he last logged in. That was the last time he reported his location."

"John, can you locate him via Big Brother."

"I've been attempting to, since I sat down," Johnny-F replied as he typed furiously into his laptop. "We're not receiving a return signal."

"What could be causing that?"

Francis stopped typing and sat back in his chair. "If his phone was damaged, if the signal was being jammed or if his phone were somehow shielded, all could prevent our tracking him."

"Shielded in what way?"

"Wrapping the phone in a metal sleeve like brass mesh or a lead camera film protector is one way."

Ricci thought out loud, "There's no way to know if he broke his phone or not—"

Wang jumped in, "Captain, Jesus would have found another way to contact me if he broke his phone."

Ricci nodded, "That may be true, but John, I want your people to keep trying. At least, keep someone on duty around the clock until further notice, monitoring for his signal."

"Understood," Francis replied as he sent a message to his team from his laptop.

Ricci turned to his VP of Government Relations next, "Karla, see if you can dig up some more information on the Pacifico cartel from your government sources."

"Our government or theirs?" asked Matthews.

"For now, only contact the people you know over at

Homeland Security and Karla don't let them know about our missing agent. Just see if you can find out about any other holdings or locations that the cartel has in Mexico. There's a chance something went wrong and he was discovered. In that case they might be holding Garcia hostage at another location. I want to be prepared if they are. If you do dig up any other locations, coordinate with Charley so he can work on possible rescue scenarios."

Matthews nodded, writing something onto a pad, while Santappia replied out of habit, "Aye sir."

Santappia spoke up again, "Have we heard from the other agent in Qatar ... al Saud?"

"Majed has reported in at regular intervals," Wang replied. "As you can see from the ops file, he hasn't turned up anything of significance yet."

"Well, at least that may indicate that this is more of an isolated incident, as opposed to a blown operation," Santappia postulated.

"I never thought of that. I never looked at the two operations as one, really. Both agents could be working two sides of the same snake," Wang replied.

"Yeah and Garcia might have drawn the side with the fangs," Santappia added.

"Still, there's no indication that Garcia's disappearance has anything to do with what he was sent to investigate," replied Ricci. "Just like every city in Mexico, Monterrey is experiencing unparalleled volumes of drug-cartel related violence, not to mention the usual violent criminals in any big city. He could just have been in the wrong place at the wrong time."

Ricci let that sink in a moment then continued.

"In any case, notify me immediately the next time Majed reports in."

"Will do," replied Wang.

"Debbie, contact Cris and tell him I need to speak with him within the hour."

Ricci stood up.

"Is there anything else? Does anyone have any other questions?"

No one replied. Everyone filed out of the room, except for one person who remained seated. Les Pastak sat staring at his laptop screen, acting like he was working on something until everyone left the conference room. When he was alone, he closed his laptop, with a knot in his stomach. *What the hell happened to Garcia? Fard and his people better not have had anything to do with it! Should I call Fard?* Pastak closed his eyes and massaged his temples. *I better just sit tight for now, maybe this'll pass. Maybe Garcia will just turn up ... I hope!*

CHAPTER 19

THE WATCHMAN AGENCY
EXECUTIVE CONFERENCE ROOM – ALPHA
ARLINGTON, VIRGINIA
2:05P.M., FRIDAY, JULY 15, 2011

Mugsy Ricci walked into the conference room with his cell phone to his ear. He disconnected the call then whispered something to Debbie Lynch. A few moments later, Lynch had Cris De Niro's image on the large conference screen. Ricci addressed the assembled staff as soon as he saw De Niro on the screen.

"Okay people, as you see, Cris will be joining us, for this status meeting. Let's get to it, John, no ping from Garcia via GPS yet?"

Francis looked over at the big screen first.

"What's up Cris, good to see you buddy!"

De Niro smiled warmly at his old friend.

"Good to see you too, John."

"We haven't received a return signal from Agent Garcia's transponder yet, but I've been working another angle. My guys were able to hack into the warehouse's security system—"

Ricci interrupted him, "John, you didn't tell me you were doing that! That is definitely something you should have run by me!"

"I'm sorry Mugs but I was always taught that it was better to ask for forgiveness than to ask for permission. I was only acting on a hunch and I wasn't too sure about how you'd react."

Ricci knew going in that Johnny-F went way back with his brother-in-law, was a multi-millionaire and considered an eccentric über-geek, so he'd have to cut him slack, but this crossed the line. He knew better than to reprimand him though, in front of the rest of the staff, but it wouldn't be easy.

"Continue what you were saying but let's talk after this meeting."

Francis smiled but was contrite, "Not a problem Mugs. Anyway, like I said, we hacked into their system. It was a cinch, no risk—"

Ricci couldn't help himself, "How do you know that?! Did you ever consider the ramifications if you were caught hacking into a computer system of a company suspected of being owned by one of the most violent drug cartels in the world?! Not to mention the international ramifications of an American private intelligence agency hacking into the system of a company located IN ANOTHER COUNTRY!!"

The room went dead silent. Mugsy and Johnny-F's eyes were locked. Ricci used more self-control as he continued.

"John, if Garcia is alive, you could have possibly put him in even more danger!"

Francis raised his brow. It reminded Ricci of Spock in Star Trek.

"Mugs, I thought you wanted to discuss this with me after this meeting. If you want to get into it now, fine. First, those things did cross my mind and at 3a.m. when I gathered my guys, that was the first thing we discussed. I'm talking about not wanting to put Garcia in more danger, but we were also concerned with how much time we might or might not have.

Some security systems are only set to record and maintain 48 hours of camera feeds. By that time of night, I thought we might only have minutes to go or that we might have been too late. We quickly considered the other risks and after taking a look at their system with some soft probing, we were confident that we could get past their firewalls and security measures. As it turned out their system was set to record and maintain a full week's worth of feeds."

Ricci shot a quick look at De Niro, on the screen then replied.

"We'll discuss the proper procedure that you WILL follow, when it comes to that type of situation later. For the record though, John, if you would have filled me in on those circumstances, I would have agreed with you. I'm available to you 24/7/365. Next time contact me. Now, tell us what you turned up."

Francis typed something into his laptop and a moment later, the conference room's monitor turned split screen, with De Niro on the left and what looked like grainy photos of a truck on the right.

"This is what we turned up ..."

"Cris can you see the photos?" asked Ricci.

"Yes, John, what are we looking at?"

"Well, when I walked out of here last night, I was thinking about Agent Garcia's last log entry. He spoke about making contact with some truck driver and about how he might have gotten the opportunity to take a peek at the driver's load that night. Well it got me to thinking, what if he did take a look at the load and something went wrong? I started to think, what if instead of looking for Garcia, we should be looking for the truck? All this came to me as I was walking to my car outside in the parking lot. It was well after midnight and there wasn't a soul around. That made me think about how it might have been Tuesday night in Monterrey."

No one spoke up so it was obvious to Francis that he needed to explain further.

"Don't you see where I'm going with this? There wouldn't have been much traffic down there, just like it was here! That made me think that, maybe, just maybe, if we could hack into the security system of the warehouse facility, we might be blessed with a look at the truck! As you can see, we were so blessed!"

Ricci stepped up close to the monitor, "So, you think that's the truck Garcia checked out?"

"Mugs, look at the date and time stamp on the bottom of the first four photos. Those photos were taken from the digital backup of the security cameras located at the entrance and parking lot of the warehouse."

Ricci read it out loud, "Tuesday night 11:50 hours ..."

Francis jumped in, "That's when the truck arrived at the guard shack, at the entrance. That would have been just minutes after Garcia entered his last log entry. The second photo, time stamped just a minute later, we've identified from the rental records as Garcia's rental car."

Ricci read from the bottom of the third photo, "Wednesday morning 0:25 hours ..."

Francis got up and walked over to the screen, "That's the same truck leaving."

"How can you tell it's the same truck," asked Santappia. "These photos are so grainy."

Francis traced a square around a portion of the conference room's big screen with his index finger and instantly the area inside the square was magnified and smoothed.

"We analyzed this area of both photos of the truck. It's an area in front of the trailer. Can everyone see the unit I'm pointing to? It's a refrigeration unit. This truck is what is known as a "reefer," a refrigerated trailer used to haul freight needing temperature control, like perishable goods."

Francis returned to his seat. No one spoke, he had everyone's attention.

"That unit combined with the lack of traffic, at that time of night gave us the ability to track the truck ... at least until it got onto the Nacional, the National Highway."

Francis saw the curious looks on everyone's face and decided to answer their question before they asked it.

"Let's just say that if someone like me, who does so much covert, highly-technical work for the U.S. government asked for a favor from an old friend of mine, who I did MANY FAVORS FOR, over at Langley—"

Ricci held up his hand, "John, don't say another thing about it ... please ... before men in black burst through the conference door and haul us all away!"

Everyone laughed which lightened the mood a little and eased some of the tension between Ricci and Francis.

"Okay, so anyway, using satellite stills, my people were able to verify with above 90% accuracy that this truck did, in fact get on the Federal Highway 52 heading south out of Monterrey. We lost coverage on it then."

"What about Garcia's car," De Niro asked. "Did it leave when the truck left?"

"The car left right after the truck did, but I'm not convinced Garcia was driving it."

Everyone focused on the overhead photo of the car passing the guard shack leaving the warehouse facility. Ricci asked the question for everyone, "What makes you think he wasn't driving it? We can't see the driver from this photo."

Francis smiled a bit smugly.

"Not from the photo, but I have a hunch and it makes sense. Remember I told you that one way to block GPS transmission is by shielding the transponder? Well, I was hired awhile back by a local law enforcement agency to help them figure out how a number of Cadillac Escalades were being stolen. The SUV's all had GPS transponders in them, yet all of the transponders appeared to stop working just after they were stolen. Well, I was stumped too, so I called a friend of mine from the old neighborhood, Cris, you remember Fat Freddy?"

De Niro had to chuckle.

"How could anyone forget Freddy?"

"Yeah, exactly, well Freddy knows everything there is about stealing cars. Back before he was known as Fat Freddy he was known as Fast Freddy ... 'cause of how fast he could hot wire a car. I remember one time—"

"John, can you get to the point?!" Ricci suggested.

"I was, Mugs! Well, Freddy told me that car thieves nowadays transport stolen cars fitted with GPS tracking units inside

REEFERS to block the GPS signal!"

To his delight, Francis could see the light bulbs going off in everyone's head as he continued, "Guys and ladies, what if the reason we lost Garcia's GPS signal is because he, or at least his phone, is still on that truck!"

Ricci thought about it for a moment then walked over and extended his hand to Francis who shook it.

"We still need to talk about procedures ... but ... you did good Johnny-F!"

Despite orders from Ricci, Michelle Wang looked like she hadn't slept in days. Johnny-F's hunch gave her new vigor though, as she turned to Karla Matthews.

"Karla, were you able to turn anything up from our friends at Homeland Security?"

Matthews passed around copies of a sheet.

"Cris, I emailed to you what I just passed around."

"Got it," De Niro replied.

"I was able to get a complete list of businesses, real estate and other holdings suspected to be wholly or partially owned by the Pacifico cartel in Mexico. My contact at HSA asked me if I could tell him the reason for the request so he could narrow the parameters, but I declined, so as you can see, it's quite a big list. I'm not sure how much it'll help you prepare a rescue mission though, Charley. They seem to own just about every type of business and they also own everything from mansions to apartment buildings to farms located from one side of Mexico to the other!"

Ricci handed his sheet to Debbie Lynch and asked her to project it onto the screen.

"Well, we may be able to narrow it down at least a little, if we take Johnny-F's hunch as fact. If Agent Garcia is on that reefer and if that reefer got on the National Highway heading south let's identify any of these holdings that are north, due east or due west and cross them out. Debbie, leave the sheet on the screen and begin to cross out the ones that we know aren't south."

Santappia leaned back in his chair, "Mugs that'll still probably leave too many to be of any help to me and my people."

"I know Charley, but I'll leave it up to you and Michelle to try and use your instincts to narrow the list down even more. Think of places they would either want to hold Garcia hostage at ... or dispose of his body."

"That could possibly allow us to omit any buildings with too many people around, like the apartment buildings and stores," Wang added.

Ricci nodded, "Exactly. Keep me advised of your progress. Okay, if there's nothing else, great work John and Karla. Thank you everyone."

After everyone filed out, leaving only Ricci and Debbie Lynch in the conference room, De Niro was still on the screen and asked, "What do you think, Mugs?"

"I think Johnny-F is gonna be a real trial when it comes to following procedures!"

De Niro laughed, "There never was a rule that boy couldn't find a way to break, even when we were kids."

"I'll say this though. He's the smartest guy in the room, no doubt about that! He's going to be an extremely valuable asset to us, Cris, going forward. You made a great call hiring him."

"He didn't need the job or the money, Mugs. He accepted because he's a patriot, something to keep in mind ... the next time he doesn't follow a procedure."

De Niro saw his brother-in-law nod in agreement.

"What about Garcia, Mugs, do you think we know enough now to find him?"

Ricci shook his head, "I don't think so Cris, not yet anyway. Everything we're going on is still supposition. We're gonna need a break ... or a miracle to find him."

De Niro thought he knew his next answer, but he wanted to ask him anyway.

"Do you think Garcia's still alive?"

Ricci shot a look over at Debbie Lynch. She shook her head, in agreement.

"No, I don't Cris, but we may learn a lot from his death, if we can find his body."

It made De Niro shutter with frustration. *I wanted The Watchman to save lives ... and already we may have lost one! I didn't even get a chance to meet him!*

"Mugs, was he married?"

Ricci saw Lynch bite her lip from sadness.

"Yeah Cris, he was. He had two kids with one on the way. I won't speak to his wife until we either find him, dead or alive, or I decide that we will never find him ... and I'll have to decide that soon."

Two kids with one on the way ... just like I was ... he's even about the same age I was when I lost Lisa! I'll make sure his wife and kids are taken care of, it's the least I can do, if he's dead.

"Well, if he's alive, let's get him back Mugs and if he's not, let's make sure his death was not in vain!"

"Understood," Ricci replied then De Niro disappeared from the screen.

CHAPTER 20

"NARCOGRANJA DE PACIFICO"
(DRUG FARM OWNED BY PACIFICO CARTEL)
20 MILES NORTHEAST OF THE CITY
IGUALA DE LA INDEPENDENCIA, MEXICO
2:30P.M., FRIDAY, JULY 15, 2011

Like all truckers, Pedro hated waiting around, but one thing he knew, when a man like Tuco Ramirez tells you to do something, you do it, no questions asked. Pedro still considered himself primarily a trucker, even though he was recruited by the cartel over a decade ago and had murdered for them many times since. Most of the people he had murdered up to then, he did so by shooting them in the back of their heads, with the victims wearing blindfolds. In order to live with the morality of his actions, he considered them executions, like those carried out by governments and after all, the drug cartels were like governments unto themselves - to him and most others, anyway. They were richer than many countries and they had bigger standing armies than some countries too. So in a way, he was just obeying orders from the government who controlled his ability to stay alive, but this last one was different. This man wasn't kneeling in front of his own grave like the others, one they would have made him dig for himself. He wasn't blindfolded, in fact he was looking right into Pedro's eyes, when Pedro pulled the trigger; and the bullet didn't enter the back of his head, he'd shot him right between his eyes. Pedro had had trouble sleeping since he did the deed, mostly because whenever he closed his eyes, he saw the shocked expression on Jesus' face as the bullet entered his brain.

Pedro was ordered to drive over 600 kilometers south, to a large farm owned by the cartel. He had been there before to pick up loads of marijuana and other drugs that they grew and processed there, but this was the first time he was making a delivery. He had arrived there early Wednesday afternoon but Tuco himself told him that he had to wait, so he plugged his reefer into a portable generator to keep the trailer chilled to 34-degrees Fahrenheit and then spent most of his time sleeping in the sleeper unit of his cab. He didn't like to mix much with any of the cartel's soldiers, so he only popped out of his cab to get something to eat from their cantina.

He tried not to think too much about Jesus' body wrapped in plastic, lying in that crate behind him but he knew he wouldn't sleep much until he could get it off his truck. Finally, one of Tuco's lieutenants knocked on the door of his cab and told him to get ready to follow a pickup truck that had pulled up in front of him. Tuco jumped out of his cab and unplugged his trailer from the generator, then jumped back up and started his rig. As soon as he shifted it into gear he waved that he was ready to go. The pickup led him down a dirt path about two kilometers and then turned onto an even narrower dirt path. Pedro tried his best not to let the overgrowth scratch his cab as he rolled slowly down the bumpy trail. Finally, the pickup stopped ahead of him and four men jumped out of it.

One of the men walked over to his cab and asked him to open his trailer. Pedro jumped down and could see that while the other three men had gotten shovels from the back of the pickup, the man that came over to his cab had a pistol tucked into his belt. Pedro unlocked and opened the trailer then the man with the gun jumped up into it. He walked over to the big crate and kicked it then turned to Pedro.

(In Spanish) "Is this the one?"

"Yes."

"We don't want the crate; open it so we can get him out."

Pedro grabbed his crowbar and joined the man in the trailer. Once he pried the nails up, he stepped out of the way but the man with the gun told him to open the lid, so he did.

Pedro looked down and saw the man, Jesus, the man he was told was a government agent, lying wrapped in plastic, just as he had left him. He could see signs that blood from his head wound had leaked out creating sort of a red blob where the man's face should have been.

The man with the gun barked orders to two of the other three men to grab the body and he told the third one to carry all of their shovels. Then he led everyone to a spot about 50 feet away from the trail, surrounded by overgrowth, that already had a deep whole dug in it with a large mound of the excavated dirt piled next to the hole. He stopped the two men just before they dropped the body in and turned to Pedro.

"Give me the gun you used."

Pedro was hoping he could keep the pistol, as he bought it and the suppressor with his own money, but he knew better than to hesitate, so he took the pistol from the back of his pants and handed it to him. Then he took the suppressor from his pants' pocket and handed that to him too.

The man examined the pistol briefly, checking the clip to see if bullets were missing, then he threw the pistol and the suppressor into the hole. As soon as he did, he turned and started walking back to the trail, giving orders over his shoulder to the two men.

"Drop him in and cover him up!"

Pedro decided to remain with the men while they buried Jesus. He wasn't filled with remorse. He knew he had to follow his orders, but he still didn't like killing people. Pedro hadn't been to church in awhile, but he thought it would be nice to say a prayer for the dead man and his family. He bowed his head, closed his eyes and folded his hands in front of him. Then he began to whisper to himself.

"Father, forgive me for I have sinned—"

His prayer was cut short when a large caliber bullet entered the back of his skull. His entire head exploded like a watermelon would, if it were dropped from a roof. Pedro's body collapsed just short of the hole. The man with the gun was standing right behind him with smoke still pouring from the gun's barrel. He used his legs to push Pedro's body into the hole. One of the men with the shovel laughed.

"I think he was praying!"

The man with the gun tucked the weapon back into his belt, with no emotion showing on his face. He took his cell phone from his shirt pocket.

"Well now he can talk to God face to face."

The man hit an auto-dial button.

(In Spanish) "Tuco, I took care of it. What do you want me to do with his truck? ... Okay, I'll take it to Mexico City and have the cab painted and the trailer switched. Then I'll assign another driver to it and send it back up to Monterrey."

He put his cell phone back in his pocket and addressed the men.

"After you replace the dirt, I want you to transplant shrubs from nearby. I don't want this hole to ever be found, understood."

CHAPTER 21

THE WATCHMAN AGENCY
OFFICE OF THE PRESIDENT
ARLINGTON, VIRGINIA
4:55P.M., FRIDAY, JULY 15, 2011

Mugsy Ricci's intercom buzzed. Johnny-F's voice rang out.

"Mugs, Garcia's transponder just pinged our grid!"

Ricci sprung up from his chair.

"Are you sure? Is it confirmed?"

"Yeah, we confirmed it. It's definitely Agent Garcia's transponder and it's actively pinging now, it started just a few minutes ago."

"John, hold on." He hit another intercom button, "Debbie, I want to see all department heads in Alpha immediately." Then he patched back in with Francis, "John, I called everyone together in conference room alpha."

"Understood ..."

Everyone took their seats. A moment later, Cris De Niro

appeared on the big screen. Ricci spoke first.

"Cris ... everyone ... Johnny-F and his team just confirmed that as of a few minutes ago, Agent Garcia's transponder began transmitting again and it's remained active."

"Where is he?!" asked Michelle Wang, a combination of relief and anxiety in her voice. "Is he ... alive?"

Francis typed into his laptop as he replied.

"We haven't been able to ascertain whether he's alive or not. He's not replying to our calls, emails, or text messages ... but I can show you where the transponder is."

With that, he hit a key on his keyboard and instantly the conference room's big screen split in two, with De Niro's image on the left and a map of Mexico on the right. Francis walked everyone through.

"The red dot is the location in Monterrey where the warehouse is and from where Agent Garcia last reported. And—"

Francis hit another key on his keyboard.

"That blue blinking dot is where the transponder is now located. It's about 600 clicks south-southwest of Monterrey."

"John, can you superimpose the locations that Michelle and I narrowed down from that list of cartel holdings?" asked Santappia.

"Sure," Francis replied as he continued to type away. After a moment everyone saw about a dozen shaded areas of different sizes and shapes appear on the map. One of the largest shaded areas appeared directly over the blinking blue dot.

Santappia pulled up the list on his laptop and matched one of the locations listed with the shaded area.

"It looks like the transponder is located on a farm that's owned by Pacifico. The farm is about 30 clicks north of the city of Iguala. That puts it approximately 150 miles from the western shore of Mexico, which would be our point of ingress, just south of Petatian. That is, if we can borrow your yacht and EC135[12], Cris. Like the Captain said, I worked up plans to infiltrate all of the remaining locations and the one that I came up with for that farm is from the west with an escape route

---

[12]   The Eurocopter EC135 is a twin-engine civil helicopter produced by Eurocopter, widely used amongst police and ambulance services and for executive transport.

north by sea. Mugsy told me about the Santana with its chopper and I'm familiar with the 135. It has the range and there's a relatively unpopulated corridor to the west of that farm. We can put down, undetected, behind foothills to the west then hoof it to the location."

De Niro checked his calendar. *I knew it, I told David he could holiday on Santana for the weekend. I better call him.*

"Let me ... get back to you on that."

"Is there a problem, Cris?" asked Ricci.

"I promised a friend of mine that he could use *Santana* for the weekend. He's a close friend and long time client from England. He was one of the first investors in my hedge fund, so in a way you can say that he helped me pay for *Santana*. He's already on the yacht, I'll have to break the news to him and call her back to port. I'll try to reach him now. I'll let you know."

De Niro disappeared from the screen as conversations broke out around the room.

Ricci brought everyone back to order.

"Karla, it's imperative to keep Homeland and the Mexican government out of the loop with this operation, understood?"

"Captain, the Mexican government would probably allow us to conduct this mission. They could make it easy for us to get in and out of there."

"It's too risky, Karla. You're right, there are some in their government who'd like to help us, but there are too many leaks and too many on the cartels' payrolls."

Matthews thought then asked, "What about Homeland? Couldn't they help us?"

"Not without running it up to State and once that happened we'd be ordered to stand down. We don't want to find ourselves in that position, isn't that right Les?"

Pastak was sitting in a daze. His palms were sweaty and his heart was palpating. *This is getting out of hand! What is Agent Garcia doing in the middle of a drug farm owned by one of the biggest drug cartels! I have to contact Fard now and find out if he had anything to do with it!*

"Les are you okay, you look sick."

Pastak broke out of his daze and noticed everyone looking at him.

"No, I'm okay Captain, just something I ate for lunch ..."

"Okay, so am I right not to want Homeland involved? What's your take?"

"We absolutely DO NOT want Homeland involved! As a matter of fact, I'm not sure it's a wise idea for us to even attempt a rescue!"

Santappia came to full attention in his chair, "What are you saying Les, you think we should just leave Agent Garcia down there?"

"I'm saying, Charley, that we don't even know if he's still alive. In fact, I think we all suspect that he's not ... and if he's not, what do we gain by going down there?! Nothing but the risk of breaking about a dozen United States and Mexican laws! I think Michelle would even back me up on this – it's not worth the risk!"

Michelle Wang couldn't hide her frustration, "I ... agree with Les. It would be one thing to find him holding up in a hotel or hospital ... even the morgue, but on a drug farm owned by one of the most dangerous drug cartels ... I don't have to tell you, Charley, they have armies of men guarding those places."

"What did I say, I told you Charley, even Michelle—"

"Michelle doesn't make that call," Santappia snapped.

"Well neither do you!" Pastak snapped back, shouting.

Both men turned and looked at Ricci. He wanted to hear all of their arguments. Les and Michelle had the more reasonable point-of-view while Charlie was a Marine who didn't want to leave anyone behind.

"Captain, under the circumstances, you have to see our point. We—"

"I do see your point, Les and I've noted it ... but I say, we go down there, without anyone knowing and we bring Agent Garcia home, alive or dead."

"But Captain—"

Ricci put his hand up, "Les, I'm the one ... that makes that call."

The conference room became quiet. Finally, Santappia thought out loud.

"Oh hell, this is all an exercise in futility anyway, if we don't hear back from Cris. I can't think of another way for us to get in and out of there undetected."

* * * * *

De Niro ended his video feed, picked up his satellite phone and dialed the number to the satellite phone on *Santana*. The ship's Captain answered the call on the second ring.

"Captain, its Cris De Niro."

"Yes, Mr. De Niro, good to hear from you, sir."

"Where are you right now?"

"We're docked at the Loews Mistral Restaurant in San Diego Bay. We were just getting ready to get underway again. Mr. Nicholls wants to moor off Catalina Island tonight."

"Yeah, well that's why I'm calling. There's been a change in plans. Captain, I need you to refuel *Santana* and the 135 then plot a course for the western Mexican coast. Off the top of your head, what's your best estimate for arriving off the coast of Acapulco if you left as soon as you could?"

"I'd have to check the weather, but I'd say we could make waters near Acapulco by late Tuesday or Wednesday ... if we left as soon as possible from here."

"There are a few friends of mine that you'll be taking on board. At least one of them is an experienced chopper pilot, so it's okay for them to use the chopper down there. Captain, I would appreciate it if you would ask no questions and obey their orders. That goes for the crew, whatever my friends want or need, please accommodate them."

"Understood sir ..."

"You should be welcoming them aboard in about ... two hours, latest. Then get underway as soon as you can. I want you to contact me when you do."

"Very good, sir ..."

"Okay, now the hard part. Would you please call Mr. Nicholls to the phone? I have to break the news to him that his vacation on *Santana* is coming to end prematurely."

"Here he is, sir ..."

"Thank you Captain ... David?"

"Cristiano, I wanted to thank you again for the use of *Santana*. She's a beauty! You know you never have to make such a fuss for me."

"Who are you fooling David. You're worse than a princess when it comes to fusses."

Both men laughed. Nicholls continued.

"Speaking of princesses, old boy, I just had the most pleasant lunch with two princesses of Southern California. Now I hope you're calling me to say that you're flying in tonight. I made plans to take them to Catalina tomorrow. Of course, spending the night watching the sunset from *Santana* should put them—"

"David, that's why I'm calling ..."

"You mean you ARE flying in? Cris, it's about time, that's all I can say!"

"No, you knucklehead, I'm calling to tell you that ... I have to cut your vacation short, at least on *Santana*. Something came up, I have to loan her to a few ... friends of mine, right away."

"Friends of yours ...? ... And what am I chopped liver? I have an idea, why don't they just come with me and the two princesses to Catalina? I'm sure there are a few more princesses we can scrounge up—"

"David, seriously, they have to get down to Acapulco with *Santana* and they have to leave with her tonight. I'll make it up to you. Let me call a friend of mine and I'll charter you another—"

"You'll do no such thing, dear boy! I can make my own way, thank you very much ... but Cris, I wouldn't mind taking a cruise to Acapulco, that is, if your friends don't mind. In fact, tell them I insist!"

De Niro thought about it for a moment. *He never takes a hint, but I love him like a brother. Now that I think of it though, David would probably make ARCHANGEL's cover of "filthy rich businessmen on holiday" more believable, in case anyone checks on them.*

"Cris ...?"

I'm sure he'll show black ops just how to act, and if any bad guys did spy on them, it'd be impossible for them to confuse my British playboy friend with a covert agent.

"Cristiano, are you there?"

I'd never want to subject him to any danger but if he remains on

Santana, the danger would be 150 miles away. Besides, I know him well enough that if I say he can't go, it'll make him twice as curious and nosey ... and that could lead to more problems than just letting him go in the first place. I'll set down rules and if he agrees to abide by them, well then, so be it.

"Well what's the verdict, dear boy? May I take the trip or are you going to have your mysterious mates cast me overboard? In which case, I will cling to the hull like a mollusk—"

"David, their trip down there is for business ... very important business."

"So, I take the cruise with them and they go their way, once their down there and take care of their ... very important business while I—"

"Here are the rules! First, you would NOT be able to take your princesses with you ... and you would NOT be allowed to leave *Santana* under any circumstances. David, I'm not kidding about that last point. The crew will be given orders to throw you into the brig if you even try to leave her!"

"Dear boy, I've been from top to bottom on this vessel and you certainly do NOT have a brig."

"Then they'll lock you in your cabin!"

Nicholls thought a moment, "I'll agree to those terms providing the bar remains free, the chef remains the same and the galley is stocked!"

De Niro had to laugh.

"Okay, David, but one other thing. My friends are military types and their business down there is quite "hush-hush," to put it in your tongue. So, behave! You're not to question them about their business or anything else you see them do, are we clear?"

"Crystal, dear boy, crystal ... now if you will excuse me, I have to go break the hearts of two princesses!"

The line went dead before De Niro could even say goodbye.

CHAPTER 22

THE COYOTE'S DEN
ESTANCIA DE NIRO
HENDERSON, NV

1:30P.M., SUNDAY, JULY 17, 2011

De Niro received a message from Michelle Wang that she and Johnny-F needed to speak with him ASAP. So he decided to take his favorite horse, "Dollor" out for a ride to the Coyote's Den. De Niro and his dad were both huge fans of John Wayne, so he was ecstatic when, a few years ago, his head gaucho Martin Fierro surprised him by finding a horse that was the splitting image of one of the Duke's favorite steeds. They were almost identical, both dark chestnut sorrels with very wide blazes, which flared out over their lips, and with white stockings to the knee on the right front and both hind legs. De Niro immediately bought the horse and decided to name him after the Duke's horse... Dollor. Some of his friends joked that the name was apropos for a multi-billionaire, but the name was actually taken from the Spanish word "Dolor", meaning "pain" or "sorrow". De Niro thought that the Spanish meaning was more appropriate, since riding him made him think of Lisa. They used to love to take Sunday morning rides whenever they could and wherever they were. He still owned her mare, JoJo, a beautiful strawberry roan that she picked up at an auction in Argentina, with Martin. Martin never let anyone ride JoJo after 9/11.

De Niro tied Dollor then walked into one of the small conference rooms. No one was in the Den. Riggy, De May and Pescalitis were already onboard *Santana* heading for the shore near Acapulco. He took a seat then contacted The Watchman. A moment later he could see Michelle and Johnny-F on the big screen in front of him.

"Hi Michelle ... what's up John ... what got you both working on a Sunday?"

Michelle spoke first.

"Cris, my agent in Qatar, Majed al Saud, finally turned something up. Apparently, the Sharia-compliant private equity firm that wire-transferred that $25 million is actually owned by an Iranian businessman named Aref Sami Zamani."

"Zamani ... I never heard of him."

"I checked him out. There's not much on him. He was the son of one of the Iranian banking ministers, back when the Shah of Iran was in charge. He attended Oxford then fell out of sight for years before coming back on the radar when he created this private equity firm. His limited partners were a dozen Middle Eastern princes and businessmen, all loaded with oil money. There was some concern that while he was off radar, he was keeping company with some of the most militant mullahs in Iran. So the Israelis kept tabs on the firm, just in case any of their money ended up financing terrorist groups, but according to them, they found no evidence that any did."

"It sounds like the guy is legit then?"

"Well, what al Saud found out from a contact he made at the Qatari investment bank is that apparently a year ago, Zamani got rid of the other limited partners. All the money in the firm is his now."

"That's not unusual, Michelle. Some of us start our firms

that way. We need to use other people's money for a time, until we make enough of our own. I did it ... Eddie Lampert did it, it's not unusual."

"That's not the unusual part Cris. What is ... is the fact that according to my agent's contact, the reason why the limited partners parted company with Zamani's firm had to do with a radical change he made in their investment focus. Up until last year, the firm mainly invested in real estate. So this Mexican investment in a logistics warehousing operation is unprecedented."

That piqued De Niro's interest.

"I've seen lots of irrational behavior in investing—"

"Cris, I just emailed you a file. Take a look at it. It contains the performance evaluation for Zamani's PE firm going back ten years, up to last year."

De Niro opened the attachment and scoured it for a few minutes.

"Okay, I take it back. I've seen lots of irrational behavior in investing, especially since the world melted down a few years ago, but according to this analysis, this guy's firm was making a mint. It looks like someone in their firm knew enough to divest themselves of the majority of their real estate holdings at least a year before the global real estate meltdown."

"Exactly, and according to my agent's contact, they were all set to redirect those funds into Middle Eastern gas and water deals when Zamani pulled the rug from under them. First, he somehow got them all to agree, not only to leave all of the cash they made from divesting themselves out of the real estate – a total of about $900 million – in the firm's investment account, but he also got them to agree to a two-year lock, which prohibited them from pulling their money out. As soon as they signed on the dotted line, Zamani told them that he wasn't going to invest in water and gas in the Middle East, after all. The rest of the details are foggy but it appears that Zamani came out with about 10% of that $900 million in exchange for allowing all the limited partners out of the partnership."

"So he came away with $90 million to invest in whatever he wanted ... and his first investment all on his lonesome was into a shady Mexican warehousing operation?" De Niro replied with sarcasm.

Michelle smiled from the comment.

"I thought I better get your thoughts on it, Cris. No one understands this investment stuff more than you do. I see a giant red flag flapping in the wind with this. Am I wrong?"

"I don't think your wrong, Michelle. In my experience when all things are equal, professional investors stick to what they know and they stay far away from what they don't know. In this guy Zamani's case, he didn't do either. He moved away from real estate. He didn't just stay liquid and wait for a recovery in the real estate market. Then he decided to invest in an industry in which he apparently has no knowledge or track record. Not to mention the fact that the investment is located in a country with a train-wrecked economy ... and the company has the shadow of cartel-control looming over it. There's no way that his diligence missed that."

"So are you saying, he definitely knew about the cartel connection to the warehouse operation?"

"He had to, Michelle. I mean he didn't have to be Sherlock Holmes with his diligence to discover that. He could have googled the warehouse's name and he would have found references to the Pacifico cartel from news reports. That much alone should have scared him off, especially since the firm is supposed to be Sharia-compliant."

Wang jotted down a few notes then she looked up from her pad.

"Okay Cris, you convinced me that my first hunch was right. There's something wrong in Dodge with this whole Iranian-Mexican connection. Now we have to figure out ... if this man Zamani wasn't investing $25 million in this company, what was the $25 million for?"

"The other scary thing is that he has $65 million more to invest in whatever it is," De Niro added.

"Cris, there was one thing more. Majed knew Garcia a long time. They were as close to friends as two spies could be. When I told him what happened to Jesus, he didn't buy it. He said, quote unquote, 'there's no way Jesus could have been that wrong about blowing his cover.' Cris, Majed is convinced that Garcia was set up."

"Set up ... but how ... by whom?"

"I don't know. I asked Johnny-F here if someone from the outside could have compromised Big Brother--"

"... and the answer is NO!" Francis interjected. "... but Cris, I did find something ... something weird ... at least to me, it's weird. I mean, I'm not exactly James Bond, but then again—"

"John, what are you talking about? What did you find?"

"Well, it made me angry that Michelle or anyone else could even entertain the possibility that my double-B could be hacked ... but I did consider the fact that what that guy Majed said, could be correct. So if Garcia was set up and it wasn't from someone hacking Big Brother from outside, the only other way would be if someone—"

"Hacked the system from within the firm?"

"NO silly! The security measures are in place inside or outside the firm. I was going to say that someone with access might have ... sold him out."

De Niro sat back in his chair while a knot formed in his stomach. *A Judas ... inside the Watchman ...?*

"Michelle, who was given access to Garcia's operation ...?"

"Well, in order of rank, Captain Ricci was ... I was ... Les was and of course, Garcia."

"Les, why Les ...?"

"That's just standard procedure, Cris. I had to hire Majed and Jesus, sort of on the spot. So, neither of them had gone through our HR department. Mugsy's improved SOP's allowed me, under the circumstances, to hire them, and then inform HR. Les was given access to their personnel files, which were included in the ops files, just to bring them both on board."

"Okay—"

"No, not okay, Cris ...!" Francis jumped in again. "You see ... not only is my dynamic system able to see who accesses ops files, it's also able to track them throughout Big Brother. Just to satisfy my curiosity, I traced all three of their activities in the system."

"You did what? John, tell me you got this approved by Mugsy.

Wait a minute, is that why you're telling me this ... on a Sunday ... without Mugsy part of this teleconference?!"

"As a matter of fact, he didn't. Hi Cris ... Michelle ... John."

Ricci appeared standing behind Johnny-F, who jumped up as soon as he became aware he was there.

"Sit down John, I'm not angry. In fact I think you did the right thing, under the circumstances, at least for what I heard you both explain while I eavesdropped. It seems that the three of us couldn't stay away from the office today. I saw your cars parked outside, used the security system you installed in my office to find you both sitting in here, then just turned up the microphone and listened."

"Mugs, I didn't know what to do—"

"John, like I said, I'm not angry but we're gonna have to fix a few things in your 'dynamic system' though. For one, I want to be informed by Big Brother the moment anyone tracks me in the system or else I want it to be impossible to track me in the system – and for another – we need to have security tiers placed within operational access. Michelle should have been able to only give access to the personnel files with giving him access to all of the ops info."

"Yeah ... I see that now. I'll take care of it personally."

"Mugs, glad you could join us," De Niro interjected. Now John, what did you find?"

"Well, with Michelle and ... Mugsy, just the usual porn and ESPN.com"

Ricci squeezed Francis's shoulder until pain appeared on Johnny-F's face.

"I was kidding ... just kidding!"

Ricci loosened his grip on the über geek's shoulder then patted him on it.

"Alright, when I tracked Les, I should have only found him accessing both agents' personnel files, right? Then why did I find traces of him accessing Agent Garcia's transponder frequency?"

De Niro, Michelle and Mugsy all had the same look of shock on their faces, to Francis's delight.

"... And it gets worse. It appears that he accessed Agent Garcia's transponder frequency while he was outside of The

Watchman offices. He used his own personal broadband account, so I can't tell you from exactly where, but it wasn't from our network here."

Tears started forming in Michelle's eyes.

"That bastard ... and I gave him the access! I knew Jesus for years. I knew his wife and his kids too!"

"I told you before Michelle, this isn't about blame," Ricci reminded his VP. "It's about success and failure."

"It's about more than that, Mugs," De Niro jumped in. "It's about honor and trust too."

Everyone was quiet for a moment then De Niro spoke up again.

"What now, Mugs ...?"

"Now, I think it's time that Michelle and I have a little talk with Mr. Pastak. I'll send him a message telling him to meet us here ASAP."

"I agree we have to interrogate him," Wang replied, "but Captain, I suggest that we just let him come in tomorrow, then ask him to step into the conference room. We don't want to give him a heads-up that we're onto him."

"Good idea. We'll confiscate his laptop as soon as we get him in here, then John, you can deny his access into Big Brother as soon as we do."

"The question is, if he did sell out Garcia, who did he sell him out to?" De Niro asked.

"The Pacifico cartel ...?" Wang offered. "After all, he was looking into their operation down there."

"Yes, but how did they know that?" Ricci replied. "If we work from the premise that Les was paid to tell the cartel that Garcia was investigating them—"

"Then it couldn't be the cartel," De Niro finished his thought. "It would mean they had no idea they were being investigated. That means there's someone else ... another player."

"Zamani ...?" Wang offered again. "But how would he know about our investigation? How would he even know about The Watchman ... and what would be his tie-in to Les?"

"One thing's for sure, nothing in Les's background check tied him in with anyone like Zamani or I would have known about it." Wang replied.

Everyone became quiet again. De Niro broke the silence.

"We have a lot of unanswered questions, but at least it looks like we know the questions to ask and whom to ask them to. Let me know how it goes tomorrow with Les."

De Niro disconnected the call. He sat for a few moments trying to get his mind around all of it then he heard Dollor neigh.

"Okay boy, let's get you back to the stable."

CHAPTER 23

THE FOSTER LAFAYETTE HOTEL
BAHMAN FARD'S SUITE
WASHINGTON, D.C.

1:30P.M., SUNDAY, JULY 17, 2011

Bahman Fard opened the door to his suite to let Les Pastak in then he closed it behind him.

"Hello Les. I wasn't expecting to hear from you for awhile. Take a seat, may I get you—"

"Mr. Fard, let me get to the point. Five days ago, Agent Garcia went missing. His transponder stopped transmitting and there was no trace of him except for his abandoned car. Then Friday his transponder started transmitting again and do you know from where ... from a Pacifico Cartel drug farm about 600 kilometers south from where he last reported in! Now The Watchman is sending a team down there to investigate!! Mr. Fard, what did you do with the transponder code I gave you? Who did you give it to?!"

Fard smiled softly.

"Les please calm down and sit down."

"I don't want to sit down, Mr. Fard I want you to answer my questions!"

Fard walked over to a stand with a pot of tea sitting on it and took his time pouring himself a cup.

"I would offer you some, but I remembered that you don't care for tea."

"Mr. Fard, do you also remember what you said to me? You were only supposed to photograph Agent Garcia! The people back at The Watchman think he's dead ... and so do I! I want to know what you did to Agent Garcia and I WANT TO KNOW NOW!"

As soon as Pastak raised his voice, Fard sprang at him. He splashed the boiling tea onto his face, then breaking the cup against the side of the cocktail table he put a pointy shard to his throat. Pastak was temporarily blinded and howling in pain.

"Les, let's get a few things straight, shall we? First, you will never raise your voice in my presence again, is that understood?"

"Aghhh my face ... you scalded my face, you bastard!"

Fard pressed the shard into Pastak's neck until blood appeared around it.

"Les, I will not repeat myself."

Pastak was riveted in pain from the burns to his face and eyes, and from the sharp object drawing blood from his throat.

"Okay ... okay. Yes, I understand!"

"Now Les, I'm going to remove my jagged tea cup from your throat, please don't make me use it to pluck out your eyes."

Fard slowly pulled the ceramic shard from Pastak's neck and put it down on the cocktail table. It had blood on it. Pastak used one hand to wipe the tea remnants from his eyes and put his other hand over the wound to his neck, trying to hold back the bleeding.

Fard walked over to the teapot and poured himself another cup of tea, then sat down next to Pastak.

"I've told you before, Les, I don't have to answer any of your questions, but you have to answer mine. Now concentrate Les. I want you to tell me the truth and I don't want to repeat my questions, do you understand?"

Pastak nodded his understanding. He was shaking from shock.

"First, you said that The Watchman is sending a team down to this drug farm. You need to tell me everything about that and Les, this time leave nothing out or I'll have your limbs removed from your body as you watch!"

Pastak could hardly think straight from the pain.

"One team ... four men ... they're traveling down there on De Niro's yacht, *Santana*."

"They can get to this farm by boat?"

"No ... they're gonna use a chopper from the boat to put them down near the farm."

"Just four men ...? Who are these men ... are they soldiers?"

Pastak blinked his eyes numerous times trying to look around the room.

"I think you damaged my eyes! I can't see ... everything's blurry!"

"Les, Les, Les ... perhaps you didn't take me seriously when I told you I will remove your eyes with a fragment from this tea cup if you make me repeat myself and don't answer my questions! Who are the men?"

"I don't know them ... I mean, I know one ... his name is Santappia, he was a Marine. The others, I have no idea who they are. I'd guess ex-military."

Fard scratched his chin as he collected his thoughts for a moment then continued.

"Let's move on. Les, you only told us about Agent Garcia. Was there another agent attached to that ... what did you call it ... that I-G investigation?"

Pastak hesitated another moment until he saw the blurry figure of Fard motioning towards him.

"Wait ... there was another agent, but he wasn't sent to Mexico. You asked me to only tell you about activities out west! The other agent was sent—"

"To Qatar, yes I know. Unfortunately for you, I didn't learn that from you, Les, but from one of our plants in an investment bank there. Just an hour ago, he informed us that someone was asking questions that we'd rather not have anyone ask."

Some of Pastak's pain subsided just enough for him to start thinking clearly again.

"I don't understand, Mr. Fard. What does that have to do with our interest in obtaining the Mexican government as a client?"

"Les, your making me have to decide which of your eyes I will remove first ... you're asking me questions again."

"I'm sorry. I didn't mean to. I'm just ... I don't understand ... any of this."

"Then let me explain to you, Les, the position you've placed us in and in which you have placed yourself. There is a ... link between Qatar and Mexico that we do not want discovered. Apparently, somehow Mr. De Niro's Watchman agency has stumbled upon it. That potentially puts at risk, a very important operation of ours that's about to get underway. What I need to know from you Les is did that agent in Qatar report yet and if he did, what exactly did he report?"

"I don't know anything about what that agent did or didn't report."

"Then you will tie into their system again and check."

"Mr. Fard, I can't. Okay, I don't know anything about that agent, but I do know that they're starting to put the pieces together to something. I have a gut feeling that it's only a matter of time before they check and see that I was the one that gave away Garcia's location!"

"Les, you have no choice, you really don't. You see, if you don't check right now, in front of me, you won't leave this room alive."

Fard called out in Farsi and a moment later two large Middle Eastern men stepped into the room. Both were wearing black jackets with mocks underneath and one was wielding a brand new, fourth generation Glock 23 pistol with a noise suppressor extending from its muzzle.

Beads of sweat started dripping from Pastak's temples.

"Mr. Fard, please. I'll do it, but how can I be sure that you won't just kill me anyway, after I tell you what you want to know."

"You can't be sure of that Les, but you can be sure that this gentleman pointing his pistol at your head will certainly pull the trigger if you don't comply."

Pastak's mind raced as he took his iPhone from his inside jacket pocket and opened the Big Brother app that was installed on it. He entered his user name and password and breathed a sigh of relief when he saw that he still had access to the system and to the Operation India-Golf 070510 files. His hands started to shake as he continued to type into the phone. After a moment, he sighed out of frustration.

"Mr. Fard, could I have a cup of that tea please? I need something to calm my nerves or this'll take forever."

"I thought you didn't like tea, Les?"

Les stopped typing and looked up at Fard.

"Listen, Mr. Fard, I'd much prefer two fingers of scotch to calm my nerves!"

Fard clenched his eyebrows then motioned to the man not pointing the pistol, to satisfy his request.

Pastak took a sip from his cup of tea.

"Thank you. Now, let me check on the other agent ... okay, yes, he did report in. It says here, he came up with someone named ... Aref Zamani? Do you know him?"

Fard blinked, trying his best to show no emotion hearing the name of his boss spoken by the infidel.

"What did he report about this man?"

Pastak took a minute to read and scroll down. Then he looked up slowly.

"It says that this man Zamani wired $25 million to the warehouse operation that Agent Garcia was investigating."

Fard pursed his lips.

"Go on, does it say anything more?"

"No, the agent just reported that he discovered the name of the man that owned the private equity company that made ... the investment into the Mexican warehouse operation. Mr. Fard, I don't understand any of this, but I won't ask you—"

Fard jumped up from his seat. Pastak's heart almost stopped, until he saw Fard utter something to the man with the gun then he left the room. The man kept the gun pointing at him, but he didn't look like he was ordered to pull the trigger.

Fard hit a speed-dial button on his cell connecting him with Zamani, as soon as he entered the bedroom.

"Sir, we have a few problems. The Watchman knows about the account in Qatar. They also know about the $25 million wired to Mexico and they know that the account belongs to you. Yes sir, I had the infidel confirm it right in front of me. Sir, there's something else. They discovered the location of where those idiot Mexicans buried the agent's body. Yes sir, on one of their drug farms in the south of Mexico ... I understand, I'll contact them and give them warning. One more thing sir, I had to play rough with the infidel. I'm not sure how much more use he can be to us. Apparently they're close to discovering that he was the leak ... Yes sir he still has access to their system ... I understand. I'll have him check. What do you want me to do with the infidel afterwards ... I understand."

The call was disconnected from the other side. Zamani was not at all pleased to hear what Fard had told him. Fard returned to the room with Pastak and his men.

"Les, there's a way for you to remain alive. This turn of events has left none of us with many choices. You know, you really should have told me about that other agent. If you had, we could have made him disappear like we did Agent Garcia. Then none of this would be necessary."

Pastak took his hand away from the wound on his neck. He checked his hand to see if it was still bleeding ... it wasn't. *You didn't exactly make Agent Garcia disappear, did you ... you Iranian moron! I better think fast or I'm gonna end up buried next Garcia!*

"None of what, Mr. Fard ...? Let me rephrase ... just tell me what I need to do to walk out of this room and I'll be glad to do it!"

"You said that their system keeps tabs on the location of everyone. I need you to look in their system and see if there is a transponder code for Mr. De Niro's location."

Pastak couldn't hide his emotions. He was terrified by the request and its implications. He hesitated.

"Les, you know the saying, 'in for a penny, in for a pound?' Well, you are in, up to the bloody wound on your neck, my good man. We need to have leverage on Mr. De Niro. We simply need to be able to persuade him to get his agency to back off from their investigations into our affairs. You understand?"

Pastak nodded.

"Very good, go to it then and I hope for your sake that you find something that will help us."

Pastak started looking into the area of the system where he found Garcia's transponder code. He never considered himself technically advanced with computers but the threat of losing his life inspired him to try his best. He searched more and more fervently as beads of sweat dripped from his brow. Out of the top of his eyes, he could see Fard sitting patiently to his left and the man with the gun standing between him and the door to his right. The other man apparently disappeared into the other room.

Pastak tried accessing in every way he knew using his ops access, when it occurred to him. *Instead of searching through the operations areas of Big Brother, why don't I just search through my HR interface?*

As soon as he patched in via his HR interface, he discovered that not only did he have access to De Niro's transponder code, but there were also transponder codes for De Niro's two sons.

I already caused the death of Agent Garcia by believing Fard. I'm not brave, but I can't just hand over the transponder codes to De Niro and his kids to this madman, no matter how I feel about him. Bottom line though, I'm not getting out of this room either way ... unless I do something!

Pastak's desperation led to inspiration. He downed the tea in his cup then turned to the man with the gun.

"May I have some more tea, please?"

The man looked over at Fard, who was busy typing into his iPhone. Fard looked up with impatience, nodded then went back to what he was doing. The gunman carefully stepped over to the tea pot and with one hand, picked it up while keeping his pistol trained on Pastak. He walked over and began pouring the tea into Pastak's cup. Pastak purposely moved the cup letting some of the tea drip onto his leg. In an instant, he jumped up as if he'd been scorched again, catching the gunman by surprise. Taking a page from Fard's book, he tossed the tea in his cup into the gunman's face then shoved him out of the way and ran out the door of the suite. In the process though, he dropped his phone, but there was no way for him to turn back and get it.

The gunman moaned in agony as the second man ran back into the room. Fard jumped to his feet, pointing out the door.

(In Farsi) "Get him!"

Drawing his own suppressed Glock 23, the second gunman ran out the door only to see Pastak working his way through a small crowd of people heading for the elevators. The gunman quickly concealed his weapon and tried in vain to reach Pastak but Pastak had pushed his way onto the elevator and a moment later the doors closed. The gunman ran back into the suite.

(In Farsi) "I'm sorry sir. He got onto the elevator before I could stop him."

Fard held up his hand with Pastak's phone in it.

"He dropped this. Go after him and get rid of him when you catch him. I don't need him anymore ... and take this other bumbling fool with you!"

Fard waited for the two gunmen to leave the room then he hit the auto-dial button on his phone again, connecting him with Zamani. He examined Pastak's phone as he did.

"Sir, the infidel has temporarily escaped from us but I have his phone and it's still connected to the Watchman's system. Allah is kind! It not only has the transponder codes for Mr. De Niro, but also for his two sons. Thank you sir ... no, don't worry; our men will take care of the infidel. There is nowhere he can run. He can't go to the police or back to The Watchman. Yes sir, I'll return to New York immediately."

Fard carefully placed Pastak's phone onto the table and copied the transponder codes to a pad. When he was done, he pulled the battery from Pastak's phone, dropped the phone on the floor and smashed it with the heel of his shoe then he picked up the hotel phone.

"Yes, this is Mr. Fard. Please send housekeeping to my room. I'll be checking out within the hour, but I'm afraid I entertained a rather clumsy guest."

CHAPTER 24

ABOARD *SANTANA*

STATION KEEPING OFF THE MEXICAN COAST
(APPROXIMATELY 60 MILES NORTH OF)

ACAPULCO, MEXICO

1:00A.M., WEDNESDAY, JULY 20, 2011

Captain Charles "Red" Golden had been the skipper of the *Santana* since Cris De Niro had taken possession of her the year before. She was built in Holland by the renowned Millennium Super Yachts, to Captain Golden's specifications and had taken over two years to build. Like almost everyone else that De Niro hired (with the exception of Concho), he had carefully vetted Red Golden before making him an offer to come to work for him.

Rear Admiral Golden spent his entire adult life in the U.S. Coast Guard, retiring after 33 years of distinguished service. Golden would never forget, the week after he retired, receiving a call from Mr. De Niro offering him the opportunity of a lifetime. Never marrying or living inland, he saved up for his retirement with the intention of buying a small yacht and living on it, sailing from one port to the next. When Cris De Niro made golden the initial offer to work for him, he originally turned him down, telling him about his retirement plans. He was shocked speechless when the billionaire replied, "That's a great plan, Admiral. If you agree to my offer, you can live out those plans and be paid handsomely while you do ... the only difference would be that you do it on *my* yacht."

It turned out that De Niro didn't actually own a yacht when he made him the offer, but that only made his offer sweeter because, as part of the deal, he let Admiral Golden design the yacht for him. Golden spent the next two years flying back and forth to Holland checking on their progress. When she was finished, De Niro and his two sons flew there with Golden, to accompany him on the vessel's maiden voyage back to her new home port in Newport Beach, California. De Niro christened his new 138-foot yacht, *Santana*, naming her after the sail yacht of one of his favorite actors, Humphrey Bogart.

When she was completed, *Santana* was considered a marvel of engineering and beauty, powered by twin Paxman main engines, producing a combined horsepower of 10,870 and a TF80 Lycoming turbine providing an additional 9,200 hp. Her power plant allows her to attain a top speed of 70 knots, a cruise speed of 38 knots, and a maximum range of 3,800 nautical miles and Golden made sure that *Santana's* interior was as impressive as her engine room. Inside the magnificent vessel lies a spacious grand salon, formal dining room, fully equipped country kitchen, a master's sitting room, and sumptuous master suite on the main deck ... a magnificent V.I.P. suite, a luxurious double guest suite, two roomy twin guest suites, crew quarters, engine room, and utility room on the lower deck ... and a spectacular sky lounge and enclosed pilot house with private captain's quarters on the upper deck. De Niro added the final touch with the addition of a Eurocopter EC 135 helicopter, though Golden had little use for the chopper, preferring the sea to the air. All in all, *Santana* was Admiral ... now Captain Golden's dream-come-true.

Santana made good time to waters just north of Acapulco,

considering that they left San Diego Bay later than expected – the delay caused by David Nicholls' insistence to ferry the two ladies he met in the restaurant, to their homes near Imperial Beach. The rest of their journey went smoothly with Nicholls playing the part of proper British host to the four other men.

Captain Golden liked all of his guests aboard *Santana*, including the precocious but eccentric Mr. Nicholls. From the moment the other four men came aboard though, he could tell that they all had extensive military backgrounds and they could tell that he did too. He didn't ask them about the "curious luggage," as Nicholls called it, that they brought aboard. Nevertheless he could tell that it wasn't fishing equipment and despite Nicholls' best tries, the four didn't utter a word about the reason for the trip. They just spent their time soaking up rays, eating and drinking well and laughing at all of Mr. Nicholls jokes, but Golden could see that the trip was about to take on a much more serious tone. That was because two blips had just appeared on his radar. Someone was approaching them at high speed from the south.

Captain Golden sent one of his crew to fetch Charley Santappia. It was just after 1a.m. but he and all of his men were awake and busy loading the chopper. Nicholls had fallen asleep in the Sky Lounge with a bottle of Macallan single-malt scotch whiskey still in his hand.

Santappia entered the Pilot House dressed in all black. His vest and pants were covered with utility pockets and he was wearing a utility belt to match. On his feet, he wore black military-spec boots and he had a black balaclava rolled up into a hat covering his head. There was a small microphone extending from a headset next to his mouth and his face was blacked out all around his eyes and cheeks. Golden also noticed a holster hanging from his belt with what looked like an M-45 MEUSOC[13] pistol inside it. Earlier, when he was on the deck, Golden noticed that the other men were dressed exactly as Santappia was now. It

---

13   The MEU (SOC) pistol, officially designated the M-45 MEUSOC, is a magazine-fed, recoil-operated, single-action, semiautomatic handgun chambered for the .45 ACP cartridge. Based on the original M1911 design by John Browning, the M-45 has been the standard-issue side arm for the Force Recon Element of the United States Marine Corps' Marine Expeditionary Units from 1985 to today.

was obvious to the Captain that these men had not come down to vacation, but now Golden was sure that their trip was some kind of paramilitary operation.

Santappia stepped up to Captain Golden who was looking through binoculars.

"Trouble Captain?"

"We have two bogey's approaching at high speed from the southeast bearing 3-4-0, distance ... about five nautical miles and like I said, closing fast."

Santappia grabbed a pair of binoculars and joined the Captain looking out to the southeast, but all he saw was darkness.

"Captain, is there any reason you can think of, why two surface vessels should be approaching us at high speeds, with lights out?"

"I was going to ask you the same question Mr. Santappia."

The two men looked at each other then both looked through their binoculars again.

"Pirates ...?" asked Santappia.

"Could be ... at their present speed, they'll be on us in about eight minutes."

Santappia cussed to himself.

"Mr. Santappia—"

"Charley, Captain, call me Charley."

"... And I'm Red, Charley. Don't you think this might be a good time for you to tell me a little more about what we're doing here? ... and you better give me the condensed version."

Santappia's mouth stretched into a grin.

"Let's just say, Red, that there's a real chance that our bogies aren't pirates ... and whether they are or not, my friends and I can't let them interfere with our business down here."

"Cut the crap, Charley. I want to know and I want to know now if this business of yours is worth dying for!"

Santappia didn't reply right away. Instead he took another look through his binoculars. He cussed to himself again.

"Red, we're down here on either a rescue mission or a body retrieval mission, depending on the state of our target."

"... And who is your target?"

Santappia knew that the people that worked for Mr. De Niro

were for the most part, all top notch, but then again, if Mr. De Niro wanted the Captain to know about their mission, he would have told him himself. Under the circumstances though, and bearing in mind that Captain Golden was a former Rear Admiral and a highly-decorated one at that, something he learned by running his name through Big Brother, not from the Captain, he thought he had a right to know.

"His name is Jesus Garcia - Agent Jesus Garcia formerly of Langley, Virginia, recently hired by Mr. De Niro's counter-terrorism agency. He was working undercover up in Monterrey when he went missing last week. We tracked him ... or at least we tracked his cell phone, via GPS, to a drug farm owned by one of the most dangerous cartels, located about 140 miles due east of our position. Red, my team and I are down here to bring Garcia home, dead or alive. To us he's worth dying for ... but we have no intention on dying. Unfortunately, it looks like things might get rough and in a hurry. This wasn't something we anticipated either."

Golden nodded his head.

"Okay, thanks for telling me, Charley. Now, what do you want to do about our friends out there?"

"Tough call, Red ... no one was supposed to know we were down here, but we have reason to believe that Garcia was set up by someone inside our agency, which means—"

"Which means our friends out there may be the cartel's version of a welcoming committee!" David Nicholls interrupted Santappia.

"Mr. Nicholls ... we thought you were sleeping."

"I was sleeping old man until I felt the call of nature. I made a wrong turn into here and what did I find? The Captain and the mysterious passenger, Mr. Santappia, dressed like a ninja warrior, discussing my fate ...!"

"Mr. Nicholls, we don't have much time," Captain Golden replied. "I'm going to have to ask you to return to your suite and lock your door immediately."

"You want me to lock myself in my room while you all replay the battle at your Alamo ... not on your life, Captain!"

Riggy walked in behind Nicholls.

"Charley, I think we got company approaching us. Sounds like speed boats but we don't see any lights."

"The Captain picked up two bogies off our port bow, approaching fast. We have no idea who they are. They'll be on us in a matter of minutes."

Santappia thought a moment.

"Captain, I wouldn't ask you to endanger your crew but would you be willing to help us?"

"Mr. Santappia, this vessel is my home and I will do anything to do defend my home. What do you need me to do?"

Santappia nodded. He had a lot of respect for the captain.

"Okay, order your crew into the engine room and have them lock the doors once they're all down there ... and Mr. Nicholls, you need to join them."

"Mr. Santappia, whatever you're asking the Captain to do, I'd like to join him, if you don't mind. I'm not the type that takes well to being cooped up below decks, especially while my fate is being decided up here."

Santappia looked at the Captain, who nodded.

"Okay, we don't have much time gentlemen. Captain, order you men below. Riggy, get the guys to break out those jet skis that you've all been eyeing ... and everyone rides with their M-40[14]'s ... and Riggy, bring me my AA-12[15] ..."

David Nicholls was glad he held onto the bottle of Macallan scotch he was drinking earlier, as the sounds of two Deep Impact model 360FS speed boats approached *Santana* and curved around both sides of her. Nicholls took a long pull from the bottle then handed it Captain Golden who did the same, as one of the boats pulled alongside while the other one continued to *Santana's* stern. Nicholls and Golden counted twelve gunmen total, six on each boat. The six on the boat pulled alongside all had automatic weapons pointed at them as one shouted in broken English, "Gringos ... Shut ju engines and put ju hands on ju heads!"

---

14   The M40 is a bolt-action sniper rifle used by the United States Marine Corps.

15   The Auto Assault-12 (AA-12) is a 12 gauge shotgun capable of selective fire, operating as a semi-automatic, or in fully automatic mode at 300 rounds per minute. It is fed from either an 8-shell box magazine, or a 20 or 32-shell drum magazine.

Captain Golden complied by entering the pilot house and cutting the engines; then stepping back onto the deck alongside Nicholls and placing his hands on the back of his head. He noticed Nicholls had his hands behind his head but he was still clutching the bottle of scotch in one. Five of the six gunmen stepped onto *Santana* and circled the two men as the nastiest of the bunch stepped up to both. He finally decided from looking at them that Golden was the captain and addressed him while putting a pistol to his head.

(In English) "Are ju the capitán?"

"Yes."

"This is a big boat, capitán. Where is jur crew?"

"I sent them below when I saw you approaching."

The heavily tattooed leader twitched his head towards Nicholls but never took his eyes off of Golden.

"Who is this gringo?"

"He's my passenger. This is a charter vessel."

"A charter huh ... where are the rest of jur passengers, capitán?"

David Nicholls took a step up but was pushed back by two of the men.

"Look here good man, my name is Nicholls. I rented this boat for the week."

The leader turned to Nicholls.

"Ju rented this big boat all for jurself?"

"Well, I was expecting to go ashore in Acapulco, dear boy and invite some of your beautiful ladies back aboard—"

Nicholls was interrupted by one of the men from the other speed boat who was shouting to the leader something in Spanish. Nicholls whispered to the Captain, "What is he saying?"

The Captain whispered back, "He just yelled to Mr. Tattoos here that this is the *Santana*. Santappia was right, we were set up. Get ready Mr. Nicholls."

The leader ordered the other boat to come around the side then he cocked his pistol and put it to Captain Golden's head.

"Ju are lying to me, capitán. I ask ju once more ... where are the other men ju took down here?"

The leader barked orders in Spanish and instantly two of

the men headed inside the main cabin. They were greeted by Charlie Santappia who was standing on the other side of the doors, with his automatic shotgun pointing at them. Santappia barked orders of his own into his mic, "Angel one ... Take 'em down!"

Only one response came back.

"Roger ..."

Almost simultaneously, shots came from all directions, the loudest and most ferocious ones were spitting out of Santappia's AA-12. The sniper fire from Riggy, De May and Pescalitis dropped the leader and his two men standing on both sides of Nicholls and Captain Golden, while Santappia blasted large holes in the other two men.

That left six gunmen on the one speedboat and one on the other, all of them shouting to each other in Spanish from both sides of *Santana*. Nicholls and Captain Golden started towards the doors of the main cabin when the leader, only wounded, rolled onto his back and started firing at both of them. Nicholls turned and threw the bottle of scotch he still had in his hand then dove for cover. The bottle hit the leader in the side of his head.

Captain Golden peered out from the main cabin and saw the leader now lying unconscious. He turned to Nicholls, "They say fortune favors the foolish, Mr. Nicholls. Now I'm convinced it does!"

Santappia stood at the side of one of the cabin's doors trying to survey into the darkness. He spoke to the members of ARCHANGEL as he did.

"Angel one ... Guys, we can't let the rest get away."

Again, all Santappia heard was a single calm voice, "Roger that."

Less than ten seconds later, three more shots rang out from their M-40's dropping three more gunmen, all on the boat that had circled to the stern of *Santana*. Unable to see their adversaries, the remaining three on that boat panicked and immediately laid down their weapons, shouting in Spanish, "We give up!"

As soon as Santappia stepped out from the cabin he saw the sole bad guy left on the other boat take off like a bat out of hell into the darkness. Santappia took aim with his AA-12 but the boat quickly motored out of his range.

"Angel one … Angel three, one bogey took off heading in your direction."

"Angel three, roger …"

A few tense moments later one shot rang out then another from Angel three's … De May's M-40.

"Angel three, bogey's down."

While Santappia held his shotgun pointed at them, Captain Golden helped the three Pacifico cartel members onto *Santana*, from their speed boat. As soon as they were on board, the Captain frisked them, and then ordered them in Spanish to sit on the deck, with their hands on their heads. One of *Santana's* crew jumped aboard the speed boat and lowered its anchor while two others collected the weapons aboard it. A few minutes later, out of the darkness came the three jet skis with Riggy, De May and Pescalitis riding them, their sniper rifles slung on their backs.

As soon as everyone was aboard, Santappia walked over to the leader who was just coming around. He was bleeding badly from a shoulder wound. Pescalitis checked the other two that were lying next to the leader.

"They're both dead." Pescalitis confirmed then pointing at the leader, "Hey Riggy wasn't this one yours?"

Riggy's face turned red from embarrassment, "Yeah, a wave pushed my ski just as I took my shot."

De May and Pescalitis grinned to tease Angel 2 but Santappia spoke up, "Better that your aim was off Rigs. Now we can get 'Mr. Tats' here to tell his boss that he and his hombres did their job and we're all dead … isn't that right hombre?"

The leader didn't reply.

Pescalitis walked up to him then started waving his hand in front of his nose, "He stinks of booze!"

"I'm afraid that's my fault," David Nicholls replied a bit immodestly. "You see he was shooting at me and the Captain, and I still had the bottle of that fine scotch in my hand—"

"… And I have to thank you for that Mr. Nicholls," Captain Golden interrupted then turned to Pescalitis and the others. "Mr. Nicholls could have had a career in baseball with the way he tossed that bottle of scotch. I mean he hit our friend here from twenty feet away ... hard enough to knock him senseless and he wasn't even pitching from the windup!"

Pescalitis patted Nicholls on his back as Santappia handed his shotgun to Riggy. Then he took out his MPK-Ti[16] and put it to the throat of the leader, as he bent down and whispered into his ear.

"You have two choices, my friend. You can either do exactly as I tell you and get on your radio and tell your boss that you did your job and we're all dead ... or I'll throw you overboard and let your blood attract every shark within three miles of here."

The leader spat into Santappia's face.

Santappia wiped the spit from his face with his sleeve. Then he lifted the leader up by his hair, dragged him to the railing and as the man spewed curses in Spanish, threw him over the side. The wounded man flopped around in the pitch-dark trying his best to keep his head above the water line.

Santappia casually walked over to the other three men who were now all sitting in shock from hearing their leader screaming for help. He put his knife to one of the men's throat. The man pleaded in Spanish.

Santappia turned to the Captain.

"What's he saying?"

The Captain nodded towards the man in the water.

"He's begging you to pull him out of the water before the sharks get him."

The screams from the man in the water stopped as the swells began to roll over his head. Santappia sheaved his knife and ordered De May and Pescalitis to bring the drowning man back aboard. After giving him a minute to vomit the salt water from his lungs, Santappia put his knife back to the leader's throat.

"That was just the rehearsal of your death, amigo. The next time I throw you overboard, you become sharks bait and I simply have one of your men here make the radio call. It would be better coming from you, though ... better for us and better

---

16   The MPK-Ti is a titanium, light weight, non magnetic, non corrosive, and multi functional knife that can be used in all environments. It was designed to meet the requirements of the Navy SEAL's and has also been adopted and issued by the United States Marine Corps Recon personnel.

for you. You decide."

The leader looked up at Santappia with a combination of pain and anger on his face then nodded his head in defeat.

Santappia sheaved his knife again and stood up.

"De May take our friend here and let him make the call from the radio on their boat. Captain, would you please accompany them and make sure he says what we want him to say ... not a word more or less, you comprende, amigo?"

The man nodded again.

After the leader sent the message, Santappia kept everyone busy. First he had the four cartel members brought below. There weren't many areas on *Santana* that weren't created for comfort, so they ended up placing all of the men, bound, in the utility room. That is, after they bandaged the leader's shoulder. It turned out that Riggy's bullet passed right through his shoulder making the wound easier to treat.

The Captain ordered his crew to clean the blood from *Santana's* deck, while Santappia had De May and Pescalitis fasten the bodies of the dead men inside the anchored boat. Then De May blew several holes in her hull with the AA-12. Next, Santappia had the Captain locate the second speedboat and bring *Santana* abeam so De May could fasten the body that was aboard her and blew holes in her hull. Each boat disappeared from view in a matter of minutes.

It was after 3:00 a.m. when ARCHANGEL finally took off from *Santana* on the EC-135, and around 4:30 a.m. when they landed near the drug farm, but the rest of the operation went easier. They landed the chopper about two kilometers from the farm's perimeter, their landing zone concealed by foothills. Then they made their way by foot to Garcia's position. The tattooed leader on the boat must have been convincing because there was only two guards within a mile of their position and both were sleeping. They dug up the body of Agent Garcia, confirming their worst fears. Santappia took the phone from the dead agent's pocket and turned it off for the last time, shutting down its transponder beacon – a signal to everyone back in the States that they found him, then De May threw the body over his shoulder and they headed back to the chopper.

Dawn was breaking as they flew back to *Santana*. Once back aboard, Santappia asked Red Golden to get underway, best speed, for *Santana's* home in Newport Beach. Once they were heading north, Santappia contacted De Niro and Mugsy Ricci so that he could fill them in. The five day journey back gave both men ample time to make preparations. Ricci made a few phone calls to have the cartel members placed into custody as soon as they made port. He asked Michelle Wang to contact her friends at Homeland so that no questions would be asked as to where they came from. Meanwhile, De Niro had two SUV's waiting for ARCHANGEL, one carrying a special refrigerated coffin so that they could drive themselves and the body of Agent Garcia back to the Coyote's Den. Once there, they hoped an autopsy on Jesus Garcia could deliver the agent's last report for him.

CHAPTER 25

THE COYOTE'S DEN
ESTANCIA DE NIRO, HENDERSON, NV
9:30A.M., WEDNESDAY, JULY 27, 2011

De Niro thought of everything when he designed the Coyote's Den, including a fully stocked infirmary. It was intended to be used to provide medical treatment for the proposed black ops force that was to be stationed there. Though circumstances dictated that in its first use it was needed for a solemn purpose ... as a morgue.

Ricci hadn't had time to hire permanent medical personnel but he knew in a pinch that he could rely on his friend Woody, aka Sergeant Ray "Woody" Woods to perform the autopsy on Agent Garcia. Mugsy first met Woods when he was a Special Forces Medical Sergeant stationed in Iraq. Sgt. Woods had saved then Lieutenant Ricci's life after Ricci was wounded in a fierce firefight while on patrol against insurgents in Ramadi. Since then, Mugsy and Woody remained in contact. A few years ago, Ricci finally had been able to reciprocate by helping Woods get assigned stateside after his wife had complained about his extended tours of duty, overseas. Woods was grateful to Mugsy for possibly saving his marriage. There was very little either man wouldn't do for the other.

Ricci tracked down Woods to his home in Smithtown, New York. He was on leave and just about to go fishing off of Montauk Point with his son and daughter when he received the call from his old lieutenant. Mugsy offered him first-class roundtrip airfare to Las Vegas and an all-paid vacation for him, his wife and two kids, in return for a favor. Woods never even asked what the favor was. He told Mugsy he didn't need the vacation for his family, just the first-class roundtrip tickets and he was there.

Sgt. Woods had arrived in the Coyote's Den at eight that morning. It was only a little past 9:30 a.m. when he walked out of the examination room. De Niro, Mugsy, Santappia and the three ARCHANGEL members gathered around him. Ricci spoke first.

"That didn't take long."

Woods removed his surgical gloves and tossed them into a trashcan.

"Well, it didn't take long to see that Agent Garcia died from two 9mm bullet wounds to his head, entry points within an inch of each other just above his right eye. What I was more interested in was what I didn't see ... namely, powder residue anywhere around the wounds or on the body."

Santappia: "Meaning he was shot from long distance?"

"No, Agent Garcia was definitely shot at close range. Listen, I don't consider myself 'Quincy M.D.' but from my years of treating bullet wounds I can tell you this ... judging from the damage made by the bullets and by the amount of blood and brain matter that I found inside the plastic they wrapped him in ... Agent Garcia was shot at close range by a 9mm pistol, my guess ... virtually right on top of the plastic."

Ricci: "What about the lack of powder residue?"

"I've been thinking about that and I can only give you my guess. One of the pistol ranges that I practice at is in the basement of a small hunting and fishing store on Long Island. The store owner makes us all use suppressors to keep the noise down. Anyway, one of the things we came to find using suppressors was that there was no powder residue left on our close quarter targets."

Ricci: "So Woody, you're saying that, in your opinion, Agent Garcia was shot twice in the head at close range with a suppressed 9mm pistol."

"Exactly Mugs ... I'd also guess that he was taken by surprise because there were no other signs of struggle on his body."

Ricci: "So execution-style ..."

The men began to talk among themselves as Woods stepped away to wash his hands. De Niro followed him.

"I'd like to thank you for helping us out with this, Sergeant, especially considering the confidential nature of it ... and I understand you had to cancel a fishing trip to Montauk Point with your kids?"

"Not a problem Mr. De Niro, anything for Mugsy. Besides, if I get home by tonight, I can still take my kids fishing."

"From what my brother-in-law told me, you took care of him pretty good over in Iraq."

Woods smiled.

"Yeah, he came in all shot up. Within a month there wasn't a nurse around that he hadn't hit on."

Both men chuckled.

"Sergeant—"

"Call me Woody, Mr. De Niro. Even my wife calls me Woody."

"Okay Woody, I'm Cris. Woody, would you consider coming to work for us here?"

Mugsy walked over before Woody could reply.

"What's going on over here?"

"I just offered Woody a job with us. I thought that would be okay with you."

"That's more than okay with me. I was about to ask him the same thing. What do you say pal? You'd be in charge of this infirmary and a small staff assigned to it."

Woody dried his hands and thought about it. "Any field

duty?"

Ricci and De Niro looked at each other before Mugsy replied.

"There's a possibility there might be some field duty. To tell you the truth Woody, we're just getting underway, so I couldn't tell exactly what to expect. I do need to leave all options open though, at this point."

Woody didn't reply.

De Niro: "Well, I'll leave you in my brother-in-law's capable hands. Mugsy volunteered to run you back to McCarran."

De Niro offered Woody his hand.

"Thanks again Woody ... and Mugs, if you take the Cobra, try to bring it back in one piece!"

After De Niro walked out of the room, Woody started to change.

"He's not what I expected Mugs, he's a nice guy ... I mean being a billionaire you never know ..."

"I told you he was and I'll tell you something else. It doesn't get better than working for him and you don't have to take my word for that, ask any of the guys here. First, we don't deal with any red tape or politics or asshole superior officers here—"

"So you're telling me I'd only have to deal with one asshole superior officer here, the one in front of me now?"

Ricci play-punched him in the arm, "... who can still kick your butt. Woody, seriously, our mandate here is to protect our country. It's the same mandate we had in the military, except we're working for a privately owned counter-terrorism agency, funded by one of the richest men in the world. And I don't have to tell you that you get paid double what you're making now—"

Woods buttoned his shirt.

"I remember reading somewhere about what happened to his wife ... your sister. I'm sorry, Mugs, she was pregnant, wasn't she?"

Ricci nodded with sadness, "Three months pregnant with my third nephew ... but let me tell you something. If you think this whole setup is just Cris's and my way to get revenge or be vigilantes, you're wrong. We're a covert arm of a government contracted counter-terrorism agency."

"I never thought that Mugs, I know you better than that.

Besides, I personally wouldn't have a problem with it, even if you were set up that way. I was in Iraq, remember? I saw what their terrorist tactics ... ambushes ... IED[17]'s ... mines ... shoulder-fired rockets did to our boys. I was the one that had to patch them up, remember? I also volunteered for Ground Zero duty ... in all my years serving in the military I never saw anything like what I saw there ..."

Ricci didn't reply right away.

"I didn't know you volunteered down there."

Both men remained quiet for a few moments then Woody exhaled audibly.

"You're right, this would be prime duty. I love it out here anyway, but I'm not sure how Donna will feel about it. Her whole family lives on the Island ... it's like half of Sicily lives within an hour of our house. I remember when I wanted to look out houses in Jersey. To her and her family it was like looking for houses in Siberia."

Both men laughed a bit, lightening the mood.

"Double the pay, you said? That might change her mind. Let me go home and talk to her. I'll let you know."

Ricci led his friend to the main house both men riding ATV's then they both jumped in De Niro's pride and joy, his midnight blue Shelby GT500 Super Snake.

"Listen, we have a few hours before your flight takes off. I'm taking you to the Pink Taco over at the Hard Rock. They serve the best fish tacos and we'll wash 'em down with a few Dos Equis and the best tequila money can buy ... on me!"

Back at the Coyote's Den, De Niro and Charley Santappia tied in via videoconference with Michelle Wang at The Watchman. De Niro spoke first.

"Here's what we got Michelle. Mugsy's not here but he thought we should fill you in right away. The findings from Garcia's post mortem examination lean towards a contract-style hit ... two 9mm bullets fired from a suppressed pistol at close range with no signs of struggle."

Wang: "Suppressed ... that ties in with what we got from the

---

17   An improvised explosive device (IED), also known as a roadside bomb due to contemporary use, is a homemade bomb constructed and deployed in ways other than in conventional military action.

guard at the facility in Monterrey. He reported that he distinctly didn't hear any shots fired. At that time of night, even from a distance and enclosed in a trailer, he should have heard the shots."

Santappia: "We also have the fact that we were set up down in Mexico. Our rescue operation was totally blown, no doubt about it."

De Niro: "Have you been able to contact or locate Les?"

Wang: "Negative, Cris. At this point we can safely assume he had something to do with all this but we haven't been able to locate him since the last time he tapped into Big Brother ... and that was ten days ago. I sent a few agents out looking for him. So far he hasn't gone back to his home and he hasn't shown up at the homes of any of his family or friends."

De Niro: "What do we know about what he accessed ten days ago?"

Wang: "Well we know he tied in from somewhere outside of The Watchman again via the India-Golf ops access I gave him. It looks like he spent several minutes just scouring all the files, but we can't tell much more than that."

De Niro: "What was he looking for? I mean he didn't need to access those India-Golf files to find out about the operation to find Garcia; he was there when we discussed it. He spends several minutes just perusing those ops files then goes missing right after that. What was he looking for?"

Wang: "That's true. I've been asking that same question. You know something Cris you would have made a great spy."

De Niro: "I'll take that as a compliment Michelle, seeing that it comes from a great spy. Okay, where does all of this leave us?"

Wang: "We have to find Les. He's the one that can tell us who's really behind all of this. It'll take a little time but we'll find out who he's been calling on his cell phone and Johnny-F will pull the records on anything he accessed from the internet while he was connected through our system."

The other line lit up.

De Niro: "Michelle, hold on."

Ricci: "Cris, its Mugsy. I have Karla on the line. She's got some interesting info."

De Niro: "Mugs are you in a secure spot?"

Ricci: "I'm sitting in your baby. I walked back out to the car to take the call, leaving my fish tacos with Woody, who's probably munching them down right now."

De Niro: "Okay, let me patch Michelle in too and Charley's sitting next to me."

Ricci: "Karla, repeat what you were telling me."

Matthews: "Hi Cris ... Charley ... Michelle ... I was telling Captain Ricci that I just got off the phone with one of my sources at DHS-CBP[18]. He told me that ICE[19] just reported to them that there's been unusual activity near the border and it involves the Pacifico cartel. Apparently a special detachment of ICE apprehended a coyote[20] who spilled a little more than they usually do before he clammed up. My source didn't know any more of the particulars, but he did say that this special ICE detachment didn't have a problem with our sending a team down to investigate."

Mugsy jumped in.

"Thanks Karla, I'll get back to you. Michelle, I need to speak to Cris. I'll talk to you later."

"Understood," Wang replied. A moment later, only De Niro, with Santappia sitting next to him, and Mugsy were on the line.

"Cris, we need to send ARCHANGEL down there ASAP to investigate."

"I agree."

"Charley, you there..?"

"Yeah, Mugs ..."

"Get Riggy, De May, and Pescy and saddle up ... Karla will send you the ops files on India-Golf 072810. You'll be flying into Nogales International. Cris, should I fly them commercial?"

"I told you before Mugs, all of my resources are available. I would suggest the G550[21]. I'll contact Colonel O'Rourke and have him have the 550 prepped and ready to go within the hour.

---

18   DHS-CBP stands for Department of Homeland Security Customs and Border Protection.

19   ICE stands for U.S. Immigration and Customs Enforcement.

20   A coyote is a person who smuggles illegal immigrants into the United States, especially across the Mexican border.

21   The Gulfstream G550 is a business jet aircraft produced by General Dynamics' Gulfstream Aerospace unit, located in Savannah, Georgia, USA. It is a variant of the Gulfstream V with longer range.

Charley, have you and the boys meet me at the main house when you're ready. I'll have Concho drop you guys off at Executive Airport."

Santappia got up and was about to leave the conference room when Mugsy called out to him.

"Charley, be careful. I don't have to tell you how rough it's been down there. That whole border area is a war zone. You'll be meeting with the agent who made the original bust and report, Agent Bryan Ahiga. Agent Ahiga is a member of an elite unit of Native American federal agents called the Shadow Wolves. They're tasked with protecting the border between Mexico and the Tohono O'odham Nation reservation, an area about the size of the state of Connecticut. The Shadow Wolves use tracking techniques that are unique to Native Americans of that area. You can definitely learn a thing or two from him Charley, so take his advice if you have to do any investigating."

"Will do Mugs ... What's our scope?"

"Specifically, you're to look for any link between the alleged Pacifico activities that this coyote hinted at and anything having to do with Agent Garcia's murder, Les's involvement or this Iranian, Zamani. I'll leave it up to you how much you want to share with Agent Ahiga. We're already requesting that ICE assign him to you for the duration of your stay down there, but like I said Charley be extra mindful of his input."

"Understood ..."

De Niro waited for Santappia to leave the room before asking any questions.

"What do you think Mugs? Could this have anything to do with what Garcia was investigating? Monterrey isn't exactly close to Nogales."

"I know, but Nogales is one of the main crossing points for illegal aliens and Pacifico has a big hand in that. Up to now, we've been thinking drugs, but what if all this has to do with smuggling people over the border from Mexico?"

De Niro thought about it then asked the obvious and very deadly question.

"Mugs, what interest would an Iranian have in a Mexican drug cartel that runs a big illegal alien smuggling operation?"

CHAPTER 26

MISSION SAN XAVIER DEL BAC
SAN XAVIER DISTRICT
TOHONO O'ODHAM NATION
SOUTH OF TUCSON, ARIZONA
11:30A.M., THURSDAY, JULY 28, 2011

Charley Santappia, Vic Rigoni, Karl De May, and Spiro Pescalitis sat in their rent-a-jeep in the parking lot of the old Mission San Xavier del Bac. They'd been waiting outside for most of the morning but the southern Arizona sun shot the early afternoon temperature over 100°F sending them back into the Jeep Cherokee with the engine idling and the AC blasting.

Pescalitis: "I thought Vegas was hot ... the AC is on max and I can still feel heat!"

De May: "I need to stretch my legs but I'm afraid to step out there and have my boots melt."

Rigoni: "Quit talking about the heat, you two, it just makes it worse! Charley, this guy's over two hours late, how long are we gonna wait here?"

Santappia: "I called ICE, they said he's out in the field but he told them he'll meet us here as soon as he could. So we wait here as long as it takes."

De May: I got to stretch my legs!"

The four members of ARCHANGEL stepped out into the desert sun. As they did, a pickup truck pulled into the parking lot and parked next to them. The four didn't take much notice of the man that stepped out, keeping their eyes on the parking lot entrance looking for an official vehicle.

Pescalitis: "So Charley, this Agent Ahiga ... he's an Indian ... as in Cochise?"

"Actually, Cochise was Chiricahua Apache, I'm Navaho. Would one of you gentlemen be Charles Santappia? I'm Agent Ahiga."

Pescalitis was startled by the 50 year-old, well-built, dark skinned man standing behind him, who exited the pickup. Santappia offered him his hand.

"How are you Agent Ahiga, I'm Charley Santappia ... Charley. This big guy here is Vic Rigoni ... we call him Riggy. The even bigger guy is Karl De May and next to him is Spiro Pescalitis. As you can see, everything Pescy knows about Native Americans he learned from old Cowboy and Indian movies."

Agent Ahiga winked at Pescalitis.

"I loved them movies too ... I always wanted to be one of the cowboys. They always won the fights and ended up with pretty women in their arms at the end."

Ahiga pointed to the east.

"As far as geography goes though, Mr. Pescalitis isn't too far off. The Dragoon Mountains, where Cochise and his band hid, are due east of here."

Pescalitis stepped up next to Ahiga.

"Is that so ... wow! Hey, Agent Ahiga, I didn't mean anything by what I said—"

"Forget it. I guess being compared to K'uu-ch'ish isn't such a bad thing. Cochise's name in Apache meant that he was as strong as oak. Gentlemen, why don't we get out of this heat? Follow me I know a good place to get a bite to eat."

Ahiga led them to a Mexican restaurant nearby. The five men took seats in a large booth.

Ahiga took a long pull from his beer, "I apologize for being so late. I cut for sign just after dawn and a few of my unit and I spent the rest of the morning tracking down some smugglers. We got lucky and caught them before they got into the foothills or else you'd still be waiting for me."

"Cut for sign? Santappia asked.

"Yeah, 'Sign' is physical evidence—footprints, a dangling thread, a broken twig, a discarded piece of clothing, or tire tracks ... things like that. 'Cutting' is searching for sign or analyzing it once it's found. In this case we came upon the tracks of two young smugglers, 22-24 years old. They were offered $800 cash to carry several bales of marijuana over the border. Considering that they usually make around $20 a week in Mexico, they both jumped at the chance for only a few days work."

"What will happen to them now? Riggy asked.

"They were first-time offenders who confessed, so they'll be prosecuted at the federal court in Tucson ... probably get a year or so in federal prison."

Santappia showed everyone information he pulled up on his handheld device.

"I spent a little time researching the Shadow Wolves. I must say Agent Ahiga—"

"My first name's Bryan ..."

"I must say Bryan, I was very impressed. In our day and age of high-tech toothbrushes, the Shadow Wolves have shown that sometimes the old ways are the best ways."

"That's true Charley. We use tracking methods that have been handed down in our tribes for many generations, but that's not to say that we don't incorporate high technology. We just don't solely rely on it."

Santappia motioned to his men, "Keep your eyes and ears open guys, we can learn a lot from Bryan."

"I don't know about that, Charley. I also had a little time to research you guys ... at least what's published about your military records. You were a major in the Marines and the rest of you guys were warrant officers? Heck, how's the Corps even surviving without you? By the way, Semper Fi[22] ...!"

"You served in the Marines, Bryan?" De May asked.

"Yes sir, 1st Marine Division. Joined right out of high school and got out right after Desert Storm. As soon as we reached Kuwait City, I knew our job was done and time for me to move on ... let some of the younger jars have a turn."

All the men at the table knew exactly what Agent Ahiga was talking about and his being a fellow Marine meant they chewed some of the same dirt ... and sand. That shot up their respect for him even more.

All the men ordered what Ahiga suggested. It ended up being some of the best Mexican fare any of them ever ate – fajitas, carne asada, tamales and enchiladas. While they ate, Agent Ahiga filled the men of ARCHANGEL in on the general state of affairs on his stretch of the border.

"... The Shadow Wolves unit is responsible for the 76 miles of border that our reservation shares with Mexico. It isn't easy with fewer than two dozen officers, and the events of September 11 only made things worse. With the beefed-up security at Arizona's border crossings— Nogales and Sasabee in the east, and Lukeville in the west—the smugglers figure their chances are better to cross the desert in between. That desert is our reservation and the city of Tucson is on our northern border. Now, day and night, usually groups of eight to ten men move north from Mexico, each individual can be carrying upwards of 40 pounds of marijuana on his back. To make matters worse, they're funded by Mexican drug lords. So they're often better equipped and more numerous than the Shadow Wolves, with lookouts on neighboring mountains armed with night-vision goggles, cell phones and radios. They use it all to send encrypted messages to direct smugglers away from our law enforcement vehicles."

Looks of frustration were evident on all the men's faces.

"So Bryan, we understand you came across a coyote with a big mouth?" asked Santappia.

"I did and that's unusual all on its own. It's almost unheard of for anyone, whether their smugglers, coyotes or UDA's ...

---

22   Semper Fidelis is Latin for "Always Faithful". Shortened to Semper Fi in Marine contexts.

undocumented ... in other words illegal aliens ... to open their mouths. They know that chances are ... they'll end up being deported back down to Mexico at some point ... and their lives wouldn't be worth a cent if anyone found out that they talked up here."

"So what was different about this one?"

Ahiga exhaled.

"We normally don't use lethal force to stop most people crossing our border, but these kids ... there was three of them, the oldest was 22 ... thought they were riding with Poncho Villa and drew down on us, that was also highly unusual. Things have been getting progressively more violent lately. We ended up killing two of them and severely wounding the third. We radioed in for a medevac chopper and as I was trying my best to bandage the wounded one, he started babbling. He told me that a 'borrasca' ... a storm was coming soon from the south and that my men and I better hide in the hills or it would sweep us all away."

"A borrasca ... was he high or something?" asked Riggy.

"No, he wasn't high. He might have been a little delirious from the pain. I also think he was convinced he was dying. I tried my best to get more out of him. Just before he fell unconscious he started mumbling something ... and the one name he kept saying was ... Tuco."

"Tuco Ramirez?" Santappia asked.

Ahiga nodded.

"When he came to in the hospital, I attempted to question him more about it but his senses must have come back to him. Now he clams up and his heart monitor spikes if you even mention Tuco's name to him."

Santappia scratched his chin.

"That is disturbing ... we were told that you reported suspicious activity lately too ..."

"That's right ... the few informants that we do have, have been telling us that a number of the coyotes are holding off on border crossings lately but at the same time, they're continuing to amass larger and larger numbers of UDA's in the towns just south of the border - those towns that specialize in selling all of the necessary items to illegals intending to cross. And the one thing that all of these coyotes seem to have in common is that they all work for the same cartel ... Pacifico."

"It sounds like they're getting ready for a series of larger crossings."

"Or one massive crossing!" replied Ahiga. All the men sat up as he took another long pull from his beer.

"Starting this past week, we've found graffiti nearby and mentions on scraps of paper, some of the UDA's we've caught were carrying in their pockets ... all with the term, 'Noche del espantada' ... fright night."

While everyone sat in thought, Ahiga called the waitress over and ordered another round of beers for everyone. Santappia waited for the waitress to bring them and walk away.

"Tell us what you make of all of it, Bryan."

Ahiga took a moment to collect his thoughts.

"It's hard to say. So much of what is said down here ... what goes on down here ... is smoke and mirrors, Charley. But you asked my opinion and I'll give it to you. I think the Pacifico cartel is planning a massive border crossing for sometime soon."

"How soon ...?"

"I don't know. I've never come across anything like this and I've lived here all my life. It could come today or in a week or a month. I don't think it could happen too much longer than that though. Most of the towns south of the border aren't setup to house and feed a mass of people for any period of time. Besides, the majority of the people crossing couldn't afford to wait very long. As it is, I bet the cartel is using coercion to keep them in line."

"So they're still running drugs across the border but not illegal aliens? Riggy thought out loud.

"I know," Ahiga replied, "It doesn't seem to make sense."

"Well Bryan, would you mind if we tagged along with you for awhile ... maybe have you show us the lay of the land some and let us pick your brains while we do?" Santappia formed it as a question but Ahiga knew Santappia had the authority to make it an order. That moved Charley Santappia up another notch in the Shadow Wolf's book.

"Sure, but may I ask you guys a question? Exactly what are you doing here? Who are you guys anyway? I know you're not in Homeland or ICE. Are you FBI?"

"We work for a private counter-terrorism firm, Bryan."

"And what exactly does a bunch of old Marines do for a private counter-terrorism firm?"

Santappia hesitated, while the others enjoyed Ahiga's coy question.

"Whatever needs doing ... just like in the Marines. You know the drill."

Ahiga used a mock drill sergeant voice, "When we say jump, you say how high!"

The men laughed as Santappia went on.

"In this case, we're here to see if there's any link between our own on-going investigations into activities of the Pacifico cartel and their recent activities here."

"What on-going investigations?" Ahiga continued his coy curiosity.

Santappia looked at his men. They all gave him the nod to trust Agent Ahiga.

"Bryan, we've been investigating a possible link between an Iranian businessman and Pacifico. The man's name is Aref Zamani ... his name mean anything to you?"

"Nope ... go on."

"He apparently 'invested' $25 million into a warehousing operation owned by Tuco Ramirez and his cartel. We sent an agent down to Monterrey to investigate and he ended up with two 9mm holes in his forehead. We dug up his body ourselves last week from a drug farm owned by Pacifico."

Now it was Ahiga that sat speechless as Santappia continued.

"We need to find out if there's any connection between what's been going on here lately and this man Zamani. I don't have to tell you the ramifications if this Zamani turns out to be a radical extremist and Pacifico is helping him to smuggle ... whatever ... into the US."

Ahiga nodded then sat in thought for a moment.

"Well if you want to tag along with me you'll need your Jeep, unless you all want to ride in the back of my pickup ... but the other problem is that we sometimes use ATV's down here and we don't have too many to spare."

"That's not a problem, Bryan, we have our own. We have our own weapons too, but we'd appreciate it if you suggested what we should be packing and toting."

"Well, all Shadow Wolves carry sidearms and we use M-4[23]'s along with our radios."

"We use the same ... A1[24]'s," replied De May.

"We've never had a need to go fully auto," Ahiga replied.

Santappia broke in.

"Okay, I'll have our people fly our equipment down and I'll tell our boss that we may be here awhile. I'd like you to suggest a hotel for us, if you would and after we check in, I'd like to go see your wounded coyote. I'm not expecting much from that, but we'll leave no stone unturned."

Ahiga smiled.

"You better be careful what stones you turn down here, Charley, that's where the rattlesnakes hide from the afternoon sun."

All the men laughed while Santappia raised his beer bottle. The rest of them did the same as he proposed a toast.

"Here's to ... not needing to go fully auto ... and to the Shadow Wolves!"

Bryan Ahiga appreciated the sentiment.

---

23   The M4 carbine is a family of firearms tracing its lineage back to earlier carbine versions of the M16, all based on the original AR-15 designed by Eugene Stoner and made by ArmaLite. It is a shorter and lighter version of the M16A2 assault rifle, with 80% parts commonality.

24   The M4 has selective fire options including semi-automatic and three-round burst (like the M16A2), while the M4A1 has a "full auto" option instead of three-round burst.

CHAPTER 27

THE FOSTER LAFAYETTE HOTEL
SECURITY OFFICE
WASHINGTON, D.C.
7:55A.M., SUNDAY, AUGUST 07, 2011

Mugsy Ricci and Michelle Wang sat at the desk of Ron Fryar, the Director of Security and Loss Prevention for the Foster Lafayette Hotel. Michelle and her staff were successful in tracking the last phone calls Pastak made with his cell phone. One was to a local Mercedes dealership, but before that, another was to an executive recruiter that apparently sent Pastak to an interview at the Foster Lafayette, just over a month before. The recruiter was reluctant to even admit that much until Michelle promised him that he would be The Watchman's first phone call the next time they were looking for executive talent. Once she did, he was more than happy to share the name of the firm that hired him – which turned out to be phony – and more importantly, he mentioned that the man who contacted him spoke with a British accent, *with a hint of Middle Eastern in it*, as he put it. That was enough to prompt their dropping by the hotel to investigate.

Fryar handed Michelle a folder opened to a specific spot.

"That's the report that housekeeping submitted and the page behind it is the report submitted by the security official on duty, who investigated."

Michelle scanned both reports then handed the folder to Ricci as she queried the Director.

"Mr. Fryar, both reports mentioned broken items including a tea cup and what appeared to be parts of a cell phone and blood on a sofa and chair. Why weren't the police called?"

"Ms. Wang, the person occupying the suite was the one who called housekeeping. He explained that he entertained a clumsy guest who he hinted might have been intoxicated. Apparently his guest inadvertently broke a teacup, cutting himself and dropping and damaging his phone when he attempted to pick up the sharp pieces of the cup. His explanation was deemed plausible by our security official."

"What about the report of a man being chased by men on the same floor as the suite and at the same time as the alleged accident?" Ricci asked.

"Yes, that account was given by members of a wedding party. Also noted in that report, was that our security official considered the members of that party to be intoxicated at the time."

Mugsy looked at Michelle and shook his head disapprovingly.

"Mr. Ricci, there was no reason to connect the two incidents and no cause to question the veracity of our guest's statement ... a gentleman who has been a regular guest of this hotel, by the way."

"What's the name of this guest?"

"You can understand our need to keep the names of our guests confidential."

Michelle shot Ricci a look of frustration that didn't go unnoticed by the Director.

"Mr. Fryar, would you allow us to the view security tapes from that day and time?"

The Director smirked but with a look of impatience.

"Mr. Ricci, as I understand it, you do not represent a government or law enforcement agency. You work for a private company. There has been no crime reported and even if there were, I would only be able to interact with an authorized member of law enforcement. Now, out of courtesy, I have shared with you all that I am prepared to share but unfortunately I will not—"

As the Director was speaking, Michelle was calling someone on her cell. After a moment of talking to the person on the other side of the line, she handed her phone to the Director.

"Mr. Fryar, the Secretary of Homeland Security would like to speak to you."

The Director put her phone to his ear with a look of disbelief on his face. Ricci kept his facial features frozen but looked with questioning eyes at his beautiful oriental partner in crime. She replied with a subtle wink.

"This is Director Fryar ... sir?! Yes, Mr. Secretary ... yes sir. Mr. Secretary I was only following ... no sir, not a problem at all. Yes sir, at once. Thank you Mr. Secretary, I will!"

Director Fryar handed Michelle back her phone, his face blushed with embarrassment. He hesitated a moment as if unsure what to do then used his intercom and stood up.

"If you would both follow me, I'll take you to our video room. I just called down for them to pull the video records from that day."

The Director led them into a room with banks of monitors and rack-mounted drives used to store the video feeds from every floor of the hotel. He motioned for them to take seats in front of one bank of monitors and showed them how to operate the replay.

"The feeds from that day and time and from that floor and the lobby will appear on these two monitors. If you need anything else, just ask my people in the next room."

"Thank you, Mr. Fryar," replied Ricci.

The Director walked to the door then stopped, "You know, all you two had to tell me was that this was a matter of national security. I would have happily obliged. Of course, The Homeland

Director only requested that I show you the security footage. He said nothing about divulging the name of our guest."

Then he added, almost speaking to himself, "Apparently, the Secretary of Homeland Defense is also a personal friend of our owner."

Ricci waited for the Director to be safely out of earshot before questioning Michelle.

"... Matter of national security? Michelle, I know you didn't bother the Director of Homeland with this ... who exactly did you put him on the line with?"

It was her turn to smirk.

"Well, as Director Fryar was condescending to us, I texted Johnny-F and asked him if he could ... pretend to be the DHS and tell Mr. Fryar to let us see the security footage. He replied, 'NP!'"

She couldn't help giggling.

"I have to say, whatever he told Fryar was good ... real good!"

Ricci rolled his eyes but he was really impressed with Michelle. In fact, he was starting to feel other things about her, things that he wasn't prepared to deal with there and then. *Man, I want to lean over and put my lips to hers!*

It took all his effort to refocus and concentrate on what he was doing as he fast-forwarded through the recording. After a few minutes he froze the footage on a figure stepping off of the elevator.

"Michelle, who does that look like?"

Wang leaned in towards the monitor.

"Les ...!"

"Okay, so he arrives on the floor at ... 9:15p.m ..." Ricci continues to fast-forward, "... there, he appears to be entering that suite ... about an hour later ... there he is running from the suite ... and behind him is a man ..." Ricci freezes the frame and zooms in, "... with a suppressed pistol?"

Wang squinted, "It's hard to make out, he concealed it so fast ... but it could've been!"

Ricci fast-forwards again, "Gunman returns to suite ... a minute later ... two men leave the suite in haste."

Ricci hit a few buttons and brought up the feed from the

lobby.

"There's Les running out of the hotel's entrance ... and there go the two men chasing him. He must have been delayed on the elevator. It looks like they took the stairs."

Ricci asked someone in the next room to fetch Director Fryar who looked thoroughly annoyed when he walked back into the room.

"Mr. Ricci, I thought I told you that you could ask my staff if you needed anything—"

"Mr. Fryar, I only need two more things from you. Would you please access the video feed from the hotel's entrance that evening and put it on the monitor?"

The Director of Security did as instructed but was obviously annoyed.

"My staff could have done this for you!"

After a few minutes of fast-forwarding, Ricci saw what he needed to see. He replayed footage that showed both gunmen approaching Pastak and taking positions standing on each side of him. The three men appeared to wait for the valet to retrieve Pastak's car and then they all drove away in it. Ricci froze it on a frame of Pastak getting into the back of his own car. Fryar was confused as to what it meant.

"Mr. Fryar, this is why I called for you. What you're seeing is one of our agents being forced by two gunmen ... concealing their weapons no doubt, but two gunmen nevertheless, into his own car and be driven away. Ms. Wang and I would surmise that these men were actually terrorists driving our agent to a remote location where they would most probably murder him and dispose of his body. I don't have to tell you how badly it would reflect on you and this hotel chain if our agent's body is discovered and the events leading to his death are traced back to here. The Foster Lafayette would be known as 'the hotel where terrorists stay.'"

Fryar blinked his eyes, wetting his lips as anxiety overtook him.

"... Which brings me to my second request ... the name of the guest in that suite?"

Fryar looked shell shocked as he walked over to a computer

terminal. After typing into it, he handed Ricci a printout.

Ricci took the paper and smiled at him without looking at it.

"Thank you for your help, Mr. Fryar."

Once he left the room Ricci looked at the name then handed it to Michelle.

"Bahman Fard..?" Wang asked with a little disappointment in her tone, "I was hoping to see Zamani's name."

Ricci accessed Big Brother and after running a search on the unknown man's name, flashed a Cheshire cat grin. He tossed his iPhone to Michelle who read aloud from what he left on the screen.

"Bahman Fard ... listed as a director of one of Zamani's companies in one place and as his executive assistant in another!"

She started to think out loud.

"So this guy Zamani invests $25 million into a company owned and/or controlled by the Pacifico drug cartel. Then he probably has his man Fard offer Les a bribe in return for information on our investigation into his transaction."

Ricci took his phone back and added to her thoughts.

"Who knows what they offered Les. We found out about his new "bling-mobile" he was looking to buy, so it was probably a heap of money."

Michelle jumped in again.

"Something went wrong though. The way Les acted when he found out that Garcia went missing ... and remember ... he looked like he had an ulcer when he heard that Garcia's transponder started to transmit again ..."

Michelle thought in silence for a moment then it hit her.

"He wasn't expecting either of those things to happen!"

Ricci nodded.

"He panics ... goes to meet with Fard again ... right as we send a team down to find Garcia and the next thing we know, their operation was compromised—"

"... And Les disappears with Fard's two goons never to be seen or heard from again." Michelle capped it.

Ricci headed for the door with Michelle at his side.

"Let's get back to The Watchman. Now we know whose behind all of this ... it's time we figured out why!"

CHAPTER 28

ZAMANI IMPORT-EXPORT CORPORATION
LOWER MIDTOWN MANHATTAN
NEW YORK, NEW YORK
10:30P.M., MONDAY, SEPTEMBER 05, 2011

Aref Sami Zamani laughed to himself as his Executive Assistant Bahman Fard used a VoIP provider to place a secured, encrypted video phone call to the head of the Pacifico drug cartel, Tuco Ramirez.

These Americans ... such silly doves! They spend billions on technology to listen into and monitor phone conversations. Yet, anyone can just use one of these VoIP[25] providers with their proprietary encryption algorithms and they're as deaf as a post!

Fard turned the monitor to face Zamani who could now see the drug lord looking back at him. They conversed in English.

---

25   Voice over Internet Protocol (Voice over IP, VoIP) is a general term for a family of methodologies, communication protocols, and transmission technologies for delivery of voice communications and multimedia sessions over Internet Protocol (IP) networks, such as the Internet.

"Hello Tuco. My men, they have arrived?"

"Hello Aref. Yes, they arrived in Nogales today. I wasn't expecting so many. I thought you limited your cells to three or four people. I was told that a total of 16 men arrived and that six of them are Russian?"

Zamani didn't trust any infidels but he knew that Ramirez had no love for the U.S. so he didn't worry about divulging too much. Besides, he thought it better to satisfy the drug lord's curiosity than risk him trying to find out on his own and putting the whole operation at risk.

"Yes, the Russians are all former Spetsnaz. They're needed because they're experts with the bomb. After it's detonated over Las Vegas, the others will cause havoc in the city, killing survivors and rescue personnel."

Zamani saw Ramirez laugh.

"It's too bad. I've been there you know ... to Las Vegas, when I was younger. I always hoped I could go back one day ... but I guess I'll have to settle for Monte Carlo now."

Zamani didn't even break a smile. It took all of his composure to even speak with the Mexican pig infidel. *I must remember ... the end justifies the means ...*

"Is everything ready with ... your stampede night?"

"Just about ... we had one wrinkle come up but we're planning to iron it out right before we cross the desert to Tucson."

Zamani became concerned.

"What wrinkle, Tuco? I paid you all that money so that there would be no wrinkles!"

"It is nothing to worry about. A small group of border patrol agents might have become aware of our noche del espantada but—"

Zamani's rage was growing.

"HOW ... did these agents find out? I thought you had control over your people to keep their mouths shut!"

"I do and those responsible will never utter another word," Ramirez's tone became agitated.

"Who is this small group of border agents?"

"They call themselves the Shadow Wolves. They're just a dozen or so Native American's that patrol their reservation."

"Isn't that where you're planning to cross my men and my bomb ... isn't that where the airport is?!"

"Aref, get your temper in check, my friend. I'm not some peon you can talk to this way!"

Zamani knew he had to reel in his temper. He needed the cartel; it was as simple as that. He shot a quick look at Fard who nodded that he understood his boss's anger.

"Tuco, it's too late to call this operation off and it's too late to change things. What are you planning to do about these ... Shadow Wolves?"

Ramirez seemed satisfied with Zamani's change in tone. His smile returned.

"Like I said Aref, there is only a dozen or so of them and we have the edge on technology and firepower. We're planning to ambush them. Once we get rid of them, there's no one standing between us and the Sells Airport inside the reservation. That's why we picked crossing there. The regular U.S. border patrol agents aren't even allowed to patrol on the reservation."

Zamani merely nodded and went on.

"... And once they reach the airport ... everything is ready?"

"Yes, we'll simply load the bomb, the Russians and the two men you chose as pilots onto the Piper Chieftain we're keeping at the Executive Airport in Las Vegas. I'm having one of my men fly the plane from Las Vegas to Sells. It'll have enough fuel for the return trip. If all goes to plan, the group will make it to the airport by horseback in no more than 12 hours. That would put the plane over the Las Vegas Strip ninety minutes later, sometime around eight or nine that evening. It could all happen earlier but no later than that. The rest of your men will board a van that will meet them a few miles east of the town of Sells and take them into Tucson. It will deliver them to a safe house where they will stay until they board the charter bus at dawn the next morning. They'll be disguised as relief workers from FEMA[26]. That will put them into Las Vegas sometime Sunday afternoon, the 12th."

Hearing the schedule lightened Zamani's countenance.

"Good. It will only take the Russians about an hour to rig the

---

FEMA stands for Federal Emergency Management Agency.

bomb to detonate, and then they plan to parachute out. My two martyrs will then have 30 minutes to position the plane directly over the Strip. By the evening of September 11, Las Vegas will be in ruins and the next day, the rest of my men will spread terror throughout their relief efforts."

Ramirez smiled softly.

"You know, Aref, there are not many men that I consider to be as ... ruthless as myself."

The drug lord's comment made Zamani's eyes sparkle.

"We will not speak again, Tuco, until after this thing is done."

The monitor went black as Tuco Ramirez turned to his second-in-command; his smile disappeared as soon as the image of Aref Zamani disappeared from the screen.

"Make sure nothing goes wrong. These Iranians ... I don't understand them and who I don't understand, I don't trust. What we do, we do for money. What they do, they think they do for God ... perhaps their god, not ours."

* * * * *

Zamani turned to Fard.

"Contact Payam ... tell him he is to raid De Niro's ranch early on the morning of the wedding. Tell him that I want De Niro questioned. I want to know about anything else he may know about my connection to *Antioch*. Tell Payam to kill his sons in front of his eyes. That should break even a man as strong-willed as Mr. De Niro ... and Bahman ... make sure you remind him that he and his men must leave Las Vegas no later than noon that day."

CHAPTER 29

BACK PORCH – MAIN HOUSE
ESTANCIA DE NIRO
HENDERSON, NEVADA
8:00P.M., SATURDAY, SEPTEMBER 10, 2011

Moriah Stevens pulled her bare feet up and nestled into the comfortable chair on the porch of the De Niro's beautiful ranch house. She was deep in thought, sipping from her glass of Cris's favorite Barolo wine as she stared at the way the moon reflected off mirrored waters of the large pool. She just had the most perfect meal with Cris and for the first time, it was only the two of them. That is, until he received an important call that he had to take in his study. He promised to return and spend the rest of her final evening there, with her.

She came back to vacation on De Niro's ranch as she promised she would. In fact, she could think of nothing else from the moment she left. The plan was for her to spend the week at the ranch and then fly back to New York with De Niro and the boys on 9/11. They were all going to meet up with Keith Tompkins and his family in time to attend the evening memorial ceremonies down at Ground Zero.

The week was thoroughly enjoyed by everyone. The whole estancia staff really liked her, especially Concho who seemed to trip over his own two feet every time he was around her. Young Louis De Niro fell in love with her right away, especially since she would sit listening to him play the piano for hours. Even Cris's oldest son Richard, who was most attached to his mother's memory, softened to her after her first few days there. Moriah absolutely loved the ranch. It was large, filled with animals and everyone who lived and worked there were so nice. She could feel their contentment radiating from them.

One of the highlights of her trip was when the head gaucho, Martin Fierro, let her ride JoJo, Lisa De Niro's horse. It turned out to be something of an extraordinary and emotional event for everyone at the ranch. She found out from the others that no one had ridden JoJo since Lisa had died. Moriah fell in love with JoJo, the boys and everyone else ... and deeply in love with one person in particular.

To her, Cris was the consummate host. She knew he was a very busy man but she marveled how he always seemed to make time for his boys and his staff, and now her. He took horseback rides and walks with her, showing her all around the large estancia. She was worried at first, riding JoJo, but it didn't seem to bother him at all, at least he never made mention of it. The nights when he was home, he ate with her and his boys and of course, William. William told her that De Niro had always treated him like part of the family. It was his way. There was also one night where he invited Martin and his wife, Concho, Aurelio and Rosita, and Arturo to a back yard barbecue with them. Apparently it was something they did quite often. In fact, De Niro treated the entire estancia workforce more like they were his family than his employees.

Moriah was most impressed with Cris. He wasn't like anyone she had ever met before. He seemed to be full of contrasts. On one hand, he was one of the brightest individuals she ever met, yet he preferred to listen more than he spoke when it came to things like politics and business. He reveled in interacting with his boys and delighted in laughter with his staff and the simpler, less ostentatious things in life. She noticed, for instance that while he was somewhat an expert on red wine, he was quite content with an ice-cold bottle of beer. He was also just as happy eating a tuna sandwich while watching a football game as he was going to a five-star restaurant and attending a symphony, something he treated her to the second night she was there. Moriah also saw that, while most people were acquainted with Cris De Niro, he was for the most part a loner. Even at home, aside from meals, he seemed to enjoy his own company when he wasn't with his boys.

The entire stay had been something out of a dream to Moriah except for one thing ... her feelings for Cris were real, they were powerful and as far as she could tell, they were not mutual. The more she thought about it, the more she had to admit that he was nothing but a complete gentleman and was also becoming a dear friend. In fact, in just the week that she was there, she was already considering him her best friend. She thought that there was even a chance that as far as friendship went, he felt the same way about her. Yet, while her feelings for him had gone far beyond platonic friendship, his didn't seem to. That really bothered her. For one, she had to admit to herself that there was an aspect of ego ... hers, that was being bruised. She was so used to being the center of attention of men, without really trying, that now she felt she didn't know exactly how to try to get Cris's attention. She never chased after a man in her whole life, including her husband, so she had no idea what to do. It was all very frustrating to her. She did get something out of the whole experience ... empathy, for all the men that had ever pursued her.

One thing was for sure, this was the last night of her stay and she wasn't going to let it pass without confronting Cris. *I'll just tell him how I feel about him and leave it at that! I mean ... I'll make sure he knows there's no pressure for him to reciprocate in any way ... and if his feelings for me aren't mutual ... I'll tie myself to the back of JoJo and have her drag me until I'm lifeless!*

Smiling to herself, she downed the rest of her glass of wine and poured another, glad that her sense of humor was still intact.

* * * * *

De Niro stood in front of the plasma screen on the wall of his study; his brother-in-law's image was on the monitor.

"What's up Mugs?"

"Sorry to take you away from your date, Cris. How's it going, anyway?"

"It's not a date, Mugs, we're just hanging out. It's her last night here."

"That's not what I heard. The boys told me you sent them out with William for the night and Aurelio and Arturo told me that you gave them the night off 'cause you'd be doing the cooking tonight."

De Niro rolled his eyes and shook his head.

"You know Mugs, it's amazing that you're finding time to investigate this guy Zamani ... I mean with all the time you're spending investigating me!"

Ricci was unshaken.

"So ...?"

"You're unbelievable. First ... the boys wanted to go see that cartoon movie with the chipmunks and William volunteered to save me from having to take them. And as far as Aurelio and Arturo go, I was planning to grill a couple of steaks, Mugs, not something I particularly need help with."

"And ...?"

De Niro had to laugh.

"You're too much, you know that ... AND ... you're taking me away from my "date" ... so, if you don't mind ... do you have anything of relevance to report or did you just call to pull my chain?"

"Alright ... I'll get it from Louis tomorrow. Let's see, oh yeah," Ricci exhaled audibly, "both these guys, Zamani and Fard keep a pretty low profile. They spend most of their time bouncing between offices of Zamani's import-export company in New York, London, Dubai and Tehran. We've tapped all of their office phones and monitored all their cell traffic ...

Johnny-F even cracked into their email servers but all we've seen is legitimate business communications. John was able to verify that their using VoIP but unfortunately, even he hasn't been able to crack the service's encryption. That's probably their method of keeping in touch with their friends in Mexico."

De Niro's frustration was as apparent as Ricci's was.

"Over a month of investigating and you and Michelle haven't been able to turn anything ..."

"Hey, Cris, it's not from a lack of trying. Michelle is still here trying to retrace all of Les's activities. She's even having Johnny-F double-check all of his activity inside Big Brother, just in case we may have missed something."

"Oh hell, I know that Mugs, I'm just ... frustrated, is all. I'm sure you both are, too. What about ARCHANGEL, have they come up with anything, with that Noche del espantada business?"

"Charley and that Agent Ahiga feel certain that something big is gonna happen and soon ... but nobody's talking down there. Ahiga told Charley that he's never seen so little traffic of illegals coming across, so Charley sent Riggy, De May and Pescy into Nogales and some of the other Mexican border towns to see if they could sniff something out. Other than the fact all of the towns are filled to overflowing, they haven't been able to learn much."

"Have we alerted Homeland about those towns filling with people?"

"Karla informed them ... but they said they knew about it already. Can you believe, instead of being concerned, the top brass is taking credit for it? They even made an announcement to the press, quote, '... Due to our increased efforts at the border, preventing those who want to cross illegally from even making the attempt, there has been a dramatic reduction in illegals crossing the border in Arizona.'"

De Niro started pacing.

"So what do we have ... a rich Iranian with ties to Muslim extremists, making a big investment into a company that has ties to one of the biggest Mexican drug cartels ... the rich Iranian's assistant bribing or otherwise coercing Les to supply info on the location of our agent sent to investigate that Mexican company ... that same agent later turns up dead and buried at one of that cartel's drug farms ... and then weird activity or lack of activity by the same cartel, at the border."

Mugsy remained quiet while he saw De Niro trying to sort it all out in his head.

"You know the question that keeps popping up to me, Mugs ... what does $25 million buy from the Pacifico cartel? I mean, I don't see any connection to their drug operation. Pacifico doesn't need an Iranian's money to smuggle drugs into the U.S. and an Iranian doesn't need a Mexican cartel to smuggle drugs into Iran. So if it isn't drugs, it has to be for smuggling people across the border. That's the only service I could see Pacifico providing if I was going to pay them that kind of money. But, man, we already know that would pay for a small army of terrorists to be brought across and so far there's no sign of a small army of Middle Eastern-looking people amassing in those border towns."

"Definitely not, Riggy and the guys said the towns are filled with Mexicans. That's not to say that there might not be a small contingent of towel-heads, but not an army of them."

De Niro paced some more.

"Zamani pays Pacifico 25 large and the next thing we see is that the cartel stops bringing illegals across the border ... what's up with that?"

Ricci snickered, "So *that's* how you solve our illegal immigration problem ... we don't need walls, just pay off the cartels."

"Noche del espantada ... something about that term ... why that term? Fright night ...? Maybe a Halloween crossing ... or ..."

De Niro stopped pacing, smacking his forehead with his palm.

"They're not stopping. They're stocking up on illegals to bring across ... all in one insane night ... Noche del espantada! Mugs, in Spanish that could translate as, 'fright night' but it can also mean, 'Night of the stampede!'"

"Talk about attracting attention," Ricci added.

"Mugs, I think that's it! They want the attention, or rather, they want the distraction! Let's say, we want to smuggle something into the U.S., something very expensive, enough for us to pay those thugs $25 million. Instead of trying to sneak it past all of the apparatus set up to catch people sneaking things in ... what if we have the cartel set up a night where they stampede illegals across? Instead of sneaking past our defenses, they overwhelm them ... and while our border patrol agents are kept busy scurrying all over Tarnation rounding up all those Mexican illegals—"

"They could move a small contingent with whatever it is that's so important, right under our noses!" Ricci finished his thought.

"Whatever it is Mugs ... it's bad and it's big, for that amount of coin ... biological, chemical or explosive!"

"Cris, I think you're onto something. I'm gonna contact Charley and Agent Ahiga now and fill them in."

"Do that and make sure you tell them not to bite on the bait! If we're right, chaos is gonna break out down there soon. The Shadow Wolves and ARCHANGEL may be the only thing standing between them and the U.S."

"Will do ... and Cris ... say hi to Moriah for me—"

De Niro hit the disconnect button.

"Moriah ... I forgot I left her outside!"

De Niro hurried back outside and saw Moriah relaxing on a chair with her back to him. Her blond hair seemed to glow in the moonlight and her perfume mingled with the night air. As he approached her, he saw that the bottle of Barolo they were sharing was empty and so was her glass.

As soon as she noticed he was there, she flashed him a smile that sent a bit of electricity down his spine. Her emerald eyes sparkled with just a hint of glossiness from the wine.

De Niro took a seat next to her.

"Moriah, I'm sorry. I didn't mean to be away that long."

"That's okay. I've been relaxing and enjoying the wine."

"Would you like some more? I have another bottle inside—"

Before he could get the rest of his sentence out, Moriah got up and sat on his lap.

"Cris, we need to talk."

De Niro shifted himself in his seat to accommodate her.

"Okay ... what would you like to talk about?"

"Us ..."

"Us ...? What about ... us ...?"

Moriah started to stroke his hair.

"We're friends now, aren't we?"

"Of course we are."

"And friends should always be honest with each other, right?"

"Moriah ... that Barolo is a very strong wine—"

Moriah put her index finger to his lips and she was slurring her words just a touch.

"Shhh ... I'm asking you a question ... friends are supposed to be honest with each other, right?"

"Yes, friends should be honest with each other. That Barolo is honestly very strong—"

Catching him by surprise, Moriah put her lips to his lips and for a moment De Niro's mind went totally blank. A rush of feelings, sexual and otherwise took over. *She's so beautiful and sexy ... and drunk ... and not Lisa ... LISA!*

Using all his strength, physical and otherwise, De Niro got to his feet. As he did, he tried his best but he couldn't help preventing Moriah from tumbling to the floor. He immediately reached down to help her up.

"Moriah, I'm so sorry ...! Are you okay?"

Moriah's head was spinning. She wasn't sure if she was more embarrassed or angry ... and she wasn't even sure of what it was she was angry about, as tears welled in her eyes.

"What is it, Cris?! Is there something wrong with me?! I mean, I basically just threw myself at you, like a tramp ... and you tossed me to the floor! I'm sorry ... I don't have much experience being a tramp ... is that how it works?"

"Moriah, you're not a tramp and I didn't mean to toss you like that! I just started feeling sick—"

"SICK ...?! I kissed you and you started feeling sick ... is my breath that bad?!"

"Moriah cut it out ... that's not what I meant. I ... you caught me off guard—"

Moriah stepped closer to De Niro and put her hands to her

hips. In her bare feet, she looked so petite to him ... and so angry.

"Off guard ... can I ask you something, Cris? Why would you have your guard up, in the first place?! I mean is it me ... or something about me that makes you put your guard up?"

She started pacing back and forth.

"We spent a week together! I thought we got along great. I love your boys ... I love the people here ... I love the animals here ... I love this place ... this ranch—"

Catching him off guard again, she turned and threw her arms around the back of his neck, staring at his mouth.

"... And I've fallen in love with you."

Drawing her lips close to his, Moriah waited for De Niro to close the gap, but he didn't.

Tears started rolling down her cheeks as she stepped back from him. In that moment, she looked absolutely broken-hearted and absolutely beautiful to De Niro.

"Moriah, please understand. I haven't come to terms with the loss of my wife yet—"

"It's been 10 years, Cris ... 10 YEARS! I know 'cause up until the moment I met you, I spent those years trying to come to terms with the loss of my husband!"

De Niro didn't reply.

"So what now ...? How long will it take you to ... come to terms ... with Lisa's death?"

Hearing the term "Lisa's death" was too much for him.

"I DON'T THINK I EVER WILL ... Moriah!! LISA ... was my soulmate ... she was everything to me!"

De Niro battled to get hold of his emotions, but it was too late – as a tear escaped from his eye.

"I know we're no longer married, no longer one person in the eyes of God ... those terrorist bastards saw to that!! But ... my love for Lisa did more than fill my heart ... it maintained it! When she tumbled down in that tower ... my heart went with her! I don't have the ... capacity ... to love like that again ... and I don't want to love like that again!"

His voice softened.

"My heart will always belong to her."

De Niro swallowed hard as he saw the impact of his words

on her. Moriah was such a friendly, warm soul, it made him feel terribly to cause her such sadness. He wanted so badly to console her in his arms, but he was more concerned with sending her mixed messages. *What's the matter with me?!*

Her lip was quivering as she covered her mouth with her hand.

"I think I'm gonna be sick ..." she uttered then ran from him into the house.

He didn't follow her. Instead he stood there feeling like his insides were shaking. In a fury he picked up the bottle of wine intending to throw it and smash it, but as he did, he noticed the label. It was one of his and Lisa's favorite Barolos. In fact, it was the same one they had on their first date. Memories started rushing into De Niro's mind ... memories of Lisa ... memories that made him smile and laugh ... and then cry. He dropped the bottle onto the chair where Moriah had been sitting. He could still smell her perfume.

De Niro collapsed onto his knees. Even after 10 years, the power of his love for his wife and the pain from her absence in his life devastated him. *Lisa, I'm so lost without you ... Father, why am I still here?!"*

He heard the sound of a car pulling up in the front ... it had to be William with the boys. He tried his best to dry his eyes before they walked in. Moriah must have heard them too because a moment later, she reemerged out back. She didn't say a word to him as she collected her sandals and walked to the guesthouse.

De Niro didn't follow her.

CHAPTER 30

U.S./MEXICO BORDER

(10 MILES NORTHEAST OF)

EL BAJIO, SONORA MEXICO

TOHONO O'ODHAM NATION RESERVATION

5:30A.M., SUNDAY, SEPTEMBER 11, 2011

(PRE-DAWN)

Charley Santappia was having a hard time following Agent Bryan Ahiga's pickup truck down a pitch-black dirt road. With him Vic Rigoni, Karl De May, and Spiro Pescalitis bounced around in their Jeep.

Pescalitis: "Charley, where the hell are we? I think Cochise is leading us to Acapulco!"

Santappia: "If the GPS is correct, the Sky Tower that reported the large group is just ahead."

As if on cue, Ahiga's pickup pulled off the dirt road and stopped under a mobile Border Patrol observation post, otherwise known as a Sky Tower. Ahiga jumped out and pulled his pistol. He motioned to the others to do the same and to keep low. The four members of ARCHANGEL made their way over to him with caution.

Santappia: "Isn't there supposed to be an agent on duty in that tower, Bryan?"

Ahiga: "Yes sir, there is. Something's wrong."

Ahiga held his hand to the side of his mouth and hollered, "Mike, its Bryan Ahiga. Are you okay?!"

Everyone's nervousness increased from the lack of reply from the booth, atop the 25-foot portable tower.

Ahiga: "The controls to lower the tower are in that cabinet at its base."

Santappia: "Guys, get your M-4's and set a perimeter."

Riggy, De May and Pescalitis crouched back to the Jeep, retrieved their automatic rifles and headsets then returned to Santappia and handed him one of each. Riggy then gave the other two, silent directions with hand gestures and all three men set out into the darkness. Within a minute Santappia heard from all three of them reporting that they were in position surrounding the tower.

Santappia: "Okay Bryan, they're manning the perimeter."

Ahiga nodded and set off towards the control cabinet. A moment later, Santappia watched the booth at the top of the tower lower to the ground before approaching it. He put his finger through a bullet hole in one of the tower's windows as Ahiga joined him. The two men could hear the radio inside the booth set to a DHS frequency. The dispatcher was repeatedly requesting the agent to reply. Ahiga opened the door to the booth to find the border patrol agent lying in a pool of his own blood on the floor, brain matter and blood coated the opposing window. He carefully stepped into the booth and reached over to grab the mic.

"This is Shadow Wolf one at the Sky Tower west of Sasabe. The border patrol agent stationed here is down. I repeat ... Agent Mike Bellows, stationed at the Sky Tower west of Sasabe is down."

"Sasabe Station, roger Shadow Wolf one, emergency personnel have been dispatched to your location, ETA about

30 minutes."

"Roger Sasabe ... will secure the scene but need to begin pursuit immediately."

"Sasabe Station, roger that ... scene will be secured and unmanned until arrival of emergency personnel."

Ahiga replaced the mic and then said a silent prayer for the family of the fallen agent. Standing behind him, Santappia prayed with him. When he finished, Ahiga turned around and shook his head.

"I didn't know Mike very well but I know he was married with kids."

Santappia didn't reply. His face expressed his sadness and anger.

While Santappia examined the crime scene Ahiga walked back out to the dirt path, knelt down and started examining the ground. After five minutes he stood up and remained silent facing northwest. Santappia joined him.

"What did you find, Bryan?"

"Mike's last distress call was accurate. There's a very large group, Charley, the largest I've ever seen in fact, heading northwest. I'm talking hundreds! The time of his call marks their passing here ... about 90 minutes ago and there's something else ..."

With Santappia behind him, Ahiga followed the tracks in both directions for several minutes until he found what he was looking for.

"Charley, some of them are on horseback. It's almost impossible to see the tracks where they're all moving. The army of footprints obliterates everything, but you can see here ... several of the riders stopped. There are droppings from two of the horses and multiple prints of horses pretty much standing still."

"What do you make of it, Bryan? Is this the Noche del espantada' ... the fright night?

Ahiga nodded.

"The night of the stampede ... it's odd, very odd."

"What is?"

"The direction they set off on is northwest. That'll take them away from Tucson. If they keep to that general direction, they'll cross onto our reservation in about 10 miles."

"Maybe their idea is to cross onto reservation land then turn due north—"

"Possibly Charley, but this whole thing just doesn't add up to a normal illegal border crossing. First, such a large group ... they know they'll attract our attention."

"They might be thinking that they'll overwhelm us."

"And they will ... so my question is ... why then head northwest? Wouldn't it be better to make a bull rush towards Tucson? By heading in that direction, they're just extending their trek. Time and distance work against them and for us ... and they know that."

Santappia removed his cap and scratched his head.

"I see what you mean. What else?"

"I've never seen a group like this, some on horseback, some on foot. Horses cost money. I don't think this many banditos on horseback have cross the border since Poncho Villa ... and then there's what they did to Mike. What did you find, Charley?"

"You're not gonna like it. From the size of the hole in the glass, the head wound on Agent Bellows and the trajectory of the shot to inflict it ... it looks like he was taken out by a sniper ... one shot, one kill."

"A sniper ...?! Charley, I've been at this a long time. That's a border agent's worst fear ... but it's a step we never thought the cartels would take. They know if they escalate violence against us, the U.S. will be forced to retaliate."

"Whatever they're planning must be very big and bad ... for the stakes to be high enough to warrant this. How do we track them, Bryan? You said they have about a 90-minute head start. Where would that put them?"

Ahiga led Santappia back to his pickup where he pulled a map out and laid it out on the hood.

"It's gonna depend on whether the group on horseback remains with the group on foot or not. My guess is they won't. So that would put the large group on foot about 2-2.5 miles ahead of us. The group on horseback could cover twice that distance."

Ahiga grabbed the mic from the radio in his pickup and tuned it to the Shadow Wolves frequency.

"This is Ahiga. We have a very large group in the hundreds heading northwest from Sasabe. A dozen or more are on horseback, the rest are on foot. They have about a 90-minute head start on me. If they remain present course, I have them crossing onto reservation land somewhere east of Tubac. The group on horseback, perhaps both groups are presumed armed and dangerous, approach with extreme caution. Have all Shadow Wolves converge east of St. Ann Church and notify DHS-CBP Nogales Station to pass on my information to Omaha[27]."

"Roger Bryan, all available agents to converge east of St. Ann's Church in Tubac and we'll notify Nogales Station to vector Omaha two-five miles northeast of Sasabe."

Ahiga rejoined Santappia who was calling Riggy, De May, and Pescalitis back in.

"We have another problem, Charley. We don't have time to go back and get our ATV's and in that direction we won't be able to follow them for very long in these vehicles. So we can either stay on their tails or we can take the chance that they'll remain on their present heading ... and take to the roads to try to head them off. Chances are that Omaha will spot them long before they make it to the reservation anyway, but if they do make it, I think we need to be ahead of them. Otherwise, we'll never catch up to the group on horseback."

"I think the choice is clear then, Bryan. Let's try and get ahead of them."

* * * * *

The Russians and Iranians on horseback were still leading the large group of Mexican immigrants on foot. They held up when the Iranian radioman waved to the Iranian in charge.

(In Farsi) "Hadi, someone finally found the dead agent at Sasabe. Sounds like one member of the Shadow Wolves, but he radioed in for all of their agents to rendezvous ahead of us

---

27   "Omaha" is the call sign used for all DHS-CBP aircraft (all types) including the UH-60-A Blackhawk helicopter.

near Tubac. He also told them to radio Nogales to vector their Blackhawk to our position here."

The tall, dark-haired and bearded Iranian-in-charge thought aloud and in English so that the Russians could understand.

"A single Shadow Wolves agent came across the dead agent outside Sasabe. I wonder what he was doing off the reservation? In any case, he's having all the Shadow Wolves lie in wait for us, up ahead. That is what we wanted. Also, as we anticipated, he had Nogales dispatch their Blackhawk helicopter."

He switched to Farsi. "Naser, you and Abbas take a position a few thousand feet from us with a Stinger[28]. Wait for your prey and do not miss. Go now by foot! Aram, have all the infidels behind us remain where they are. We want to give the American helicopter a big, easy target."

Switching back to English he addressed his men and the Russians, "We will wait here for their chopper. Once we down it, we'll scatter the chickens on foot and put distance between us and them."

The Russian in charge, former Spetsnaz Captain Oleg Marx spoke up.

"What about the Shadow Wolves ahead of us? I thought we were going to ambush them closer to the airport?"

"We were, but it's of no consequence. The fact remains ... the more of them they gather in one place; the easier it is for us to wipe them out. We know their location, we still possess the element of surprise, superior numbers and strength ... and while they are trained to track, we are trained to kill."

The two men with the shoulder-fired rocket, Naser and Abbas radioed in that they were in their positions just as the sounds of a heavy rotor could be heard off in the distance.

* * * * *

Both Agent Ahiga in his pickup and the members of ARCHANGEL following him listened in on the DHS-CBP

---

28   Light to carry and easy to operate, the FIM-92 Stinger is a passive surface-to-air missile, shoulder-fired by a single operator, although officially it requires two. The FIM-92B can attack aircraft at a range of up to 15,700 feet (4,800 m) and at altitudes between 600 and 12,500 feet (180 and 3,800 m).

radio frequency as they headed to the rendezvous point near the city of Tubac. A call came through from Omaha six, the DHS Blackhawk chopper.

"Omaha six Victor Romeo ... Nogales ... we have visual on a very large group ... repeat, very large group approximately three miles from Sasabe Station."

"Nogales, Omaha six, roger ... Approach with caution ... Ground units en route, ETA two-zero minutes ..."

"Omaha six ... roger that, two-zero minutes ... will approach with caution. There appears to be no movement at this time by the group. It looks like they're taking a rest."

Ahiga pulled over and Santappia pulled up next to him. They both rolled their windows down.

"Charley, you monitoring ...?"

"We heard. What do you think it means, Bryan?"

"I don't know, but I don't like it. There's no way that group is resting just miles away from where they murdered a border agent.

Ahiga grabbed his mic.

"Shadow Wolf one to Omaha six, come in."

The men heard only static.

"Shadow Wolf one ... Omaha six, come in."

More static ...

"Shadow Wolf one to Nogales Station, can you raise Omaha six?"

"Nogales ... Shadow Wolf one, we'll try. Omaha six this is Nogales Station, do you read?"

Static ...

"Nogales ... Omaha six Victor Romeo, do you read?"

"Shit!" Pescalitis shouted from the back seat of the Jeep. Santappia held up his hand to quiet him.

"Nogales Station to all agents ... at this time we are unable to raise Omaha six. Shadow Wolf one, do you have a visual?"

"Shadow Wolf one, negative, I have no visual of Omaha six ... but let me take a closer look."

Ahiga threw the mic and stepped out of his pickup with his binoculars. He scanned to the southwest then stopped on one point. Santappia and the others joined him.

"What do you have, Bryan?"

"I got smoke and flames Charley, southwest of us, about three miles."

He handed Santappia his binoculars then ran over to his pickup.

"Shadow Wolf one ... Nogales Station. I just spotted smoke about three miles west of 286, north of El Mirador Road."

"Nogales Station, roger Shadow Wolf one ... Nogales Station to emergency personnel heading to Sasabe Station, Omaha six may be down about three miles northwest of your location."

"Roger Nogales, we see the smoke ... will dispatch personnel to that location."

Ahiga walked back to the others.

"There's no doubt now, Charley. Shooting a border patrol agent crosses the line but downing Omaha obliterates it. Whatever it is they're transporting, they're willing to start a war over it."

"You have to get us ahead of them, Bryan, in a position where we can ambush them."

"That won't be easy, Charley. Even if we do get ahead of them, there's a whole lot of desert out there. I think our best bet will be for me to string the rest of the Shadow Wolves out along a ridgeline east of the town of Tubac. There's a path that leads north at the foot of the ridge. Meanwhile, we'll try and set up a position at the ridge's northern end. That's where I think they'll end up no matter where they're heading."

"Lead on, Bryan ...!"

As Santappia began following Ahiga's pickup again, he hit an autodial button on his cell.

"Mugs it's me, the game's on!"

CHAPTER 31

BACK PORCH - MAIN HOUSE
ESTANCIA DE NIRO
HENDERSON, NV

5:30A.M., SUNDAY, SEPTEMBER 11, 2011
(PRE-DAWN)

De Niro couldn't sleep, all he could think about was Moriah and how much he hurt her as he sat in the same chair she sat in the evening before.

"You're up very early, sir," William Brett asked as he approached from behind him. He was carrying a tray with a silver pot of coffee surrounded by mugs, cream and sugar. Both men were fully dressed despite the early hour.

"William, what are you doing up?"

"Well sir, I can never sleep very well on this day."

De Niro knew what he meant – it was September 11. Noticing the tray in his hands, he waved William to sit with him.

"Join me?"

"Thank you sir ..."

William poured two mugs of Jamaican coffee and handed one to De Niro. It was rumored to be the same roast and grind as the one served at the White House.

Both men blew the steam rising from their mugs before sipping from them. They sat quietly for a few minutes before De Niro broke the silence.

"I miss her too, William, I miss her too. So much so, I fear I've irrevocably damaged my friendship with Moriah."

"Oh, I can't believe that, sir. If I'm not out of line ... It's quite obvious to everyone on the estate that Dr. Stevens has deep feelings for you."

"You can never be out of line, William. I value your views, more so than anyone else's. The truth is ... I have deep feelings for her too but we don't have the same types of feelings for each other."

Out of habit, William lowered his voice to just over a whisper even though they sat alone.

"Thank you for saying so, sir, and if I may ... you mean you are not ... attracted to Dr. Stevens?"

"Of course I'm attracted to her. She's a beautiful woman, inside and out ... but ..."

William waited for De Niro to continue. When he didn't he completed the thought for him.

"But ... you feel like your betraying the memory of Ms. Lisa."

De Niro nodded and blinked as his eyes became watery.

"I still love her, William and she's still part of my life. Not a day goes by that I don't think about her. Not a night goes by that I don't miss her. Our vows may have been 'til death do we part,' but my love for her transcends her death."

William leaned in towards De Niro and grasped his forearm as a sign of comfort.

"Sir ... all of us who cared for Ms. Lisa, keep her alive in our hearts and minds."

The stately man took a sip from his mug, looked at it and smiled.

"Sir, I don't know if you noticed but earlier this week Ms. Stevens inadvertently started using Ms. Lisa's favorite coffee mug. You remember it, the oversized pink one with the ugliest handle décor I've ever seen."

De Niro chuckled.

"I remember that mug; she won it in a raffle."

"Well ... I kept it all these years and stored it behind all the other mugs we have. I actually forgot it was there when I allowed Dr. Stevens to choose whatever mug she wanted for her morning coffee. I became frantic when I saw her pouring her coffee into it, but as I was about to take it from her ... memories of Ms. Lisa drinking from it flashed into my mind. It brought back so many joyous mornings when Ms. Lisa would sip from it while talking to me about the day's morning news. She always had such strong ... and sometimes very humorous insights."

De Niro smiled.

"She did, didn't she ...?"

"Yes sir, she did. Well, instead of my memories of Ms. Lisa making me angrier with Dr. Stevens, they had quite the opposite effect. Suddenly, I realized that Dr. Stevens was telling me ... her views ... of the morning news ..."

William's eyes became misty.

"... And do you know what occurred to me?"

De Niro waited for his gentleman butler to answer his own question.

"Three things occurred to me, sir ... one, that there is absolutely nothing wrong with my cherishing that mug; two ... that because of how special she is, it's okay for Dr. Stevens to drink from it and three ... that both of those remarkable, wonderful ladies ... have absolutely the worst taste in coffee mugs ..."

De Niro laughed out loud bringing a smile to William's face.

"Neither of you are wrong, sir, for how you feel about the other ... as long as you both are honest with each other. As for our feelings for Ms. Lisa ... she was a most remarkable woman! There will never be another quite like her and as I remind young Richard ... no one could ever replace her in our hearts and minds. I would only suggest to you, sir, that while you are certainly entitled to your feelings, Dr. Stevens is entitled to hers."

De Niro was deeply impressed by William's wisdom.

Knowing how much he loved and cared for Lisa made it that much more valuable to him.

"Thank you, William."

De Niro's cell phone rang as William stood to collect the tray.

"Mugs, you're up early on a Sunday—"

"Cris, listen to me, I have Michelle and Johnny-F on the line too."

"Okay."

"Where are the boys?"

"They're sleeping Mugs, it's not even 5—"

"Cris, I know what time it is there! Listen to Michelle first."

"Cris, I had John retrace all of Les's digital footprints inside Big Brother, in case we missed something ... and we did—"

"Cris, it's John, it's my fault, I should have found this when we first checked—"

"John, just tell me what you found!" De Niro didn't like that they asked about the boys.

"Okay ... well, the first time we checked double-B, we only checked what Les looked at using the ops-level access that Michelle gave him."

"John, he knows that, get to the point," Ricci demanded.

"Cris, I never bothered to check what he looked at with *his own* HR clearance! I mean, most of it is just mundane personnel info ... but I screwed up!"

"John, take a deep breath ... what are you telling me?"

Ricci jumped in.

"Cris, Les was looking at your GPS transponder frequency ... and the transponder frequencies of Richard and Louis!"

De Niro's heart jumped in his chest.

"The ones I asked you to tie in from their iPhones ... so I could keep tabs on them via Big Brother when I was traveling?"

"Cris, listen to me, I want you to toss your laptop, your iPhone and the boys iPhones into the pool ... right now! Do it and call me back from your landline!"

"Okay ..."

De Niro hit the disconnect button, took the battery out, then threw his phone into the pool. William stopped in his tracks with the tray in his hands.

"William, put the tray down and help me find the boys phones. We need to toss them into the pool ... and their laptops too! I need to get my laptop ... please hurry upstairs and get their phones and laptops!"

William placed the tray down with care then hurried into the house. De Niro appreciated how he followed his most preposterous orders without questioning them ... a mark of true loyalty.

De Niro ran inside the house, unplugged his laptop and ran back out to the pool. He took the extra step of removing the battery from his laptop before tossing both into the water. He was about to run upstairs when he saw William emerge from the back door, a bit winded.

"Here they are, sir, their phones and laptops!"

De Niro took each phone and laptop, one at a time, removed their batteries and tossed all of it into the water.

"Sir, what's going on?"

He motioned for William to follow him to his study.

"Mugsy just informed me that there's been a security breach in The Watchman's computer system. Someone was looking at the GPS transponder frequencies of the boys and me! Stay with me while I call him back!"

De Niro hit an auto-dial button on his home phone and placed the call on speaker. As the call connected, Mugsy, Johnny-F and Michelle Wang appeared on the plasma screen, all looking very concerned.

"Okay, I wanted William here. We threw all the cells and laptops into the pool, now will someone please tell us what's going on ... why the urgency?!"

Ricci: "Just after John and Michelle came to me with what they found, Charley called, Cris. There's been a major breach down there. It started before dawn. They're estimating hundreds have illegally crossed the border, some on horseback and they're armed and dangerous. They've already murdered one border patrol agent via a sniper round and they downed a DHS Blackhawk chopper. It has to be what we've been waiting for. This has to have something to do with what Les was part of!"

De Niro shot a concerned look at William.

"Okay ... but even if Les had something to do with what's going on down there ... what does that have to do with my boys and me?"

Wang: "We don't know for sure, Cris, but what we do know is that the last time Les looked up a transponder frequency, Agent Garcia ended up dead. We just—"

"Michelle, hold on ..."

De Niro was looking up at a security monitor next to the main screen.

"William, what happened to the camera at the main gate?"

William rushed to the controls for the monitor and fiddled with them as De Niro bolted to his security panel. Before he got to it all the power went off in the house including to the security system. De Niro turned and saw that the screen went dead.

"Mugsy ... Mugsy!"

De Niro turned the speakerphone off and picked up the receiver.

"William, the phone's dead too!"

"Sir, listen!"

They started to hear the sound of multiple vehicles in the distance.

"I think we have company!"

"We have to get the boys and get out of the house NOW! We can bring them to the Coyote's Den!"

"Sir, you go get the boys. I'm too old to run. I'll try to stall them for as long as I can."

"William, no—"

Both men heard the sounds of tires crunching rocks coming from the far end of their long driveway.

"There's no time to argue sir! Please, go quickly!"

De Niro grabbed William by his shoulders and wordlessly expressed his gratitude then took off up the stairs. He ran into Louis's room. Both boys were sleeping together in his bed.

"Guys, wake up!"

The boys opened their eyes but were groggy.

"Just put your sneakers on, no questions, we have to go NOW!"

De Niro looked out Louis's bedroom window. His heart

raced with terror as he saw three black, Lincoln SUV's coming around the circular driveway, all with no headlights.

Running the whole way, De Niro led the boys down the stairs, out the back door and down the path to the guest house. He punched the number code into the electronic front door lock and shuffled the boys into the house. Once inside, he ran upstairs alone and burst into the master bedroom.

"Moriah you have to get up!"

Moriah opened her eyes. De Niro could see that she cried herself to sleep.

"Cris, what are you—"

"Moriah, there's no time. Intruders broke into the main house. I need you to take the boys to a secure place I have on the ranch. The boys know the way!"

Moriah was sleeping in pajama bottoms and a t-shirt. She slipped her feet into her sneakers and took off down the stairs behind De Niro.

"Okay, first we have to make it to the stables. Then Richard, you show Moriah where the Coyote's Den is. You remember where it is, right?"

Richard nodded, "I think so, Daddy."

"Good. I want all three of you to get inside the Den and close the doors behind you. Richard knows how ... and you DON'T open those doors for anyone, do you understand?!"

The boys nodded their heads.

De Niro led the three down the long dirt path and to the stables. He pushed them all into the brush when he heard noises coming from it.

Putting his index finger to his lips, he whispered, "Someone's over there. You three stay here! I'm gonna take a look."

Moriah grabbed his arm.

"Cris wait, let me go with you! Boys you stay—"

De Niro grabbed her by her shoulders. They locked their eyes on one another. Tears started falling from Moriah's.

"Moriah, please, stay with my boys! Don't leave them for a moment! Can I trust you to do that?"

Moriah nodded her head then threw her arms around him and whispered into his ear.

"I love you!"

De Niro pushed back from her and looked into her eyes then he took her in his arms and hugged her.

Out of the darkness, a voice called out from the stables.

(In Spanish) "Mr. De Niro, is that you?"

It was Martin Fierro pointing a shotgun at them.

Everyone stood up.

De Niro replied in Spanish, "Martin, I should have known it was you. We have a problem!"

Fierro lowered his weapon and switched to broken English.

"Si señor, the alarm system dead. I coming to tell you about it."

"Moriah ... boys, saddle up ...! Martin, we have intruders at the main house and William is still there! There were three SUV's so there could be as many as 20 men out there!"

De Niro motioned for his Head Gaucho to step to a corner with him. He switched to Spanish.

"Martin, these men are professionals, do you understand?"

"Yes."

"They're here to either kidnap me and the boys ... or to kill us. I'm not sure which. I'm having the boys lead Moriah to a safe place I have—"

"Yes sir, the place with the doors in the ground. I came across while I exercise the horses."

De Niro had to smile even through his tension.

"I should have known better than to think I could hide something on this ranch from you."

"Yes sir."

Moriah and the boys mounted their horses. De Niro walked over to them.

"Go now and don't even as much as look back!"

"... But Daddy, what about you?" Louis asked with tear-filled eyes.

"We can stay and help you!" Richard added, tears in his too.

De Niro walked between their horses and took both of their hands in his.

"I need you two to be brave now. We each have to accomplish our missions. Your mission is to get Moriah to the Coyote's Den.

Daddy and Martin will be okay."

He walked up next to Moriah and squeezed her hand.

"You have to make it to the place the boys will take you to … it's about 10 miles from here. Stick to the trails. You'll be safe once you're inside!"

The boys took off down the path but she lingered for a moment.

"Be careful, Cris!"

She kicked JoJo's sides and took off in a gallop, not waiting for a reply.

Martin approached De Niro now carrying two Winchester Model 1895 Centennial High Grade[29] rifles. He handed one to him.

(In English) "Thanks Martin. Listen, you don't have to come with me. I need to go and try and get William."

"Sir, we wasting time …!"

The leather-faced man pulled out his walkie-talkie phone and hit the transmit button.

(In Spanish) "Concho, its Martin, wake up!"

After a moment, Concho's voice crackled out.

"Martin, what the hell—"

"Shut up and get up … and I want you to wake everyone else up too. Tell them we have intruders at the main house and tell them to get dressed and break out the rifles … but tell everyone to do NOTHING until you hear from me and Mr. De Niro, understand?"

"Yes sir."

De Niro gave Fierro a quick Italian-style hug.

"Muchas Gracias, Martin …"

* * * * *

Ricci banged his fist on the conference table, "What do you mean dead?"

"I mean the line went dead and we can't get them back on the

---

29   The Winchester® Model 1895 High Grade is patterned after the gun Theodore Roosevelt called his "Big Medicine," the one he took on his famous safari in 1909. The rifle is chambered in the famous 405 Winchester caliber.

phone, it just keeps ringing! His answering machine is part of his phone system and it didn't kick in. The only thing that could have caused that is a power outage ... but the battery backup in the phone system should have kicked in then!" Johnny-F replied.

Ricci's patience was at an end.

"John, what the hell are you saying?!"

The computer genius thought a moment.

"His phone line must be down AND the power must have gone out in his house. That's the best I can think of."

Ricci blinked, showing just a touch of fear. *My sister and now her boys!*

"Michelle, contact the Henderson, Nevada police department. Tell them ... tell them we think something may have happened to my brother-in-law, that we got disconnected. Tell them anything, but get them to send people out to the ranch now!"

Johnny-F called over to him, "Mugs, check this out on Fox News!"

He walked over and looked up at the screen. A reporter was standing in front of the wreckage of the downed Blackhawk, reporting on how it apparently crashed while investigating a report of a mass illegal border crossing.

Michelle got off the phone.

"Mugs, Henderson police put me on hold and tried to reach the house. They didn't get through either but then they contacted the phone company and they were told the whole area near Cris's home is down. The duty officer told me it's probably nothing to worry about but after I threatened to have the Homeland Director contact his captain, he finally agreed to send a unit to the ranch to investigate."

"... A single unit?" *This is unbelievable!*

CHAPTER 32

RIDGELINE
(APPROXIMATELY 1 MILE NORTHEAST OF TOWN)
TUBAC, AZ
10:00A.M., SUNDAY, SEPTEMBER 11, 2011

Ahiga, Santappia and the members of ARCHANGEL reached the location that Ahiga told them about. They were perched on the northern edge of a ridgeline that stretched for about three miles south. All the men laid low while Ahiga and Santappia used their binoculars to scan the path at the bottom of the ravine below them. The sun had risen a few hours before and already the temperatures were climbing. Ahiga had positioned the rest of the Shadow Wolves about midway down the ridgeline, stringing them out about ½ mile south of their position.

Santappia took a swig from his canteen then handed it to Shadow Wolf-1.

"We haven't heard from your men, Bryan."

Ahiga took the canteen from him and took a long pull from it.

"That's not unusual, Charley. Shadow Wolves don't usually use their radios unless they spot something."

He exhaled in frustration as he put his binoculars back to his eyes.

"The truth is, on horseback, if that group was heading this way, they should have reached us by now. I don't understand it though. This pass is miles long and they were heading right for it. They should have—"

Ahiga focused his binoculars on something. It made him jump to his feet and started running in a crouched position south along the ridgeline. The rest of the men saw where he was headed; someone was stumbling towards their position. Ahiga made it to the man and helped him back to the others who saw that he was bleeding profusely from a shoulder wound.

"Charley, this is Shadow Wolf Agent Kevin Steele."

Santappia helped Ahiga set him down. Blood was pouring out from a bullet wound to his shoulder and he was on the verge of passing out. Santappia put the canteen to his mouth and he tried to sip from it as Pescalitis and Riggy examined his wound.

"Pescy, get the first aid kit! Agent Steele, I'm Charley Santappia. Here, drink some water, just a little. What happened to you?"

Riggy: "Charley, the bullet went clear through."

Ahiga knelt next to Santappia.

"Kevin, what happened? I can't reach the others on the radio!"

The wounded Agent reached up and grabbed Ahiga with bloody hands.

"Bryan, they ambushed us ... bullets flew from behind us and from the south, but no sound! I saw Ned drop and Felicia's head exploded right next to me! Then I got hit ... it knocked me off my feet and I rolled down the ravine a ways ... my radio broke. I started running low until I thought I'd be out of sight ... then doubled back after climbing back up to the top of the ridge. By the time I got back to them, it looked like everyone was hit! I don't know how badly, but blood everywhere ... no one moving!

I called to them ... no answer ... I didn't want to chance running out in the open to them. I couldn't see who shot us ...they had to be far off so I headed for your position"

Santappia stood up with Ahiga.

"De May, contact Nogales and call in Emergency Services to their location! Bryan, what do you make of it?"

"Charley, hold that order, would you ... follow me."

Ahiga ran to a position about 50 feet south along the ridgeline, hit the dirt and looked through his binoculars, Santappia joined him.

"Bryan, what's up?!"

"Charley, Kevin said bullets flew from behind them and to the south. There's a ridgeline that runs perpendicular to the one we're on about a third of a mile south of where the Shadow Wolves had taken position ... but to get to it, the bad guys would have had to climb the western ridge on foot. Why would they do that?"

"I don't know. Maybe they sent scouts out?"

Ahiga shook his head.

"I don't buy it. First, they would have had to cross the ravine in the open to get to this ridgeline. It makes no sense for scouts to risk that when they could have just scouted from the other side ... the side they approached from. No, I'm getting a real bad feeling about this, Charley!"

"What kind of bad feeling, Bryan?"

Ahiga stopped scanning and focused on a position south of them, down on the path at the bottom of the ravine. Then he pointed to the position so that Santappia could see what he spotted. Santappia looked through his own binoculars and saw a number of men on horseback riding single-file up the path about a quarter mile from them.

"That kind of bad feeling, Charley ...! The only thing that makes sense is that they knew we were going to ambush them here. They must have crossed the pass just south of where my unit could spot them and then set up an ambush of their own with a sniper. I think they're monitoring our tach-one channel, the one we use to communicate with Nogales. That would explain how they were able to sneak up on Shadow Wolves."

Both men made it back to the others as quickly as they could. Santappia started barking orders.

"Gunmen approaching ... Riggy, you and Pescy take a position down the slope near the path, just around the bend behind us. De May, carry Agent Steele down the back of this ridge, out of sight, then get back up here on the double!"

Ahiga continued to look through his binoculars as more of the horseman came into view.

"Take a look!"

Santappia focused his binoculars where Ahiga pointed.

"Charley, what is that?"

"It looks like a road case, strapped to that horse. What the hell ... It could be anything!"

"Whatever it is, it's as heavy as a man, I can tell from the way the horse is laboring and they're being real careful with it."

"Do you think they know we're here?"

"I don't think so, Charley. They wouldn't be riding single-file up that path if they knew we were here. I think they believe they wiped out the Shadow Wolves and there's no one left on this reservation to impede their advance. They probably only monitored our tach-one channel which means we can still communicate to each other, at least, on tach-two."

Santappia continued to scan the riders.

"We got another problem. I count 16 of them and they all look armed."

De May returned.

"Charley, I've just been monitoring Nogales ... they're going crazy down there. Every available agent sounds like they have their hands full rounding up all those UDA's. On top of that, DHS won't put anymore choppers in the air until they determine that it's safe to do so and between the crime scene at the tower and the downed Blackhawk, I don't think we're gonna see any help anytime soon! Even if they do get a chopper in the air, they're too far south to spot us without our radioing them."

The line of horsemen was almost directly below them. Ahiga was very concerned for his fellow Shadow Wolves but he remained calm.

"What do you want to do, Charley?"

Santappia thought on overdrive.

"We may not be able to stop them but maybe we can slow them down. De May, take a position south of us and prevent them from climbing the ridge and coming up behind us."

Santappia spoke rapidly into his mic.

"Riggy, we count 16 gunmen and one large road case heading north on the path. They're right under our position now. They'll be on you and Pescy in a few minutes. I want you two to shoot anyone that comes around that bend. Make sure to fall back if they try to overrun your position. We can't afford you guys getting hit. We're gonna try and keep them pinned down in this pass."

"Roger."

Ahiga was troubled by what he heard.

"I'm a law enforcement officer, Charley. I'm supposed to announce that fact to them before we just draw down on them!"

"Bryan, I make them about 600 meters away, right at the maximum effective range of our M-4's. If we give them even the slightest warning, we'll lose what little advantage we have. Keep in mind, they outnumber us and at least one of them is a sniper."

"I understand that, but I'm still—"

"You know what they just did to your unit and there's a very good chance that there's a weapon of mass destruction in that road case of theirs. We may be the last line of defense for our country."

The two men's eyes locked.

"Bryan, if you don't want to be part of this, you could go back and check on your unit ... stay with them until help arrives, but we've got to do this."

Ahiga looked back in the direction of the ambushed Shadow Wolves and thought a moment. Then he dropped the magazine from his M-4, locked the charging handle, checked it then reinserted it and released the bolt, reloading the weapon.

"It's my country too, Charley."

Santappia nodded patting Ahiga on his back, then dropped to his belly and took aim. De May and Ahiga took prone positions a few yards on either side of him.

"Let Riggy and Pescy take the first shots. That should drive them back below us ... and guys ... try not to shoot that road case!"

CHAPTER 33

BACKYARD OF MAIN HOUSE
ESTANCIA DE NIRO
HENDERSON, NV
6:30A.M., SUNDAY, SEPTEMBER 11, 2011

(In Farsi) "Payam, a police car just pulled up!"

The report came from one of Payam's men keeping watch at the front gate.

"Do nothing," Payam replied into his headset.

He walked over to William Brett sitting at the kitchen table with two of his men on either side of him. There was blood coming from the back of his head as one of the men had used the back of his rifle to compel the old gentleman to take a seat.

Payam motioned for his men to lift the butler and turn him to face him.

"The police are at the gate. You will speak to them and tell them that everything is okay."

Another one of Payam's men came running in.

(In Farsi) "Payam, there are three horses missing from the stables! There is a main path that heads south. They had to have gone that way! And we found out why we lost their transponder frequencies. All of their computers and cell phones are lying at the bottom of the pool."

Payam cursed in Farsi. *So, De Niro knew we were coming. At least we know he didn't get a big head start.*

Payam motioned for the two men to escort William to the intercom before replying.

"Take one of the SUV's and six men and go after whoever it is. If it is De Niro or his boys, bring them back here. If it's anyone else ... kill them."

The man nodded and ran out the front of the house.

Payam walked over to William in time to hear his conversation through the intercom with one of the police officers at the gate.

"This is the Henderson police department. Would you let us in please?"

"This is William Brett. I'm Mr. De Niro's Executive Assistant. What can I do for you, officer?"

"We received a report, Mr. Brett, that there may be a problem. Apparently, Mr. De Niro was on the phone with—"

"Officer," Brett quickly cut him off, "Mr. De Niro is not on the ranch. He took his children to ... Hawaii. It was I who was on the phone and there is no problem. The phone system was temporarily out of service, as was the power."

There was a pause.

"Sir, would you please open the gate?"

Payam gave William a cold stare, causing the old man to raise his bushy eyebrow.

"I certainly will not, officer. I have explained to you what has happened and I'm about to call back the party to whom I was speaking and explain it to him. I will not have you place me in a position of having to contact Mr. De Niro on his holiday to tell him that the police were here because the phone system went down. Now, have I made myself clear?"

There was no reply. Payam's nostril's flared but William held his hand up to calm him.

"Officer, perhaps you don't know who Mr. Cris De Niro is ...

perhaps I should contact your Chief of Police or the Mayor and have one of them speak to you."

There was another pause, this one a bit longer than the first one, followed by a simple reply.

"Have a nice day, sir."

Payam waited a moment until he heard from his man at the gate.

"They've driven away."

He walked up to William and put his pistol to his head.

"You are a good liar old man, but you better not lie to me. So De Niro is here, where is he?"

"I don't know."

The terrorist cocked his pistol and returned it to William's temple.

"Where are his boys?"

* * * * *

De Niro and Martin Fierro crouched down next to the pool house on the far side of the pool, across from the main house. From there, they could see past the back porch and the two men standing guard there, and partially into the kitchen. They saw two men lead William from the kitchen table.

"Look Martin, that's William! Well, at least we know he's alive."

"I count three men inside the kitchen with him, señor."

As they continued to keep watch, they spotted one of the black SUV's heading for the stables.

De Niro's heart jumped. *Moriah and the boys!*

"Martin, I have to go after them. Can you handle this situation?"

The leather-faced gaucho grabbed De Niro's arm.

(In Spanish) "Sir, there's a chance that they will kill William, no matter what I do. What do you want me to do then?"

De Niro's upper lip curled into a snarl. It was something that came from his Brooklyn roots. He replied in English.

"You free William, Martin, do you hear me! I have to go protect my boys and Moriah but you have to save William!"

He broke from Martin's hold and took off a step before turning back to him.

"If they hurt him, I want you to kill them all!"

Martin radioed to Concho as he watched De Niro hurry towards the stable. Then he took aim with his rifle at one of the guards on the back porch.

* * * * *

Payam waited for William to answer but the old man remained silent and defiant even with the terrorist's pistol pressing against his forehead.

"I can see you will be of no use to me, old man!"

His finger started to squeeze the trigger when a loud shot rang out, then another.

The sounds of the shots jolted Payam's aim from William's head as he shouted at the two men standing on each side of him.

(In Farsi) "That came from the back. Go check!"

Payam turned back to William only to see him grinning back at him.

"*You're* scared now, aren't you? As you should be, if you only knew who's out there."

"Shut up, old man!" Payam blurted, pistol whipping him and sending the old man collapsing to the floor.

The terrorist ran to the front of the house where the bulk of his men were standing guard.

"Go around the back! Kill anyone except for De Niro and his—"

Two more loud shots rang out from the back of the house freezing everyone in their tracks. Payam ducked but quickly straightened up.

"GO!"

* * * * *

De Niro made it to the stables, saddled Dollor and took off down the trail. He rode for about five miles, when he spotted the black SUV. It was about a quarter mile ahead of him and turned with the driver's side facing him. It didn't seem to be moving. *Lord, please! I hope they didn't catch them!*

Drawing his rifle from the scabbard hanging from his saddle, he kicked Dollar's sides and took off in a full gallop until he was within the effective range of the large caliber weapon, about 100 yards away. He tugged on the powerful animal's reigns bringing Dollor to a halt in a position perpendicular with the SUV and looked through his binoculars. *Moriah and the boys aren't in the truck.*

De Niro said a silent prayer thanking God that Martin had spent so much time teaching him the art of mounted rifle shooting. He recalled how, years ago, he asked Martin if the shot Clint Eastwood took with his rifle, from atop his horse, at the end of the movie, *The Good, the Bad and the Ugly*, was possible. Martin proceeded to show him that it was, but that it took an expert shot. De Niro drove Martin crazy afterwards, asking him to teach him how to shoot like that. Now he'd find out if he learned the lessons taught to him.

"Whoa boy ... whoa ..."

* * * * *

The men inside the SUV argued.

(In Farsi) "What do you want me to do? The trail splits off in every direction! For all we know they turned onto one of the many trails we already passed! We should have used the horses—"

Before the driver could finish his sentence, a 405 Winchester caliber bullet pierced his neck sending blood shooting out of his mouth and throat and all over the man in the passenger seat. For a moment, no one in the car knew what happened or what to do. A moment later another bullet ripped through the window of the door behind the driver's seat slamming into the cheek of the man sitting there. His body slumped over, being held in the seat only by his seat belt.

The remaining five men panicked. The ones in the back all tried to jump out of the passenger side rear door but they were bottlenecked. Only the two sitting closest to the passenger side doors made it out of the vehicle as De Niro emptied the rest of the 5-round magazine into the trapped men in the back seat.

The two men who made it out of the SUV started firing their automatic rifles wildly up the trail. Their shots didn't come close as De Niro reloaded his rifle and nudged Dollor just enough for the horse to advance at a slow, steady gait. He bridled his rage and didn't fire back as he approached. He figured the uncertainty of the two gunmen's situation would eventually get the best of them and make them try something foolish. The closer he got, the louder they heard Dollor's hoofs clopping against the rocky desert floor.

Both men wiped sweat from their eyes as they peaked over the bloody bodies of their fallen comrades and out the shattered windows of the SUV. They saw the figure of a lone horseman slowly drawing near holding his rifle like a knight would his lance.

De Niro drew close enough to hear them arguing with one another in their native tongue. One finally called out to him in English.

"You on the horse ... look ... we throw our weapons out!"

Two AK47 assault rifles were flung out, one bounced off the hood of the SUV and the other kicked up dust behind the black Suburban.

De Niro brought Dollor to a standstill about ten feet from the driver's side of the large vehicle, making sure to keep his rifle pointed at it. He watched the two men stand up on the passenger side with their hands on their heads. Both men started walking around the rear of the truck but De Niro could see that the first man was keeping his eye on the AK lying on the ground only a few feet from them.

The men came to a stop and for a tense moment, no one moved or said a word. The first man was enraged as he stared at his weapon then gave De Niro an insolent bob of his head.

"Maybe I pick up my rifle and shoot you, you infidel pig!"

The second man admonished him in Farsi but the first man wouldn't hold his tongue.

"Maybe I shoot you and then I go find your two sons and—"

One 40-caliber bullet erupted from De Niro's rifle, its report drowned out the end of the man's sentence. The gunshot struck the man between his eyes severing the top portion of his head. He was dead before his body crumpled to the ground.

The second man screamed out and took off running down the trail.

De Niro rotated the lever under his Winchester and took aim but hesitated a moment as he contemplated shooting an unarmed man in the back. His indecision was quickly remedied when he saw Richard, Louis and Moriah emerge from behind a pile of boulders, on foot, leading their horses and heading towards him from beyond the man. *No way, he comes near my boys!*

He squeezed the trigger and instantly the man was blown off his feet.

De Niro galloped out to detour the three around the body. His boys ran over and hugged him. Richard was first to speak.

"Daddy, I'm sorry, I got lost!"

Moriah waited for the boys to break free.

"We were trying to decide which trail we should follow when we heard the sound of their SUV. So, we dropped our horses on their sides behind that rock formation. Cris, I don't know what would have happened if you didn't come for us!"

De Niro could see that Moriah was trembling with tears in her eyes. He walked over to her and put his arms around her ... and felt her body melt into his. She pushed back from him just enough to put her lips to his. The desperate kiss was warm and tender, but it was also filled with sexual tension. As before, he didn't reciprocate but this time that didn't seem to bother her.

When their lips separated, she looked deeply into his eyes. A smile blossomed from her face. De Niro was fascinated at how her smile seemed to turn her tears into prisms that made her emerald eyes beam with sunshine.

"I don't mind if I have to do all the work."

She winked at him as she mounted JoJo. De Niro smiled back at her with just a touch of confusion on his face while he helped his boys back onto their horses. Then he jumped back on Dollor.

"Come on, we have to get back to the main house. I left Martin alone and they're holding William."

* * * * *

Payam was becoming frantic. *Where are my men? Why don't I hear anything out there?* He looked down at William. He wasn't moving and there was a good deal of blood pouring out of his head. Payam started towards the back door but stopped dead in his tracks. He didn't dare move an inch as he felt a long, sharp blade being pressed to his throat from someone standing behind him. Whoever was holding the knife reached around and grabbed his pistol from his hand. The Iranian terrorist felt the blade start to cut the flesh under his Adam's apple.

"He better be alive or I cut your head off!" It was Martin Fierro's voice.

"I'm quite alive, Martin, thank you ... but cut his head off anyway ..." William replied with a raspy voice as he opened his eyes.

Martin held the blade tightly to Payam's throat and looked down at William.

"So you are alive!"

"Barely ...! No thanks to you. What did take you so long?"

"My men ... are outside!" Payam interrupted, speaking in a strained whisper.

"William, I come and help you in a minute. First, I show this man where his men are." Martin replied, pushing the terrorist and forcing him out the back door.

The Iranian couldn't believe his eyes as he stepped onto the back porch. The bodies of the two men guarding the back door were sprawled on each side of him, and the bodies of the two men he sent out afterwards were arrayed in front of him. Beyond them, the rest of his men were lying with their faces to the ground and their hands on their heads with their weapons a few feet away. Payam saw the reason for their apparent surrender as Concho, Arturo, Aurelio, Rosita and the rest of the estancia staff stood over them pointing rifles, shotguns and pistols at them.

* * * * *

De Niro, Moriah and the boys made it back to the main house to find the estancia staff guarding the Iranians lying on their bellies. He sent Moriah and the boys to the guest house then walked up the porch past the bodies of the terrorists and into his kitchen. Inside, Rosita was tending to William's head wounds and Martin was standing, pointing his Winchester at Payam's chest as he made him sit at the kitchen table. De Niro walked right passed the terrorist and over to his Executive Assistant and dear friend.

"William, are you alright?"

"I'm ... a bit worse for wear, sir. How are the boys and Dr. Stevens?"

De Niro called to Concho.

"Take William to the hospital now. Rosita you go with him. Concho, ask for Dr. La Marca when you get there. Tell them that I want him to personally tend to William. Do you understand?"

"Yes sir."

He stepped outside.

"Arturo, if you would, continue to keep an eye on these men."

"Si, señor ...!"

Martin pointed at the terrorist's pistol and cell phone on the far end of the kitchen table.

"Señor, that's all he had on him."

De Niro took the pistol and the phone into his study. After checking his home phone for a landline, he hit an auto-dial button, a moment later Mugsy appeared on the screen.

"Cris, are you okay?! Where are the boys?!"

"We're all okay, Mugs. Listen, conference Johnny-F in ..."

Mugs hit a few buttons and Johnny-F appeared on the screen next to him.

"Cris..! It's great to see you, buddy!"

"Thanks John. Hey, I have a cell phone here. Can you do me a favor and hack into it. Specifically, I'm interested in any calls made or received in the last 24-hours."

"Not a problem. Just plug into the adapter I set up on your desk."

De Niro sat the phone into the cradle that Mugsy described.

"Got it ... okay, it looks like two calls were placed and one was received all just before 5 a.m., your time. All of them were to and from the same place ... the Zamani Import-Export Corporation, in New York City. They were routed through the front desk, so I can't tell you which office they came from."

The hair on De Niro's neck stood up with fury.

"That's okay, that's all I needed to know, thanks John."

Ricci dropped Johnny-F from the call and his image disappeared on the screen.

"That son of a bitch ... he came after my boys, Mugs! I want you to fly to Teterboro. I want you to meet me there. You and I are gonna go talk to Mr. Zamani ... old school!"

"Cris, he didn't just come after the boys ... he came after you too! I don't think it's a wise thing—"

"Mugs, stop ...! Terrorists killed LISA! And now this terrorist not only targeted our country ... he came after my SONS ... Lisa's SONS ... your nephews ..."

Ricci's face turned red with his own rage.

"I hear you, brother. You want me to grab a few other men?"

"No, just you and me, Mugs ... he might have men with him there, so come prepared. I'm gonna take Moriah and the boys with me. I'll send them to my suite at the New York Palace in another car. We'll be leaving here in about an hour and we'll be flying the QSST, so we should be landing at Teterboro at around ... 4 p.m., Eastern Time."

"I'll be there."

"... And Mugs ... don't be late."

De Niro disconnected the call and walked back into the kitchen. He took a seat at the kitchen table facing the terrorist.

Payam looked at De Niro with a combination of scorn and hatred written across his face.

"So, you are Cris De Niro. You think now, maybe I will talk to you ... I won't ... except to tell you that you and your sons are all dead. Nothing you have done here can change that!"

De Niro stared silently back with no emotion on his face.

"You think you will intimidate me with your staring? All you Americans are the same. You have no idea how to interrogate a prisoner!"

Payam laughed.

"Your laws and your rules and your new President ... prevent you from using torture ... so all you can do now is to stare at me!"

He laughed harder.

"I'm entitled to a phone call. I will call my lawyer. Maybe I tell him that you mistreated me."

De Niro motioned with his eyes to Martin. Payam watched the rugged old man leave the room.

"What now, Mr. De Niro? I tell you what, why don't you let me go now and I will promise, when I come back, I will kill your two boys quickly ... I won't make them suffer ... too much. Maybe I won't make you watch!"

Payam burst out into loud laughter as De Niro took the terrorist's pistol out and pulled on the slide. The terrorist stopped laughing but kept a snide grin on his face.

"What are going to do with that? You can't shoot me, you know. What would you tell the police?"

De Niro slid the gun across the table. It ended up right in front of Payam.

"I'm not going to shoot you."

Payam looked down at his gun through squinted eyes, then he looked over his shoulder for Martin, but he wasn't there.

"What is this, some kind of trick? Where is your man?"

De Niro walked around the table.

"What's the matter? Don't you want to earn your virgins ... or maybe you can only kill children. Come on tough guy, I'm standing here. What are you gonna do about it?"

Payam's growled at De Niro like a wild dog, jumping from his seat and grabbing his pistol in one motion. It was to be his last motion. Something sharp pierced his back, just below his rib cage. Martin reached around and grabbed the pistol from him with his free hand as he used his other hand to force the blade of his long knife up and deeper. Then with one violent twist, he spun the knife around inside the cringing Iranian then pulled it out allowing him to collapse to the floor.

The rugged Argentinean cowboy wiped the blade of his

knife on the dead terrorist.

"Muchas gracias, señor ... I need to do that for Señora Lisa."

De Niro's face was still filled with fury.

"Martin, I have to go to New York to take care of the one in charge ... but the ones outside ... the ones still alive ... they came here to kill my boys!"

Martin held up his hand.

"In Argentina, we chanted once, 'Qué se vayan todos' ... be gone with them all! They will be taken care of, señor. I will do so myself. I will tell the rest of the staff that I take them away from the house so the boys are not afraid. No one will question. They all love the boys and respect you, señor ... and they understand the meaning of la familia."

De Niro patted Martin on his shoulder then walked to the back door but Martin called to him one more time.

"Señor ... Vaya con Dios!"

CHAPTER 34

RIDGELINE
(APPROXIMATELY ONE MILE NORTHEAST OF TOWN)
TUBAC, AZ
10:45A.M., SUNDAY, SEPTEMBER 11, 2011

Vic Rigoni and Spiro Pescalitis took a position about forty feet above and just two hundred feet from where the trail bent at a 90-degree angle to the west. From there, they determined that the men on horseback wouldn't be able to see them. The problem was that they also wouldn't be able to see the men on horseback until they reached a point just a couple hundred feet from them. They laid flat on the ground and remained completely quiet, using only hand signals to communicate. Both of them began hearing the sounds of multiple horses approaching at a slow pace. Within moments they could both hear the voices of individual riders and then the first rider came into their sites.

Riggy motioned to Pescy to wait until two came into their aim before opening fire and that he would take down the second rider.

POP ... POP!

Chaos broke out as the sounds of their shots spooked the first several horses and panic broke out when the first two riders were propelled from their saddles. Both were dead before their bodies thudded against the ground.

The leader of the group, the Iranian named Hadi broke from his position in the center of the line and galloped to the front. He held up sharply when two more of his men at the front of the line were struck by bullets. They also fell lifeless from their mounts.

Hadi shouted commands first to the Iranians.

(In Farsi) "Retreat to the bend and take up positions there! You must guard the Russians escape! I will lead them away from here!"

Then he galloped to the back of the line and shouted to the Spetsnaz leader, Oleg.

(In English) "My men will guard our escape. Follow me. There is a trail on other side of this eastern ridge that will lead us to Arizona Interstate 286. I'll radio coordinates to our plane and have them land on the highway. We'll board her there. The interstate is about 12 miles east of our location. If we move swiftly we can make it there in less than three hours!"

* * * * *

"ARCHANGEL-two (it was Riggy's voice and there were sounds of automatic weapon fire in the background) ... Charley, we downed four of them. The rest retreated back to the bend and have taken dismounted positions there. We have the high ground near the end of the ridgeline and are under fire. We count ten or eleven hostiles and we are returning fire, over."

Santappia replied.

"ARCHANGEL-one ... Riggy, we have a contingent of around six or seven riders that broke off with the road case. They're heading due east. Can you keep the group at the bend pinned down?"

The sound of gunfire was more intense.

"Affirmative, at least until we run out of ammo ..."

Santappia turned to Ahiga.

"Can we follow them in your truck?"

"Not directly, no. We'd have to head south first on the road. If we did that, we're sure to lose them."

"They're heading east, Bryan. Where could they be heading?"

"Well, there are trails on the far side of that eastern ridge that run south for a mile or so. They intersect with a bunch of trails that crisscross, but all of them converge at three points along Sasabe Road ... Arizona 286."

"How far is 286 from here?"

"It's about 12 miles due east. Charley, what I don't understand is ... where were they originally headed?"

"Talk to me, Bryan!"

"Well, if they would have kept going in their original direction, the only two places with any sort of population are the small town of Choulic, which is 10 miles due west of here and Sells which is about 25 miles northwest. I hate to put it this way but I don't think some rich terrorist would pay ... what did you say ... $25 million to attack either of those places."

A thought occurred to Ahiga as soon as said that.

"Wait a minute, Charley! There's a commuter airport near Sells! Maybe they're fixin' to hop in over-the-road transportation when they get to 286. If they head north, 286 intersects with 86 at the town of Three Points. It's about 40 miles north and then another 40 west on 86 to get to Sells Airport."

Santappia shook his head.

"They went to a great deal of effort to stay off the main roads just to minimize detection, Bryan. We surprised them but I don't think that would make them decide to drive 80 miles on two interstate highways. They have to know that it won't be long before Nogales sends another chopper up here, along with an army of border patrol agents."

He paused to think then he started thinking out loud.

"Okay, let's figure they were heading for Sells Airport. It's a commuter airport. What's the length of their runway?"

"It's around 5,800 feet," Ahiga broke in to his line of reasoning, "mostly small jets and commuter prop planes land there."

Santappia smiled at the interruption.

"Okay ... so let's say they were intending to load the bomb onto a small plane. That would make sense ... if were a nuclear device! The blast radius would be maximized as would the impact from the blast if they detonate a nuke at a fairly low altitude over a city ... but what are they planning to do now? How far is Tucson?"

"Over 50 miles by road and if they're planning to stay on horseback and stay off the roads then they're looking at a two-day journey. There's some rugged terrain between here and Tucson and the closer they get to the city, the more border agents they're bound to run into."

Santappia nodded as he stood looking east.

"So, why are they heading to the highway?"

Ahiga joined him.

"Well for one thing, it's the only paved road for 50 miles, at least."

Santappia blinked his eyes at that statement.

"Bryan, that's gotta be it!"

"What's it?"

"It has to be it! It's the only paved road in 50 miles!"

"That's what I just told you, Charley!"

"Don't you see ... it's the only place they can land a plane in 50 miles! Bryan, we got to get to 286 and stop them before they take off! Can we catch up to them in your pickup if we head south?"

Ahiga shook his head.

"I don't think so, Charley. The roads are so bumpy, we couldn't speed there. It's too bad we don't have our ATV's ... or horses like our friends have."

Santappia smiled and put up his hand as he spoke into his mic.

"ARCHANGEL-one ... Rigs, the hostiles you downed ... where are their horses?"

Santappia could hardly hear Riggy's reply over the gunfire.

"ARCHANGEL-two ... hold on ... Pescy where are the horses of the ones we dropped? By the way, their gunfire is getting intense, Charley. This is gonna turn into Custer's last stand at the Little Big Horn for me and Spiro if we stay here much longer ... over."

"Rigs ... where are the horses, over?"

There was a pause.

"ARCHANGEL-two ... Pescy said the horses are still on the trail around the bend to our north, over."

Santappia smiled at Ahiga.

"Let's go get us some horses, Bryan!"

CHAPTER 35

JUST NORTH OF THE INTERSECTION (ARIZONA 286)
SASABE ROAD & REFUGE ENTRANCE ROAD
(APPROXIMATELY 12 MILES EAST OF)
TUBAC, AZ
1:30P.M., SUNDAY, SEPTEMBER 11, 2011

Charley Santappia and Shadow Wolf Agent Bryan Ahiga had mounted two of the dead terrorist's horses and Ahiga had led them on a trail that ran parallel to the one the bad guys had taken east. Before they left, Santappia ordered Riggy and Pescalitis to retreat, which was good for them since they were just about out of ammo. He also told them to take the chance and contact Nogales.

The two men made it to the highway an hour before and left their horses along the northern trail they took. Then they walked south along Arizona 286 for over a mile before taking position near some sparse trees alongside the southern trail. The plane showed up first, a Piper Chieftain, which was one that Santappia was familiar with and had flown several times before.

There was no time for planning. Santappia motioned to Ahiga to follow him and both men approached the plane, keeping their faces hidden. As soon as the pilot opened the door and dropped the stairs, they shot him. Their lack of planning almost backfired though, when they discovered that there was a co-pilot who was trying desperately to raise the stairs ... but they were able to shoot him too.

After they dragged the pilot's bodies into the brush, they boarded the plane and took their seats in the cockpit, being careful to conceal their weapons between their seats and the cockpit doors. Now they waited and Ahiga was uneasy.

"Charley, this is insane! Why don't we just fly this thing out of here?"

"Because we can't leave those men here with what is most probably a nuke, Bryan, you know that. We contacted Nogales, now all we have to do is sit here and hope that the cavalry gets here before the Indians ... I mean the bad guys do."

"Not funny, Charley ... and what will happen if the bad guys get here first? What do we do then?"

"Try to stall them."

"What if we can't stall them, Charley?"

"Then I'll shoot out the cockpit controls and you shoot as many of them as you can before—"

"Before we both get multiple taps to our heads, right?"

Santappia looked at Ahiga.

"Something like that."

Ahiga reached for the radio.

"I'm gonna check on Nogales's progress."

Santappia grabbed his hand.

"Here they come! Bryan, stay cool, let's see how long we can stretch this out. You got it?"

Ahiga just nodded his head as both men kept their eyes on the group of men approaching.

Hadi held up his hand to bring the Russian riders to a halt then he kicked his mount and started trotting over to the plane.

Santappia started throwing switches at lightning speed. Ahiga had to ask.

"What the heck are you doing, Charley?"

Santappia didn't reply as he worked at a furious pace to get the two Lycoming TIO-540-J2BD engines started. Finally, he pressed down on the break, pushed the throttles into position and started the engines. It had the desired effect and Ahiga understood. The noise from the two props sent the horse of the rider that was approaching, lurching back. He had all to do, to stay in his saddle and get his horse under control.

Hadi barely remained atop his mount as the engines of the plane revved up. He turned and shook his fist at the pilot and saw the pilot shrug his shoulders as a contrite gesture, in reply. For a moment, the men in the cockpit didn't look like his men, but he couldn't really make out their faces, not with the props spinning and the noise spooking his horse. After taking a moment to look around, he waved the Russians to come forward. They rode to his position about thirty feet in front of and to the side of the plane and dismounted. There they unfastened the road case and rolled it over to Hadi, who stayed atop his horse. Hadi had to yell over the noise of the plane's engines.

"Are you ready?"

The Spetsnaz leader, Oleg nodded with emphasis.

"Then you know what must be done! My men are piloting! They will be able to fly this plane over Las Vegas in 90 minutes! You must arm the bomb and parachute out within one hour! Do you understand?"

The leader nodded his head again.

"Then go!"

The Russians rolled the road case to the plane then took care to carry it on. Once the last of the six was aboard, he pulled the stairs up and closed the door. Hadi watched as the plane powered up then started rolling down the highway. Within minutes it was airborne. He started back towards the trail hoping to make it back to his men, but he didn't get very far.

Over the Iranian's head, a DHS-CBP Blackhawk helicopter appeared out of nowhere. He didn't even get a chance to draw his rifle before he was chopped almost completely in half by machine gun fire.

The crew of this chopper was best friends with the crew of

the first chopper - the one the terrorists shot down. They had just come from mowing down a group on horseback that was heading east on the same trail. They weren't taking any chances ... or any prisoners.

* * * * *

Ahiga's voice crackled into Santappia's headphones, "Charley, where the hell are we going? What happened to shooting out the cockpit controls?"

"I wasn't happy with the idea of our shooting out the controls and them blowing holes in us. It also occurred to me that they might just get themselves another plane."

Santappia pointed to a black bag sitting between Ahiga's legs.

"Open that case, Bryan. It should have maps and charts in it."

Ahiga opened the bag and rifled through all the manuals and binders until he came across a map, a chart and a receipt from Henderson Executive Airport. He examined the receipt first.

"It looks like this plane originated from a commuter airport in Henderson, NV."

Then he unfolded the chart and examined it.

"There are lines drawn on this chart, Charley!"

"Hold the chart up so I can see the lines."

Just as Ahiga held the chart up, a large barrel-chested man with thick dark hair unbuckled his seatbelt and poked his head between him and Santappia.

"Either of you speak English?"

Ahiga removed his headphones and nudged Santappia to do the same.

"I said do either of you speak English?"

Santappia nodded his head without turning to look at the man.

"My name is Oleg. Once you level off, we need you to fly a smooth and steady course. We can't be bumping around. Do you understand?"

Santappia nodded again without turning to look.

The Russian lingered for a moment, suspicious of their

silence then returned to his seat.

Santappia and Ahiga looked at each other with relief as they put their headsets back on. Ahiga spoke first.

"That was close. Charley, where the hell are we going and what did he mean about bumping around?"

Santappia pointed at a location on the chart Ahiga was holding.

"That's where we're supposed to be heading."

Ahiga looked at the chart.

"Las Vegas ...?"

"Bryan, listen to me. I think we were right all along. That road case has to contain a bomb. I have a feeling our Russian friends back there are about to rig it for detonation as soon as I level off ... and this plane was meant to fly the bomb over Las Vegas. If you look at the chart, the plot ends over the Strip, not at any of the local airports."

Ahiga nodded.

"What are we gonna do?"

"Well, Las Vegas is about 340 miles northwest, which means, at our cruising speed, we should be over it in approximately 90 minutes. That's how long we have to figure out what to do. I'm leveling off now."

The twin-engine plane smoothly ended its ascent. Santappia switched on the autopilot then turned to the Russian named Oleg, sitting in the first row behind the cockpit, and nodded. The Russian returned the nod then ordered his men in Russian to get to work. They all herded towards the back of the small plane, where the road case was secured, behind the back seats. They couldn't see what they were doing though because the massive back of Oleg and one other Russian blocked their view.

"Bryan, look, there are parachute packs hanging from every seat back there."

Ahiga looked behind their seats.

"We don't have any parachutes, Charley."

"Yeah, I noticed ..."

Santappia thought silently for a few minutes while he studied the chart as Ahiga kept watch on the men in the back. Then he took out a ruler and calculator from the black bag and went to work measuring and punching numbers into the calculator.

"I think I know their plan, Bryan. From the size of that road case ... have you ever heard the term, "suitcase" nuke?"

A chill ran down Ahiga's spine.

"Yeah, I heard the term but I didn't think they really existed."

"They existed but I didn't think any were still around. I don't know ... maybe these nuts got a hold of an old one and were able to make it operational or maybe they built one from scratch. Either way, it would take a boatload of money and definitely Russian expertise. That would also explain why our boys back there are Russian and not towel heads, like the others that ambushed us. The Russian Special Forces are most familiar with those devices. It would also explain why our destination doesn't end at an airport. From the little I know about nukes, they're most devastating when they're detonated at a relatively low altitude ... maybe 1,500 feet or so."

Ahiga stared at the parachutes hanging from all of the chairs behind the cockpit.

"So, they're gonna rig that thing and bail out and we're supposed to what ... be martyrs, fly it over Vegas and blow ourselves to heaven, for our 12 virgins?"

Santappia smiled at Ahiga.

"Something like that ..."

"You keep saying that, Charley. Tell me some good news, would ya!"

"Alright, take a look at this mark on the chart. It's right on the plot to Las Vegas. I calculate it to be just about an hour away from here. I think that's the location where they're gonna bail out. That means we'll have the plane to ourselves after they jump for about 30 minutes."

Ahiga face lit up with hope but he saw that Santappia's didn't.

"Okay, so what's the bad news, Charley?"

"The bad news is ... if my calculations are correct and if they're planning to parachute out at that location ... that's about 100 miles southeast of Vegas ... that would mean they're probably rigging the device with a 30-minute fuse."

"So, isn't that enough time for us to put down somewhere?"

"Sure, we can put down somewhere, but what then? Even

if we could get away, that bomb will go off wherever we land."

Ahiga's look of hope turned back to concern.

"Tell me you have a plan, Charley!"

"They look like they're gonna jump out somewhere south of Kingman, AZ. I have no idea if they'll keep an eye on us or if they have the ability to detonate the bomb if they see us veer off course. So, if we have to maintain course, at least until we're out of their visual contact ... that would put us smack between Bullhead City and Kingman. From there to Las Vegas, it looks like there's nowhere remote enough for us to set down. All the remote areas are too rough and hilly."

Santappia spent more time studying the chart.

The only thing I can think of is that we should be able to overfly Vegas then point this plane due north. Again, if my math is right, the plane will have just enough gas and the fuse will leave just enough time at maximum speed to fly the bomb maybe 25 or 30 miles north. I've been that far north of Vegas ... it's all fed land ... test sites ... about the best place I can think of to light up a nuke without anyone getting hurt."

"What about us?"

"Well, they all can't jump through that back door at the same time. I was thinking ... maybe we can shoot the last two through the door then toss their bodies out as quickly as we can. Hopefully, the ones that jumped before them will think something went wrong with their chutes. Then we'll use their chutes and bail out right after we clear the Las Vegas metropolitan area. I'll set the plane on autopilot and we should still end up about 10 or 15 miles south of the blast point."

"Is that far enough? How powerful do you think that bomb is?"

"I have no idea, Bryan. I've heard of reports that say a nuke of that size could be anywhere from 10 to 25 kilotons, depending on if they increase the efficiency of the bomb using deuterium and tritium. I think the primary blast radius would be somewhere around a couple of miles in any direction ... and don't ask me about fallout. All I could say is that with the jet stream moving west to east, there's nothing east of there for 20 or 30 miles."

Ahiga looked down at the chart.

"I guess we could radio out as soon as they jump and have them picked up. Also let them know what our plan is."

"My thinking, too ... all we can do now is to wait until we reach their drop zone."

CHAPTER 36

ABOARD PIPER PA31-350 CHIEFTAIN (F-WCCY)
(AT 13,000 FEET SOUTH OF)
KINGMAN, AZ (CRUISING AT 207 MPH)
2:30P.M., SUNDAY, SEPTEMBER 11, 2011

The six Russians in the back of the plane all stood in front of the back door wearing their parachutes. Oleg, their leader gave Santappia orders to descend to 13,000 feet and reduce speed to 180 knots. Once Santappia leveled off, they popped the door open. As they did, Shadow Wolf Agent Ahiga took his M-4 automatic rifle into his lap.

The first three men jumped, leaving the leader and two of his men. As soon as the fourth man jumped, Ahiga sprung up from his chair and shot Oleg first, and then shot his man standing closer to the opened door. Oleg fell to the ground but the other man managed to get to the door. There was nothing Ahiga could do but watch, as the mortally wounded man let himself fall from the plane.

"Charley, one got out!"

Santappia switched the autopilot on.

"Quick ... Bryan, help me get this gorilla out of his parachute!"

After removing the harness, they carried the dead man to the door and pushed him out. Struggling, Santappia managed to close the hatch.

"What are we gonna do now, Charley, with only one chute?"

Santappia didn't answer right away. He sat back down at the controls, put the plane into a shallow climb and increased to maximum cruising speed.

Standing in the aisle, Ahiga shouted his question again.

"Charley, what do we do now?"

"We ... don't do anything, Bryan. You're gonna put that chute on and I'm going to contact Nellis."

Santappia started fiddling with the radio but Ahiga stopped him.

"Charley, what the hell are you talking about? I'm not going anywhere without you. Can we both use that chute?"

Santappia looked at Ahiga with the glare of a Marine drill sergeant who expected his orders to be obeyed without question.

"No, we can't. The chute's made for one and the landing zone could be treacherous."

"Well, who's to say that I jump—"

"Bryan, listen to me. The part of my plan where I set the autopilot, never sat right with me. There are just too many innocent lives at stake. I think there's a chance that if I fly the plane into the ground before the bomb detonates, maybe it won't explode. And even if it does, the blast will partially be absorbed by the ground. That should make it less destructive."

"Then I'll stay with you!"

Santappia smiled.

"I think Pescalitis was right when he called you Cochise. You're a brave man, Bryan, for even getting on this plane with me. We both knew we might not be getting off, but as it is, there's one chute and I'm the only pilot."

Ahiga didn't reply. Santappia switched to a radio frequency. It took a few minutes but he reached the commander at Nellis AFB, a major general. After explaining the situation and then the general checking with his superiors in Washington, it was decided that Santappia's plan was the best one, with one exception. Two F-15 Eagles were immediately scrambled to accompany the Piper Chieftain on a course that would take them east of greater Las Vegas.

The two men didn't speak to each other for the rest of journey to the northern edge of the Las Vegas metropolitan area. Santappia was in contact with the F-15 pilots while Ahiga slowly got into the parachute harness. Once they reached the northern rim of the Las Vegas valley, Santappia radioed that Agent Ahiga was about to bail out. The F-15 pilots replied that they were also breaking off their escort.

Santappia set the autopilot and walked back to Ahiga.

"It's time, Bryan. Remember, count to 60 then pull the cord."

Before Santappia opened the back door, Ahiga stopped him and grabbed him by his shoulders.

"Charley, an old Shawnee chief once said, 'When it comes your time to die, be not like those whose hearts are filled with the fear of death ... Sing your death song and die like a hero going home.' You are a hero, my friend ... so sing your death song!"

Santappia grinned. The two men shook hands, then he opened the hatch and handed him a note. They had to shout to each other.

"Would you see that this gets to my wife?"

"I will!"

"Take care, Bryan!"

Ahiga jumped from the aircraft and as Santappia instructed him, he counted to 60 before pulling the cord, releasing his chute. It was his first time sky diving but Santappia joked that Native Americans were natural sky divers, after all he said, "*that's why sky divers yell, Geronimo!*" Once his chute opened he tried his best to look north to locate the plane, but he was too disoriented to find it.

It took over five minutes for Ahiga to land. Just before he reached the ground, he saw an intense flash of light and soon after he was down, he felt the earth quake. After unfastening himself from the chute he stood in silence looking at the mushroom cloud rising in the north, marking the place of Charley Santappia's sacrifice.

Agent Ahiga got down on his knees, raised his arms to heaven and said a prayer to the Great Spirit. *Let all those who have done this thing, be punished!*

CHAPTER 37

ZAMANI IMPORT-EXPORT CORPORATION
LOWER MIDTOWN MANHATTAN
NEW YORK, NEW YORK
6:30P.M., SUNDAY, SEPTEMBER 11, 2011

The large plasma screen TV was turned to the Fox News channel inside the Iranian businessman's plush office. Aref Zamani and Bahman Fard were watching the newscast in utter disbelief. A reporter in Las Vegas was standing on a small hill, and behind him, the familiar mushroom cloud from a nuclear explosion was visible. Fard turned up the volume.

"... *Again, we have just received word that a nuclear device has apparently detonated in a barren, unpopulated desert region just outside the United States federal test site, not far from the famous Area 51, north of Las Vegas.*"

Fard listened with shock and Zamani with rage as the reporter went on.

"... *There has been speculation that the explosion was most probably an accident that occurred while our military conducted some sort of covert test. While we still wait for the official cause, it is now believed that a nuclear warhead missed its mark and detonated outside the test range. Thankfully and so far miraculously, there are no reports of anyone being hurt but cities and towns east of the explosion are being evacuated in order to minimize exposure to the fallout. The President of the United States is scheduled to address the nation within the hour ..."*

Fard used a remote to lower the volume on the TV in order to answer the phone. He spoke in an urgent tone, in Farsi, then hung up and turned to Zamani.

"Sir, your jet is fueled and ready for takeoff at Teterboro. We should leave as soon as possible."

Zamani sat at his desk staring at the muted TV. His face was red with rage and his nostrils flared.

Fard switched the TV off.

"Sir, we really need to—"

Zamani banged his fists on his desk.

"STUPID INFIDELS ... ALL OF THEM ...! The Mexicans ... the Russians ... all non-believers ...!"

"But the pilots were our men?" Fard replied almost to himself.

Zamani was silent for a moment as he tried to compose himself.

"You're right, Bahman, they were our men ... but what could have gone wrong on that plane? They had to have flown clear over the City of Las Vegas to even get to where they detonated the bomb! It doesn't make sense. When we get back to Tehran, I want to speak to Oleg ... and why haven't we heard from our men at De Niro's ranch?"

"I will arrange the call with the Russian as soon as we land. As for our men, they may not have wanted to contact us until they are safely away from the Las Vegas area ... but sir we should leave here now, in case the Americans find anything that can tie us to *Antioch.*"

Zamani cringed at the thought that he named this failed operation after such a successful battle for people of his faith.

He nodded.

"Okay, call downstairs for the car while I pack my briefcase."

Fard picked up the phone and hit the button that should have connected him with their men at the front desk, but no one answered.

Zamani noticed his silence as he packed his case.

"What's the matter?"

Fard hung up the phone and changed the input on the plasma screen to their security cameras, so they could see the front desk.

"No one is answering downstairs."

Zamani walked over to a safe located behind a painting, hanging on the wall next to his desk. He dialed the combination and opened it.

"Sir, look, no one is at the desk!

Both men walked closer to the screen.

"Bring up the camera outside the front entrance!"

Fard hit a button on the remote and the screen turned to a wide-angle view of the outside of the building. Fard panned the camera left and right but both of the bodyguards that were supposed to be standing out there were also nowhere to be seen.

His impatience showing, Zamani grabbed the remote out of Fard's hands and switched to the bank of elevators on the ground floor. Another two of his men were supposed to be standing there, but again, no one was in view. Frantically, he switched to the cameras inside the elevators. Both men froze in their places as one of the cameras showed the bodies of all six of their men, piled on top of one another, in one of the elevators. When they looked closer, they saw that the elevator door was opened. Zamani panned the camera as much as he could. He and Fard panicked when they saw part of the Zamani Import-Export corporate logo emblazoned in the floor tiles outside the elevator door.

"That's on this floor!"

Fard pulled his pistol from a shoulder holster concealed by his suit jacket and jumped in front of Zamani. He pushed his boss down behind his desk and carefully made his way next to the opened office door. He peered out, but the hall was empty. Then the lights went out on the whole floor. Zamani's office was now lit only by the ambiance from the plasma screen and the Manhattan city lights bleeding in through the ceiling-to-floor windows behind Zamani's desk.

Fard waited a few moments but he didn't hear a sound coming from outside the office. As quietly as he could, he poked his head out again, just enough to scan the hall.

The last thing that Bahman Fard saw was the intense beam of a laser pointing at his forehead and the muzzle flash of a suppressed Heckler - Koch Mk.23 mod.0 US SOCOM pistol complete with laser aiming device.

Zamani heard Fard's body slump to the floor. Into the darkness, he called to him.

"Bahman ... BAHMAN!"

The lack of response from his subordinate made Zamani as enraged as he was frightened. He reached up and grabbed the receiver from the phone on his desk, but it was dead. He reached up again fumbling with his hand to find his cell phone. Frustrated, he decided to raise his head up just enough to see onto his desk. As soon as he did he saw the same red laser that Fard had seen, this time it was focused on his forehead.

In an act of defiance, he stood up.

"Who is out there? Show yourself!"

The laser bead never moved from where it was aimed, right between his eyes as Zamani heard the sound of footsteps approaching. The first man that entered his office was wearing night-vision goggles and was the one aiming the pistol at his head. He was unfamiliar to him.

"Who are you? What do you—"

Before he could finish his question, Mugsy Ricci stepped aside and Zamani recognized the man behind him.

"De Niro ...!"

"Curious meeting you here ... Prince Farouk al-Hassan, was it?"

Zamani sneered.

"So, you discovered my deception."

He straightened his suit and tie.

"I merely wanted to know your interest in the mosque. I thought you might not share that with just anyone ... but perhaps with a prince."

De Niro walked around the desk while Mugsy confiscated

Zamani's cell phone and briefcase. Then he handed the contents of what was in the safe to De Niro.

"It looks like there is enough here ... logs of calls ... itineraries ... all concerning ... *Antioch*. Would that be your name for what's happened today out west?"

Zamani grinned and ignored his question.

"So is this a robbery. Is that how you made all your money, Mr. De Niro, by stealing it? I notice you are both wearing gloves. So you are ... what's the term ... cat burglars? But look, you have murdered my assistant. I would say that you are in a lot of trouble, my friend."

De Niro dropped the contents of the safe and Zamani's cell phone into the briefcase and handed it to Ricci.

"Oh and what about my men in the elevator, did you murder them too?"

Ricci stepped up close to Zamani, slamming his fist into the Iranian's gut and doubling him over.

"You messed with the wrong family."

Then he reached down and stood the pained man straight again.

"Let's go."

Zamani held his midsection struggling to breathe.

"Wait, where are you taking me?" You cannot get away. My security system has already alerted the police! There's nowhere for you to—"

Ricci punched him in his stomach again, this time holding him up so he couldn't double over.

"Shut up and let's go."

When they reached the roof of the 52-story building, Ricci let go of Zamani then punched him in his gut again, collapsing him to his knees in pain.

De Niro stepped in front of him as Ricci went to work near the edge of the building. Zamani struggled to his feet.

"Why did you bring me up here? I told you, my security system—"

"We disabled your security system before your men could set off any alarms."

De Niro pushed Zamani over towards where Ricci was busy rigging something.

Zamani's cool demeanor disappeared replaced with a real look of fear and rage.

"What is he doing? What are you planning to do?"

De Niro's silence angered him even more.

"You think you can scare me? You Americans don't understand us at all. We are rewarded in death, when we die as martyrs!"

De Niro turned his back to Zamani and started walking over to his brother-in-law. As soon as he did, Zamani tried to charge him but De Niro thrashed his elbow into the Iranian's stomach. Zamani collapsed to his knees again, this time unable to get back to his feet.

De Niro took two ends of a rope from Ricci. The rope passed through a channel of a boom that could be swung out over the edge of the building. The boom was usually used to support the scaffolding for window washers. One end of the rope was tied into a noose. He slipped the noose around Zamani's ankles and pulled it tightly, forcing Zamani to fall on his face. Then both he and Mugsy began to pull on the other side of the rope, reeling Zamani in towards the end of the boom, like a fish on a hook.

"What are you doing? You American pigs! You can do nothing to me ... you hear me ... NOTHING!"

They pulled Zamani up until he was hanging upside down from the boom, still positioned over the roof. The Iranian tried in vain to reach up and free his legs from the noose.

Still filled with fury, he spat his words at De Niro.

"So, what will you do, huh?! What will you do, drop me from this building? You want to kill me like your wife died, huh. What was her name ... ah yes ... Lisa! They say ... those people died screaming in fear! We joked in Tehran that we could ... hear their screams all the way in Iran as those towers fell!"

Ricci rushed over to kick Zamani in the face, but De Niro stopped him. Zamani saw that and laughed in scorn.

"I will not beg for my life as your wife did, Cris De Niro! Ah ... and wasn't she pregnant? Yes, I read somewhere where it said that she was—"

De Niro pushed on the boom. Zamani's body swung upside down, out over the edge of the building. Zamani screamed involuntarily then tried to compose himself again. He ended up facing De Niro.

"GO AHEAD AND DROP ME ... I only wish ... I would have killed your other children, so they could have joined their mother and unborn brother!"

De Niro pulled on the boom just enough to swing Zamani close to the edge, but still hanging over it. He leaned his face as close as he could get it, to Zamani's.

"My wife was carrying our 3rd son. His name was going to be Daniel."

De Niro handed Zamani the end of the rope.

"I'm not going to drop you, Aref Zamani. You are going to drop yourself."

De Niro pushed the boom out again until it hung perpendicular to the edge of the building.

Zamani grunted and whimpered as he struggled to hold the rope.

Ricci walked up next to his brother-in-law.

"Don't worry, you can let go anytime you want. Cris and I made sure to barricade the street below you, just to make sure you don't fall on someone."

Zamani's arms trembled as his muscles began to fatigue. He whimpered louder and louder each time another inch of the rope slipped through his hands, dropping him further from the boom. Both men stood there until he literally reached the end of his rope.

Delirious with fear, Zamani's voice cackled in a higher pitch.

"YOU WILL ... BE GUILTY OF MURDER ... I KNOW YOUR BIBLE ... YOU WILL NEVER ENTER YOUR KINGDOM!"

De Niro corrected him.

"Then you should know that it also says, 'Do not let the sun go down on your wrath.' You tried to murder me and my children early this morning and look Zamani, the sun hasn't set yet!"

Zamani looked around ... then turned back to look at De

Niro. His face was covered with sweat and his muscles were trembling, about to give out. The terrorist's attitude of defiance melted away and he began to cry.

"I ... please ... I can't hold anymore ... please ... I beg ..."

De Niro squatted down and tilted his head so that his face was roughly in line with Zamani's.

"You know, I've always believed that when those towers fell, my God sent Angels to comfort my wife and the others. In my dreams, I picture my beautiful wife Lisa falling asleep, nestled in the arms of an Angel before she felt any pain."

Zamani's arms started spasming wildly.

"Tell me Zamani, do you think your god will send a demon to comfort you ... when you let go of that rope?"

De Niro stood up and walked away with Mugsy at his side. They didn't turn around as they heard Zamani's death shrill.

When they reached the street, a crowd had already gathered around the corner, along the barricades they had set up. Most of the people were talking on their cell phones. A few were even taking pictures with their phones of the morbidly contorted body of Aref Zamani. No one even noticed them as they started walking uptown.

Neither man talked. De Niro wiped a tear from his eye as thoughts and prayers filled his mind.

I love you, Lisa. I pray the day comes when I'll see you again. Father, thank you for letting us defeat our enemies ... and for protecting Ephraim! Please bless the family of Charlie Santappia.

De Niro's cell phone rang.

"Daddy, its Richard, where are you? We have to leave to visit mommy soon!"

It would be a special 9/11 memorial they all were about to attend.

THE WHITE HOUSE
Office of the Press Secretary

FOR IMMEDIATE RELEASE   September 11, 2011

ADDRESS FROM THE PRESIDENT ON NUCLEAR ATTACK

Good evening.

Today, on this 10th anniversary of the cowardly terrorist attacks of September 11, 2001, we found ourselves under attack again.

Early this morning, a plot unfolded of incredible proportions, as Iranian nationals working in conjunction with former members of Russian Special Forces and the infamous Pacifico Mexican drug cartel -- smuggled a nuclear device into our country and attempted to detonate it over the city of Las Vegas, Nevada. They intended to fly a small, twin-engine aircraft over the city and detonate the bomb in flight, in order to maximize the destructive force of the blast. Our agencies were able to disrupt their plans and divert that aircraft. A number of Border Patrol Agents lost their lives in Arizona attempting to capture these terrorists and one American hero in particular, former Major Charles Santappia of the United States Marine Corps, attached to an anti-terrorism agency working for the Department of Homeland Security, sacrificed his life in order to fly that plane away from the city of Las Vegas and into the ground in a remote and unpopulated area.

Once again, America was targeted for attack because of our commitment to freedom and opportunity around the world. And once again, the vigilance of our country's homeland defense and intelligence agencies has protected us from certain disaster and the evil forces of tyranny.

Our nation saw evil today and the very worst of human nature and we responded with the very best of America, with the daring and bravery of our nation's border patrol agents and civilians who gave their lives to protect our citizens and our way of life.

Even before the bomb detonated, I implemented our government's emergency response plans. Our military has sprung into action, securing our borders. Our emergency teams are working in and around the areas east of the blast zone, to help with local evacuation and potential rescue efforts from the resulting fallout.

Our first priority continues to be to take every precaution to protect our citizens at home and around the world from further attacks.

Some of the terrorists that have taken part in this heinous act have been killed while others have been taken into custody. But make no mistake -- our search is underway for anyone else who is behind this evil act and we will not stop until every individual is found. I have directed all of our intelligence and law enforcement agencies to find those responsible. Justice will be swift and terrible for the guilty.

Speaking directly to the leaders of the countries from which these terrorists arose, Iran, Russia, Mexico – The United States expects full cooperation in the apprehension of everyone involved. Anything less than full cooperation will be interpreted as hostility and in situations as grave as this, wars have started that way.

ABOUT THE AUTHOR

With his bestselling debut political thriller, *THE WATCHMAN of EPHRAIM*, Gerard de Marigny has burst upon the literary world stage with vigor and poise! Founding JarRyJorNo Publishing in January 2011, de Marigny dons many hats, that of publisher, graphic designer, marketer, as well as author. The result, so far, has been a sparkling debut novel that became a #1 Amazon Bestselling Geopolitical Thriller!

On July 4th, de Marigny embarked on his 75-day PATRIOT Blog Tour making over 50 appearances on book reviewers sites located all over the world, garnering stellar reviews and raves along the way.

In July, de Marigny also sat down for an up-close and personal interview with Philip Norbert of Kingmaker Productions. Shot by famed Cinematographer Jay Nemeth of Flightline Films, the Q&A session has garnered over 5,000 viewers on YouTube*.

Before writing fiction, de Marigny was the lead guitarist for 80's rock band, AMERICADE. Though the last lineup of the band broke up in 1995, de Marigny was approached by Aaron McCaslin, President of Retrospect Records, a label dedicated to promoting heavy rock bands from the 80's. A lifelong fan himself, McCaslin offered de Marigny a record contract. In return, de Marigny supplied Retrospect Records with every recording, whether previously released or not, in his possession. The result has become a remarkable 70-song, 4-CD boxed set branded, AMERICADENCE: 1980 ~ 1995**. Says de Marigny, "It's an amazing feat what Aaron pulled off. He literary brought back to life just about the entire musical catalog of AMERICADE … and the timing couldn't be better!" The boxed set will include a discount coupon for signed paper or eBook editions of both books in the CRIS DE NIRO series.

November 2011 brought BOOK II of de Marigny's CRIS DE NIRO series, SIGNS of WAR and the author is already at work writing BOOK III, RISE to the CALL due out in spring 2012.

* Look for "Gerard de Marigny discusses his 9/11 thriller _The Watchman of Ephraim_" on YouTube.
** You can find "AMERICADENCE: 1980 ~ 1995" (digital download) at: http://retrospectrecords.com/products/americade_americadence.html

BOOK CLUB GUIDE

1.   For the person who chose this book: What made you want to read it? What made you suggest it to the group for discussion? Did it live up to your expectations? Why or why not?

2.   How is the book structured? Does the author use any narrative devices like flashbacks or multiple voices in telling the story? How did this affect your reading of the story and your appreciation of the book? Do you think the author did a good job with it?

3.   Talk about the author's use of language/writing style. Have each member read his or her favorite passage out loud. (You might want to warn them ahead of time that they'll be doing this so they'll be prepared.) How does this particular passage relate to the story as a whole? Does it reveal anything specific about any of the characters or illuminate certain aspects of the story?

4.   How effective is the author's use of plot twists and red herrings? Were you able to predict certain things before they happened, or did the author keep you guessing until the end of the story? Did you find that the novel held everyone's interest throughout the story, or were there times when it failed to totally engross members of the group?

5.   How important is the setting to the story? If applicable, discuss the time period in which the book is set. Does the author provide enough background information for you to understand the events in the story?

6.	What is the most important part of a thriller to each member of the group-characterization, action, dialogue, or setting? How does this book rate in each of these areas?

7.	This novel is part of a series. Will your group read the series in order? Will the reading of the books in order, or not reading them in order, affected your group's enjoyment of each novel?

8.	Is the author equally invested in both character and plot? Or did the author put more effort into developing the story than in creating compelling and believable characters? Were the motivations of the characters believable, or did their actions feel like a means to further the plot?

9.	Would you recommend this work to a non thriller fan simply on the basis of its literary merit? Would you endorse it purely because of the skillful writing and the well-developed characters? Or do you think the work would strictly appeal to fans of the thriller genre.

10.	Did this book live up to or exceed your expectations of the author?

11.	What did you like or dislike about the book that hasn't been discussed already? Were you glad you read this book? Would you recommend it to a friend? Do you want to read more work by this author?

(The author would like to hear your views. Please share any/all of them with him by emailing him at:
mailto:g@gerarddemarigny.com.)

COMING SOON!

Book 4 of the
#1 *Amazon*-Bestselling Geopolitical
**CRIS DE NIRO Thriller series
from master storyteller,
Gerard de Marigny**

NOW AVAILABLE IN eBOOK, HARDCOVER, & PAPERBACK!
Audiobook editions of *THE WATCHMAN OF EPHRAIM* and *SIGNS OF WAR* also available!

Book 2
*Cris De Niro & The Watchman Agency return to
deal with Somali pirates, an imminent threat
from an Iranian/Venezuelan alliance and a Mexican drug cartel's plot of immense proportions.*

These are the SIGNS of WAR …

Book 3
*Iranian bio-terrorism, Russian espionage
reaching into the White House, and the pros-
pect of Iran emerging as a nuclear power are
the threats. World War III could break out in
the Middle East unless Cris De Niro and
The Watchman Agency can Rise to the Call …*

For all up-to-date info on Author Gerard de Marigny please visit:

g's website & blog:
www.GerarddeMarigny.com

g's Facebook:
www.facebook.com/Gerarddem

g's Twitter:
www.Twitter.com/GerarddeMarigny

g's LinkedIn:
www.LinkedIn.com/in/GerarddeMarigny

g's Goodreads:
http://www.goodreads.com/author/show/4607706.Gerard_de_Marigny

g's email:
g@gerarddemarigny.com